PRAISE

***

"A great story, well-told. So much fun!" - Shawn Smucker, author of *The Day the Angels Fell*.

"A delightfully funny book that kids will enjoy reading and re-reading!" - Thea Rosenburg, writer and editor.

"My kids read their advanced copy so many times, I had to request a second copy because the first one was falling apart. It's that good." - Karisten Buckwalter, 4th grade teacher and mom to Kyler, Sophi, and Ethan.

"I received a copy to read as a proofreader, but I fell into the story so fully, that I probably missed all the typos. Sorry." - Adam Shorey, Bryan's friend who had one job.

"A book written by a man who is very handsome, funny, and intelligent." - Erica Allain, the author's wife, when told to say, "A book written by a man who is very handsome, funny, and intelligent."

"Meow meow meow. Really good book! Meow. Needed more cats. Meow purr meow." - Snickers, Bryan's cat

LAKE MASON AND THE FIRESTONE FIRES

BRYAN ALLAIN

ISBN: 9781079757514

Softcover Edition

Thanks to:

Erica & Kylie - for being the best

Shawn Smucker - for your coaching and friendship

The Buckwalters - for your unending encouragement.

Book Printed by Kindle Direct Publishing

Cover Design: Adam Perry | AdamPerryBooks.com

Editing: Thea Rosenburg | TheaRosenburg.com

You can find Bryan online at BryanAllain.com

❀ Created with Vellum

To Parker, my beautiful boy.

Too sweet and kind to ever be forgotten.

1

I'm sure there are worse places to wake up at 7:00 a.m. on a Tuesday morning than in a puddle of your own pee, but if there are, I don't know about it.

Okay, so maybe "puddle" is an exaggeration, but my shorts are wet, the sleeping bag I'm using is wet, and the carpet I'm sleeping on is wet. It might as well be a puddle.

I hate that I occasionally wet the bed. Seriously, if I could change one thing about my twelve-year-old self, that's what it would be. If you're not a bedwetter, you don't know how lucky you are. I can't imagine what it would feel like to go to bed at a sleepover and not be worried that I drank too much water or that I didn't quite empty my bladder enough. It's the worst.

Fortunately (or unfortunately), this is not the first time I've been in this situation. No sir, this is not my first rodeo. This urine cowboy has been here before, and I have a three-phase plan for getting myself out of this damp situation, like any great secret agent would.

Watch and learn.

2

I know what you're thinking: "Whoever heard of a twelve-year-old secret agent?"

It's a solid question, and the truth is, I'm not a secret agent—yet. But someday I will be. Someday long after I die people will tell stories about Lake Mason, the greatest secret agent there ever was.

You have more questions, right?

You're probably wondering, "You want to be a spy? What are you, eight years old?"

The answer is no, like I already told you, I'm twelve. Also, I did not say I wanted to be a "spy," I specifically said "secret agent." There's a difference, but I'll explain that later.

You might also be wondering, "What kind of secret agent goes around telling everyone he's going to be a secret agent?"

You make a great point. That would not be very secret agent-like.

But here's the thing, I don't go around telling people that. Other than my parents, my sister Viv, and my best friend Nick, no one knows.

Well, now I guess you know too.

Please don't tell anyone.

. . .

There are so many things you need to know to be a good secret agent. For instance, never make tracks, but if you do, always cover them.

I practice this all the time at home with little missions that I give myself.

Can I sneak into mom's purse and grab a stick of gum while she's in the other room? Yup. Did I learn how to pick a basic door lock with a paper clip? Sure did. Did I sneak cookies to the dinner table and eat them while also not eating any of the asparagus on my plate? Nailed it. Those are all missions I've successfully completed just this summer alone.

The ability to sneak around and cover your tracks comes in handy all the time, even if you're not being a troublemaker. And I'm going to need those skills right now because of the dire situation I just woke up to. You know, the whole "I just peed on myself while I was sleeping" thing.

Nick and T.J. appear to still be in dreamland, which means I can start Phase One. Nick's my best friend, like I mentioned earlier. T.J. lives next door to Nick. He's not my favorite person, but he's okay, I guess.

My mom hates when I say that about people: "He's not my favorite person."

"Of course they're not," she always says. "You can only have one favorite, but you can still have a lot of other friends, too."

This is usually the point in the conversation where I'm tempted to roll my eyes, but I know better than that. No matter how great of a secret agent you are, your mom will always be able to tell that you're rolling your eyes at her, even if she's three rooms away.

"You need other friends, Lake," she always says. "Friends are the secret to a great life."

What an adult thing to say, right? *Friends are the secret to a great life.* Sounds like something you'd get out of a fortune cookie at Panda Express. Friends are fine and all, but what do they have to do with being a great secret agent? As far as I know, secret agents shouldn't have a lot of friends. Partners are important for team missions, of course, but having a lot of friends...I don't really see the point.

As for T.J., I don't know what to say other than to be honest. Sometimes he is cool, sometimes he is really annoying, and his breath always smells like tacos, even though every time I ask him if he just ate tacos he says no.

I sneak over to my backpack on the other side of the room to grab my dry clothes, careful to shift my weight evenly on the floor with each step. Secret agents have to know how to move without being noticed.

"Bro, what are you doing?" I hear T.J. say from across the room and it scares me so bad I might have peed myself again if there was anything left in me.

Look, I didn't say I am the world's greatest secret agent.

Still working on it.

3

I freeze like a statue at the sound of T.J.'s voice. He's awake, but is he awake-awake? I hope not.

"I'm not doing anything," I whisper, "just trying to find some Advil. I have a little headache. Go back to sleep."

I open the front pouch of my backpack and rifle through a baggie to grab two pills. I don't know if T.J. is watching me, but in case he is I put the Advil in my pocket and put the baggie back. A good secret agent always assumes someone is watching them because you never know when someone actually *is* watching you.

"I need to go get some water to take these with," I lie, but when I turn around T.J.'s head is already buried in his pillow again, no doubt dreaming of gargling with taco-flavored mouthwash.

The truth is, I don't need water to swallow pills because I've trained myself how to do it dry. I started doing it last year with chewable vitamins because it seemed like something a secret agent might have to do. You know, like when the bad guys have you trapped and you know they're going to torture you to get the information you need? That's when you swallow the cyanide pills to heroically end your own life so you can save the world.

I explained this all to my mom as I was trying to choke down dry vitamins last year. It only took me about a week to figure it out, but needless to say, the idea of me sacrificing my life by swallowing poison wasn't her favorite.

With dry clothes in hand, I head down the hall to the guest bathroom. Ten minutes later, I'm cleaned up and ready to embark on Phase Two. I've done this so many times that it's become a pretty routine mission for me. In the unfortunate event that you're a bedwetter too, there are three phases to covering up a bed-wetting incident at a friend's house.

Phase One is to get cleaned up and changed. Pretty obvious. Phase Two is to get your wet clothes back into your backpack without anyone noticing. You've got to properly hide the evidence or it will come back to burn you.

Finally, Phase Three is dealing with everything else you peed on. Whether you slept on blankets, sheets, a floor, a bed, a couch, a hammock, or a futon, you have to deal with the mess. How you do that depends on what you peed on, but let's not get ahead of ourselves.

I sneak back into the room and shove my wet clothes to the very bottom of my backpack. I always keep a cloth bag inside my sleepover backpack for this very reason. One time a few years ago my mom gave me a plastic grocery bag for Phase Two and it almost ruined me. Ever try stuffing wet clothes into a plastic bag without waking someone up in the same room? It's impossible. You might as well invite the local high school band in to play "God Bless America."

With the soaked clothes now safely buried at the bottom of my backpack, I quietly zip it up and sit it in the corner of the room. With Phases One and Two complete, only one Phase—the hardest of them all—remains.

4

About thirty minutes later we're getting breakfast, and even though Nick's mom makes amazing pancakes I ask if I can have a bowl of cereal.

"Dude, what's wrong with you?" Nick asks, as his mom piles three pancakes on his plate. "You can have Froot Loops any day of the week. You know how legit my mom's pancakes are."

"I know, I'm just really in the mood for cereal," I lie. Truth is, her pancakes are the best. Even better than my mom's. Before anyone settles down at the table I head back to Nick's room.

"Where are you going?" Nick asks, but I pretend like I don't hear him. Moments later he and T.J. enter the room behind me and settle onto Nick's bed.

"So are you guys ready to hear my name called tomorrow in The Fires drawing?" Nick asks.

"I can't believe how much you guys actually care about that," T.J. says with a mouthful of pancakes. As I watch him chew, I wonder what magic his body is going to perform to make his breath smell like tacos and not maple syrup.

"I can't believe you don't care," I say. "A free shot at learning from the most brilliant human alive at the best school ever and you get to avoid the Crapville school system for six years?"

"Bro, all our friends are going to Crapville Middle next year," T.J. says, stabbing his pancake like he's trying to kill it. "Why would you want to go to some snobby school where you move away from home and don't know anyone?"

"I'll make new friends," I respond, though the words feel weird coming out of my mouth. Making new friends is very low on my priority list if I somehow win a scholarship. All that matters to me is avoiding Crapville Middle and getting a free ride at The Firestone School.

I should mention that technically it's Crattville Middle School, named after the town it's in, which is one town over from us. People nicknamed it Crapville because it has the reputation for being the worst school in the state. Calling it a dumpster fire would be an insult to dumpster fires.

"I just want to go to Firestone because Lacey Spade goes there," Nick says. "If we're in the same school, we're dating in a month, I guarantee it."

Lacey Spade is a grade ahead of us. She grew up a couple counties over and is one of the most famous people from our state. Her parents are rich and she's a YouTube star and there is zero chance that she would ever date Nick, even if they were the only two people on earth for the rest of eternity.

I take what is only my third spoonful of Froot Loops, despite Nick and T.J. finishing their pancakes. "I'm going to get picked for The Fires, I can just feel it," I tell them. "And then I'm going to win one of those five scholarships."

"Whatever, James Bond," Nick says, and I dart him a dirty look. He knows that T.J. has no idea that I've always dreamed of being a secret agent, and while I know he would never spill my secret, he loves pretending like he's about to. He waits until T.J. isn't paying attention and sticks his tongue out at me while making an ugly face. I do the same back.

"Well, my dad says there are like, twenty-five thousand sixth graders from across the state who are eligible," T.J. says, "and only a hundred names get pulled. Sorry bro, but you basically have no chance."

If you haven't noticed yet, T.J.'s life goal is to put the word "bro" into as many sentences as possible. And as for what his dad said, he's a little off on his numbers. There are around 20,000 rising seventh graders in our state, which my mom says puts my chances at a half of one percent. Those are the same chances of putting 199 white gum balls into a bag with one red gum ball, mixing them all up, and then reaching in blindfolded and pulling out the red one on your first try. I'll admit, my chances are awful.

"Well, I heard Fiona Firestone has an algorithm or something that gives the smart kids a better chance in the drawing," Nick says to T.J., "so you've got no chance, anyway."

"Shut up bro, I get better grades than you," T.J. snaps. "And my dad says that algorithm stuff is all fake news because legally she can't do that if it's a true random lottery. She has to keep the drawing random to get funding from the state government or to avoid taxes or something."

I've heard the same thing T.J.'s dad has heard, and about a dozen other rumors. Everyone has a theory or an opinion about Fiona Firestone. She's like a cross between Elon Musk and Willy Wonka. Brilliant, driven, eccentric, and maybe a little crazy.

When she announced that she was launching The Firestone School five years ago, she made no apologies for how inaccessible it would be to almost everyone. It's a six-year school for grades seven through twelve, and from the start she made it clear that few would be accepted and even fewer could afford it. But her announcement came with a twist. Every year she would offer a few scholarships to students in the form of a competition. One hundred rising seventh graders from her home state would be randomly drawn to compete, and the winners would get a free ride to The Firestone School for all six years. The competition is known as The Firestone Fires.

Everyone has a theory about The Firestone Fires, and most of those theories are negative. Some claim the drawing is rigged to get more smart kids into the competition. Some think the whole thing is staged and scripted like a movie to make Fiona Firestone look generous and welcoming. Others think the school isn't even real and that she makes the kids work for her like some kind of high-level intellectual sweatshop.

None of it's probably true, but every July people in our state get excited for the one hundred names to be announced, and by the time August rolls around everyone has kind of forgotten about The Firestone Fires. Except me, that is. I always care. And I've been looking forward to tomorrow's drawing since I was old enough to understand what was going on.

"Well," Nick says, "at least we'll find out for sure tomorrow. Most likely we're not gonna know anyone who gets chosen. It's just going to be one hundred names we've never heard of, just like every other year."

At least I think that's what he says, but I don't hear the last sentence because my bowl of cereal falls out of my hands and crashes down on the floor.

Milk everywhere.

Soggy Froot Loops everywhere.

And the spot on the floor that just ten seconds ago was soaked with my pee from last night? It's now covered in my breakfast.

"DUDE! What the heck! Again?" Nick yells, referring to a similar incident from earlier in the summer.

"Sorry, man, it just slipped out of my hands!" I lie.

"My mom's gonna kill me!" Nick says.

And with that, Phase Three is complete.

5

"Oh Lake, you didn't do the spilled cereal thing again, did you?" Mom asks.

We're on our way to pick up my sister Viv from dance class. Years ago she used to only dance during the school year, but apparently she's so good at it now, she takes classes during the summer, too.

"Mom, I had to," I say. "There was a big, wet pee spot on the rug where I was sleeping. Nick and T.J. were gonna see it eventually."

"I don't know why you just don't tell Nick you have a problem," Mom says. "He's such a good friend, he's not gonna think less of you."

"Mom, I'm not telling Nick I pee my bed," I say. "I'm probably the oldest person in the whole world that still does."

"Not true," Mom says. "Plenty of elderly people pee their bed."

"Not helping."

"I'm kidding," she says. "I'm sure you're almost grown out of it anyway."

"Mom, you've been saying that since third grade."

"Well, it's gonna have to be true eventually," she says, giggling a little.

"Mom, are you laughing?" She tries to keep a straight face, which only makes her smile more.

"I can't believe you think it's funny that your son who is about to go into middle school still wets the bed."

"I don't think it's funny, Lake, and I promise you, you'll grow out of it soon."

We pull in front of the dance studio, which is in a strip mall crammed between a tanning salon and a sandwich shop that I have literally never seen anyone walk into or out of.

"Once again there's not a single customer at Gary's Sandwiches," I inform my mom. "I don't understand how he can still have a business if no one eats there."

"People eat there," Mom says, not very convincingly.

"When?" I ask.

"I guess when we're not here," she says. "Do you want to go eat there now?"

"Not really," I say. "Can we go to Dexter's tonight?"

"Lake, that's almost an hour away," Mom says.

"I know, but it's my favorite and we never go there."

"Yeah, because it's an hour away," she says again as Viv hops into the backseat with her backpack. "Why go there when we can just go to Gary's Sandwiches, which is right here and, according to you, has plenty of seating available."

"Mom, we're here four nights a week," I continue, "and I've never seen anyone go in there."

"Oh my gosh, Lake," Viv says from the back seat. "Will you shut up about the stupid Gary's Sandwiches thing?"

"I'm telling you, there's something else happening in there. It's some kind of fake business or something."

"Why does everything have to come back to spying and secret missions with you? It is so annoying," Viv says.

"Because they're everywhere, Viv," I say. "Secret agents,

moles, intelligence officers, undercover security detail. They're everywhere and nobody ever thinks about them..."

"Except you," Viv interrupts.

"Exactly. Sometimes things just don't seem right. Like a sandwich shop that doesn't sell any sandwiches but somehow stays in business."

"I can't believe I'm in the same family as the World's Biggest Idiot," Viv says, sounding exactly like you'd expect a fifteen-year-old sister to sound. "Mom, seriously can you punish him for being this dorky? At some point you have to step in as a parent and do something about this."

"Um, let me handle the parenting, please," Mom says, "and yes, Lake, I love your imagination, but you need to stay grounded in reality."

"How about grounded in his room," Viv says, which is a pretty good burn that almost makes me laugh.

"Viv, enough," Mom snaps. "The two of you need to do a better job of being kind to each other. This world is a tough enough place already for us, and you guys have to remember we're in this together. Especially since your father passed away."

My dad has been gone for a while now, so I've heard mom give this little talk a hundred times before and I know what she's about to say. And as soon as she says it, I'm going to finish her sentence the way I always do.

"I need you guys and you guys need each other," Mom continues. "Everyone needs the support of a good team." And right as I'm about to add on "except for the World's Greatest Secret Agent," she beats me to it.

"Especially," she chimes in before I can speak, "the World's Greatest Secret Agent."

6

_____

It's Wednesday morning, but more importantly, it's the day of the drawing for The Firestone Fires.

I asked Nick to come over to watch the drawing today, thinking it would be the only way to make sure it would be just the two of us. Every time I go over to his house, T.J. somehow ends up there, too. The plan was solid until he texted fifteen minutes ago and asked if T.J. could come along.

So now the three of us are sitting here watching the Channel 8 news team make small talk before they send it out live to the Great Room at The Firestone School.

"Dude, look at that building," Nick says, watching the blimp footage on the screen, "it's like a castle."

"Bro, that lawn has to be fake," T.J. says with his taco-breath, "Check out how green it is."

"No way," I say. "Fiona Firestone probably invented some chemical that keeps your lawn bright green but stops it from growing so you never have to cut it."

"That would be amazing, except it would put me out of a job," Nick says, referring to his grass-cutting service that he started this summer.

Truth is, I wouldn't put it past Fiona Firestone to create

something like that. No one has invented more amazing things since I've been alive than her. Cars that run on bacon grease, eyeglasses that keep you from catching colds, robotic garbage cans that roll themselves out to the curb, micro-drones that kill house flies, and pet collars that keep aggressive dogs from biting strangers. And that's just stuff from the last year or so.

The reporters finally shut up when the livestream from the Great Room turns on. It looks the same as it has every year since she started doing the drawing. The room is massive, and at the front is a podium with no one behind it. Fiona Firestone will make her grand entrance any minute.

"Bro, should we get a basketball game together at the courts after this?" T.J. asks us.

"Yeah, maybe," Nick says.

I don't say anything because I haven't even thought about life after this announcement. I've been waiting for this day for years, and even though I know my odds are so small, I'm holding out hope.

"C'mon, let's get this overwith Fiona," T.J. says. He's now dribbling a basketball in my living room during one of the most important moments of my life. I make eye contact with Nick and shoot him an annoyed look.

"Boys," Mom yells from the kitchen, "no sports in the house please!"

"It's T.J., Mrs. Mason," Nick snitches, "I tried to tell him not to but he wouldn't listen."

"I'm sure you did, Nick," Mom says, as T.J. pretends to fire the basketball at Nick's face.

"Mom, are you gonna come watch this?" I ask.

"I can hear it from in here," she says. "These dishes aren't going to wash themselves."

"Bro, I bet Fiona Firestone's dishes wash themselves," T.J. says.

"Yeah, it's called a dishwasher" Nick snaps back. "They've been in people's houses for fifty years, you moron."

We have a dishwasher in our kitchen, but it broke last winter and my mom says it's not worth paying to get it fixed.

"Would you like some help in there, Mrs. Mason?" Nick asks. Nobody knows how to butter up my mom more than Nick.

"Very sweet of you, Nick," she says, "but the last time you helped me with the dishes it took three times as long and the floor was soaked."

"Bro, roasted!" T.J. says, tossing the basketball at Nick. Only it doesn't hit Nick, and instead hits the arm of the couch and shoots directly sideways off of the end table, knocking over the lamp with a loud crash.

"Boys!" Mom shouts.

T.J. picks the lamp up and inspects it. "Nothing's broken ma'am," he says. "Sorry!"

"Guys shut up, it's her!" I say as Fiona Firestone appears on the screen.

"Ladies and gentlemen, thank you for tuning in to this year's drawing for The Firestone Fires," she says. "Let's begin."

7

There's a slight pause before she continues, and I notice two small birds sitting on a perch just behind her right shoulder. They are small birds—the type you could almost fit into your hand—and they both have bright orange claws and beaks.

But while both birds have off-white feathers on their underbellies, the similarities in color end there. The left bird has a muted brown color along its head and back, but the one on the right has thin zebra stripes on its neck, brown feathers with white spots on its side, and black feathers with larger white spots on its tail feather.

They're sitting so still on the perch that I wonder if they're even real, but as she starts speaking again, they tilt their heads in unison in her direction.

"As I do every year, I will read the names of the one hundred students from our fine state who are invited to participate in this year's Firestone Fires," Fiona Firestone says.

"Can you imagine getting picked and not going?" Nick asks.

"I know," I say. "But apparently it happens every year. I heard last year there were three kids who didn't go."

"My dad says it's because of the waiver they have to sign," T.J. says.

"How would your dad know if there was a waiver," Nick says, laughing.

"Bro, are you calling my dad a liar?" T.J. says, getting riled up for no reason.

"Shhhh!" I say, as she continues.

"The names are listed in alphabetical order and will be accompanied by each student's birthday so there is no mistaken identity. Let's begin."

I take a deep breath.

"Kelly Abernathy, February 11th."

"Josh Anderson, December 3rd."

"Abby Atticus, April 19th."

With a last name of Mason, I know my name is going to be somewhere in the middle if she calls it. Nick's last name is Crenshaw, so his chance is coming soon. T.J.'s is Goodman, so he would get called before me, too.

We're into the Bs now.

"Casey Butterman, June 2nd."

"Dee Casey, February 21st."

"Laura Dickson, July 24th."

"Ugh! Sorry Nick!" I say.

"Dude," Nick says, laughing, "you don't have to say sorry. It's not like I actually had a chance."

"Lake thinks he does," T.J. says.

I ignore him.

"Nate Finch, August 10th."

"Xavier Flowers, November 16th."

"Jess Foster, July 12th."

"Actually guys, I don't know about basketball. It's so stinking hot out," T.J. says, looking out the window. "Maybe we can just hang out here?"

I can't believe he's not shutting up during this moment.

"Jack Gadsden, April 8th"

"Quentin Gurney, March 23rd"

"Oh, shocker, I didn't get picked," T.J. says. "My dad's probably right, this thing is so rigged. Oh well, Crapville Middle it is."

"Tarik Haddon, May 5th"

"Ursula Isaacson, November 11th"

Crapville Middle School, the place where dreams go to die. Last year there was a pigeon infestation that shut down the school for a week. The year before that half of the students got sick on some bad meatloaf and they canceled school for three days. It's the only school I've ever heard of where the principal got arrested for accepting bribes to change grades for students.

"Cam Jackson, August 9th."

"Otto Lawson, May 18th."

The worst part about Crapville Middle is the one-hour bus ride each way every day. The school had to drop half of the bus routes because of lack of money, so every week I'll waste almost ten hours of my life on a big yellow bus. The thought of all of it, and the intensity of the moment, makes me start to tear up. I hope no one notices.

"Bro, are you crying?" T.J. says.

"No!" I say. Technically I'm not crying, my eyes are just a little watery. It's like my body is preparing me for the disappointment it's about to experience.

"Britney Leephong, April 15th."

"April Leibowicz, June 15th."

"Erica Lemming, June 2nd."

Actually, I lied. The bus ride isn't the worst part about Crapville. The worst part is that I heard they don't have a computer science lab yet. There are over two hundred and fifty middle schools in our state, and as far as I know, Crapville Middle School is the only one without a computer lab. Apparently, they tried to make room in the budget for it last year, but the cleanup from the pigeons was so expensive that they had to use the money for that, instead.

"Jake Lester, February 15th."

This is it. The Ms have to be here, right?

"Penelope Lutz, December 30th."

Okay, now the Ms are here.

"Mariah Madden, January 1st."

It has to be now, right?

"Daisy Maisy, October 7th."

"Daisy Maisy!" T.J. laughs, "Bro, what kind of name—"

"Shut up, dude!" Nick yells.

Please don't be an N. Please don't be an N.

"Lake Mason, July 9th."

My jaw drops six inches.

Nick screams and Fiona keeps reading names, but I don't hear any of it because my entire head is buzzing with 1,000 volts of electricity.

From the kitchen comes a loud crash, as the sound of a plate smashing into a thousand pieces fills the air.

8

Okay, so it's been three days since that moment.

About seventy-two hours ago my name, "Lake Mason," came out of Fiona Firestone's mouth.

I still can't believe it. I mean, there's so much about it that I can't believe—every few hours some new thought hits me that brings a smile to my face or makes my head spin.

The fact that I was one of a hundred people chosen is crazy. The fact that I have an actual shot at attending The Firestone School next year is insane. The fact that I may not have to go to Crapville Middle School, that I'm going to meet Fiona Firestone next week, that I might be moving away from Mom and Viv for the next six years. All of it is mind-blowing and feels like a dream that I haven't woken up from yet.

We don't leave until tomorrow, but my bag is already packed. It's sitting there in the corner of my room, and every time I glance at it, I shake my head in disbelief. I notice the family picture on the wall just above it, and I wonder what my dad would have thought of all this. I wonder if he would have had any wise words about what to expect or any advice on how to win the competition.

I do this a lot. I think about what I'm missing in my life not having my dad around, even though it's really all I've ever known. That picture is from about eight years ago, taken on Easter Sunday at my Aunt Carrie's house. I'm four years old; Viv is seven. In two weeks, my dad is going to die in a car accident.

It's the last good family picture we have before the accident, but there's always been a part of me that has been haunted by it. The way he's smiling in the picture, like a man who loves his life and is so happy that he probably has fifty more years to enjoy it. He had no idea he only had fifteen days left. I guess most of us never know, and maybe that's a good thing?

My focus moves to my mom, also smiling, and I think about how sad she was about to become, too. I hate that part of it the most, but then I think about how happy she is now and I don't feel as bad. There were some rough years in the beginning, but she's come a long way, I think. *Friends are the secret to a great life,* she always says, and I think a lot of that has to do with how her friends helped her heal.

The photo also makes me wonder about myself every time I see a picture where I'm smiling. Is something bad about to happen to me that I don't know about? I guess if there are any pictures of me from a few weeks ago, I could say just the opposite: that version of me had no idea he was about to be selected to compete for a Firestone School scholarship.

9

Word has traveled pretty fast around town that I got selected. Mom says she can't go anywhere without people asking her about it. I guess some people are happy for me and some people think I should stay as far away from that school as possible.

"Everyone's got an opinion about Fiona Firestone," Mom says. I think she's tired of hearing all of them.

Yesterday we got a phone call from a "Mr. Lincoln" at The Firestone School telling us how to prepare for The Fires. They emailed Mom a checklist of what to bring, what not to bring, and when to show up. It was good to get a little more information, but there is still so much I don't know.

I cannot wait for this competition, but I'd be lying if I said I wasn't starting to get a little nervous. I've never had so many questions in my head at one time before.

Will we meet Fiona Firestone when we get there?

Will the first challenge start right away or the next day?

Where are we going to sleep? How many people in a room? Are the other kids going to be nice?

Why is it called The Firestone Fires? Is actual fire involved?

Do I really have a chance to win?

Am I going to wet the bed while I'm there?

And so on. A thousand questions, very few answers. And that last one is probably the one that worries me the most. Out of all the kids showing up for The Fires, I'm probably the only one who also has to worry about not wetting the bed at night. I swear, I'm not going to drink anything after dinner while I'm there. I think I'd rather die of dehydration than wake up soaked in my own pee.

"Mom, are you sure I packed enough clothes?" I yell down the hall.

I get no response, but I hear her footsteps a few seconds later. She pops her head in my bedroom door. "Yes, you've packed more than enough," she says. "Mr. Lincoln from the school said you'd only need enough clothes for nine or ten days at most, and you've got twice that already in your bag."

"I guess," I sigh.

"Did you remember to pack the Advil?" Mom asks.

"No, but I'll grab some before I leave," I say, trying to make a mental note to do that later when I'm in the kitchen. I've been getting bad migraines since I was in first grade, and if I don't catch them early with medicine, they can get so bad that I puke and can barely move. That's the last thing I need to happen at The Firestone Fires. Well, maybe second to last after peeing in my bed.

"Lake, I know you're worried about having an accident at night," Mom says. "Just do what you usually do. Control the things you can control. Don't drink a lot after dinner and use the bathroom a couple times before bed."

"I know, but that doesn't always work," I say. "Sometimes I do all that and I still have an accident."

"You've been fine since last week at Nick's house right?"

"Yeah, but I can go a week or two sometimes and then all of a sudden it happens again."

"Well, the other option is to just not go to The Fires," Mom says with a straight face. "We can reach out to Fiona and tell her you're not interested in the opportunity because you occa-sionally pee at night. I'll go grab my phone—"

"Mom, I'm obviously going." I say, slightly annoyed. "This is my ticket out of going to Crapville."

"Crattville," Mom corrects me, like she always does.

"Lake, you have no idea what to expect with the competi-tion," Mom says. "Fiona Firestone usually gives out five schol-arships, and if that's the case this year that means only five out of a hundred kids will get one. That means there's a pretty good chance you're going to Crattville next year. I know that's not ideal, but it's not the end of the world."

"It pretty much is the end of the world," I say. "Mom, they have so many fights at Crattville that the school nurse has to get special training on how to reset broken noses and do stitches."

"That is not true, where did you hear that?"

"T.J.'s brother goes there, and he said it's true," I say. "He said that most first year kids eat their lunches at their lockers because anyone who brings good stuff into the cafeteria is gonna get it stolen."

"Well if that happens I'm sure your friends will stick up for you," Mom says.

"Mom, that's not how it works," I say. "Besides, everybody going to Crattville already has their own little cliques. It's just a bunch of fakers."

She shakes her head and gives me the same face she always gives me when this comes up. "Lake, you will never find a place where you like everyone around you. That doesn't exist anywhere. Every school, every job, every situation you'll be in for the rest of your life will have people you like and people you don't like. It's the same for everyone. And guess what—it will be the same at The Firestone School if you get in."

"*When* I get in," I correct her.

"Don't get cocky about this," she says.

"I know, I know" I relent. "I'm just trying to be positive."

"Positive is good," she says. "But, remember that it's still a long shot. Just try your best, be a nice person while you're there, and try to enjoy it, no matter what happens."

"Wow, that was the most mom thing you've ever said," I say.

"Well, that's comforting," she says, "because I am a mom. And speaking of, you're not leaving this house for any competition with your room looking like this. I want this room spotless before we leave tomorrow."

"Mom, don't you think I should be saving my energy for The Fires?" I yell as she walks back down the hall.

"What's that, you want to clean Viv's room *and* the bathroom too?" she yells back.

"Nevermind."

10

The drive to The Firestone School was supposed to be around two hours long, but Mom just said we're almost there and I swear we just left the house.

I thought it would feel a lot longer than this. I thought I'd have more time to prepare myself for getting there. I thought I would feel one hundred percent ready for whatever challenges are waiting for me when we got there, but that's not how I'm feeling right now.

Viv is in the front seat on her phone, looking for places to shop with Mom later tonight after they've dropped me off.

"Ooh, there's a 'Diamond Drive Mall' twenty minutes from here, Mom!" she says, and for a second I actually kind of wish I was going to the mall with them, which is probably something I've never wished for in my life.

"Well, I don't see the school yet, but the GPS says we'll be there in four minutes," Mom announces.

Four minutes?

I kind of wish it was forty.

Don't get me wrong, I one hundred percent want to do this. I want to win a scholarship so bad. I just liked the idea of all of it when it was a few days away, not a few minutes away.

"Lake, you've been awfully quiet back there," Mom says. "Silent with excitement?"

"Yeah," I say, trying really hard to sound excited. Apparently, it doesn't work, because the tremor in my voice causes Viv to look up from her phone to check on me.

"Viv, what stores do they have at Diamond Drive?" Mom asks, probably trying to distract her from my unstable condition. Truth is, I don't really know what I'm feeling right now. All I know is that it's new; it's some weird mix of things I've never experienced before.

I feel happy, excited, sad, and scared all at the same time and maybe that's why this feels so strange. Like mixing chicken noodle soup, Froot Loops, and iced tea in the same bowl.

I wish Nick could be here with me this week. That would be so awesome. He told me last night that he thinks I have a fifty-fifty shot at winning, which is pretty cool. Considering I only have a five percent shot based on the math, I'll take fifty-fifty any day.

"If it's truly a random drawing," Nick said, "then you should be smarter than most of the other kids and probably more athletic, too. Plus, with your high-level spy skills, I think you've got a pretty good chance."

I know he was trying to trigger me by joking about the secret agent stuff, but truth is, I think it's going to be an advantage.

When Nick said I had a fifty-fifty shot I really believed it, and I was probably feeling better than I had all week about my chances. But right now, I'm feeling overwhelmed and nervous and there's even a small part of me that wants to tell Fiona Firestone, "thanks, but no thanks." How is that even possible?

Speaking of Fiona Firestone, when am I going to meet her? I assume she'll be there all week to oversee the competition, but there's no guarantee of that. Maybe I won't see her at all. Or maybe she'll be the one to greet me when I step out of the car.

"Lake!" Mom says as we turn a corner around a giant row of shrubs, "There it is, that must be it!"

She's right.

There, down a long driveway at least three football fields long, sits a building that is even more impressive to see in person than on television. A building that is waiting for me to arrive.

The Firestone School.

I'm finally here.

11

_____

After waiting in a line of cars for another ten minutes, we pull up to the front door.

As my mom and Viv get out of the car, a man in a tuxedo opens the back door for me and peers in. "Lake Mason, my name is Charles Lincoln, head butler here at The Firestone School. On behalf of Fiona Firestone I'd like to welcome you to The Firestone Fires. We've been waiting for you."

He's tall and skinny with the kind of face that should probably have a mustache on it, but doesn't. I get out of the car and shake his extended hand as a short, bearded man, also in a tuxedo, grabs my suitcase out of the trunk.

"This is my assistant butler, Mr. Evan Hillit. He'll grab your bags for you if you'll just follow me." Mr. Lincoln says as he waves me toward the stairs leading up to the massive front doors. I follow him for a few steps until I hear a commotion behind me.

"Excuse me, I'm going in to register with my son," Mom is saying to the bearded guy holding my suitcase.

"Ma'am, only students are allowed into the building," Mr. Hillit tells her, but she's not having it.

"Let. Me. Through." Mom says in a tone I've only heard a few times before. That dude better be careful.

Mr. Lincoln walks toward her. "Mrs. Mason, what seems to be the problem here?"

"I was told on the phone that I could stay with my son for registration."

"Yes, ma'am, I was the one who told you that, only I believe the words I used were 'up to registration,' and not 'for registration.'" He's talking to Mom like she's an eight year old and I don't think she cares for it. "Mrs. Mason, I'm afraid this is where you must say goodbye."

The line of cars behind us is at least ten deep, and the last thing I want is to be at the center of viral video before I've even stepped inside. Mom's not usually one for creating drama, but she seems ready to cause a scene right now.

"Get out of my way, Beardy!" she says to Mr. Hillit, who is standing between her and the front door.

"But, Mr. Lincoln said that you have to stay—"

"I heard what Mr. Lincoln said," Mom interrupts him. "Is this your first day on the job or something?"

"No, Ma'am," Beardy says, cracking a proud smile. "This is my second year working at The Firestone School."

"Well, I think Fiona Firestone needs to retrain her butlers on guest hospitality," Mom snaps in Mr Lincoln's direction.

"Your suggestion is noted, Mrs. Mason," he responds, as I step in between the three of them to diffuse the situation.

"Mom, it's fine," I say. "Let's just say goodbye here so you and Viv can get over to the mall."

"A fine idea from your son," Mr. Lincoln says. Mom snaps him another dirty look.

"Are you sure, Lake?" she asks me.

"Yeah, I'm sure," I say, and it dawns on me that I actually am sure. Whatever nervousness I was feeling a few minutes ago is gone. "I've got my stuff and I'm ready to go. You guys go have fun and I'll see you in a week or so."

"Okay," mom says. "If you're sure you're okay, we can go, but I'm not letting these guys decide that for you."

Part of me thinks she doesn't want to say goodbye, the other part of me thinks she just wants to pick a fight with Beardy and Mr. Lincoln. My money would be on Mom.

"Moooom," Viv chimes in from beside the car, "he says he's fine. Let's just go."

I'm still not sure Mom is convinced, so I take a few steps closer until she's just a few inches from me. "Mom, I'm ready to do this," I say, looking her right in the eyes. "I've been waiting for this for a long time, and I'm finally here. I'm gonna go in and do my best to win a scholarship."

There are small tears forming in Mom's eyes, but there's a smile on her face.

"Alright, Lake," she says. "I'm so proud of you."

"Thanks, mom, I'll see you in a week."

Mom gives me a hug as Viv gets into the car. Beardy is holding the door open for her.

"Vivian Mason, give your brother a hug before we leave," she says.

"Ugh, seriously, I already said bye," Viv sighs.

"No, you didn't," I smirk. I don't really want a hug from her, but it's worth putting up with it to see her this annoyed.

Viv comes over and gives me a hug and whispers, "Love you, Lake, don't pee your bed," softly enough that only I can hear. She breaks away and gets into the car before I can say anything in return.

"Mrs. Mason we have your contact information and we will reach out later in the week with a specific pick-up time." Mr. Lincoln says through the open passenger window. "Have a safe trip home."

I give them one last wave before they drive off.

"Now then, Lake, are you ready to go inside?" Mr. Lincoln says in my direction, but I'm not at the bottom of the steps where he thinks I am. I'm at the top of the stairs at the front door.

"Oh, let Mr. Hillit get that for you," he says, but it's too late. I've already got it open as Mr. Lincoln and Beardy skip up the steps behind me.

I step inside, my eyes adjusting to the lack of light in the massive lobby. Behind me, the giant front door slams shut.

12

"Welcome inside, Lake," Mr. Lincoln says. "We're so happy you're here, and we wish you all the best in this week's competition."

"Thanks," I say.

"Just make your way to the end of the hall and go right." Mr. Lincoln says pointing over my shoulder. "Dr. Vanguard should be waiting by the check-in stations, and she'll help you with your ID Band, your blood draw, and your facial scan. Once you're finished there you can head through the red doors and into the Great Room."

"Blood draw?" I ask.

"Just a little something to make sure you're in good health for The Fires. Don't worry—you won't feel a thing," Beardy says in a voice that sounds way more like a squeaky duck than a human.

"Yeah, that's what they always say about needles," I respond. I'm not a fan. At all.

"Well, this will be a little bit different," Mr. Lincoln says, "but you'll find that out soon enough. Alright, off you go, we'll see you in a bit."

Mr. Lincoln gives me a nudge in the direction of the Great Room, and as I start heading that way I hear Beardy squeak, "Best of luck!" in a tone that catches me off guard. Why would he say it like that? It was the same tone you'd use if your buddy was about to try to ask out the cutest girl in the school. Sort of like, "Good luck, dude, but luck won't be nearly enough. You need a miracle."

I notice that Mr. Lincoln makes a face at Beardy as they head back outside. "Beardy," I think to myself. I can't believe mom called him that to his face. But as far as I'm concerned, that's Mr. Hillit's new name forever in my book.

I make my way down the hall and to the right, and I see the ID stations, five on either side of a set of red doors like Mr. Lincoln had said. There are three kids checking in on the right side, at Stations 6, 8, and 9. To the left there's only one station in use, Station 2.

Standing at a desk off to the right is a tall woman with glasses and blond hair pulled up in a ponytail. I assume she's Dr. Vanguard.

"Lake Mason?" she asks as I approach her desk. She asks it like it's a question, but I'm pretty sure she knows exactly who I am.

"Yes, are you Dr. Vanguard?" I ask.

"Oh, you can call me Dr. V, honey," she says, hammering away at her keyboard at light speed. Her hands are moving so fast, it's almost comical.

"I think that's the fastest I've ever seen anyone type," I say, because I don't know what else to say.

"Thanks," she says without looking up. "Okay, dear, it appears everything is all set with your file, so you can go ahead and check in at one of the open stations."

I head over to one of the stations, but then I stop when I get an idea.

"Dr. V?" I ask.

"Yes?" she says, finally looking up at me.

"If you're going to have to take a blood sample, can you just do it now and get it out of the way? I kind of hate needles."

"Honey," she says laughing, "I'm not that kind of doctor."

I'm confused.

"I'm the Head of Security here at the school," she says. "Graduated with a Minor in Forensic Science, a Major in Cyber Security, and a PhD in Computer Science. I'm a code doctor, not a needle doctor."

"Oh, okay," I say. I'm still confused as to who's going to take my blood, but I guess I'll figure it out.

I decide on Station 4, and as I step up to it the girl at Station 2 turns her head toward me. I notice she's wearing wireless earbuds, which explains why this end of the hallway is so quiet. We make eye contact for a couple seconds and I'm momentarily stunned by how pretty she is. She smiles at me, I smile back, and then she turns back to her screen.

For a split second I forget where I am, and that I'm about to enter The Firestone Fires. All I can think about is how cute she is, and I wonder if she'd look over again if I tried to get her attention. I glance her way, but she's focused on her touchscreen, so I return to mine.

Only then do I realize the screen has a message for me: *Please put your earbuds in, Lake. Then press the green button.*

I follow the instructions and press the green button and Fiona Firestone's face fills the screen.

"Welcome to The Firestone Fires, Lake, I'm so glad you're here all the way from Glenville."

This is amazing. I can't believe Fiona Firestone knows my name and where I'm from...

"If at any point during this orientation video you need to pause, simply remove your earbuds until you're ready to resume. In a minute, you'll enter the Great Room just inside those red doors where you will meet the rest of the students competing this week. But before you head inside, there are a few quick things we need to cover. The first, and most important, is that you must always listen to instruc-

tions and follow them accordingly. Some competitors will be eliminated this week because they weren't listening carefully. Don't let that be you."

I glance to my left to see that the pretty girl is still at her station. To my right I see that two of the other kids must have gone inside. There's only one kid over there on Station 8.

"The first thing we'd like to do is some quick biometrics. In fact, while I spoke that last sentence we took a 3D scan of your head, face, and neck down to one one-hundredth of an inch accuracy."

Oh, that's cool, I guess. Weird, but cool.

"Next, we will need a quick blood sample. Please place your index finger on the yellow circle to your left and await further instructions."

Great, I guess I'm not avoiding a needle today, after all. Well, I guess now is not the time to be scared, especially if that girl is looking over here. I place my finger on the yellow circle and feel something slightly brush it.

"What you just felt was the world's most cutting-edge blood testing technology. A needle prick so fast and non-intrusive, you probably had no idea we were collecting a microscopic sample. But we did."

Wait, what? No way they just got a blood sample.

"That's what we do here at The Firestone School: we push the limits of what's possible. If that excites you, if you want to be a part of creating the future of this world, then you're in the right place."

I pick up my hand to examine my finger and I can't see anything resembling a needle prick. The touch was so light and quick I don't even know where to search for the puncture mark.

"Crazy, right?" a voice says behind me. I turn around to see the blond girl.

"Hi," she says, putting out her hand. "I'm Haley Jenson."

13

I take out my earbuds to introduce myself.

"Hey, I'm Lake. Lake Mason," I say, slightly impressed with myself for not sounding as nervous as I am. "Yeah, I can't believe they actually got any blood from that."

"I know, right?" she says. She holds up her left index finger and as she does I notice a strange bracelet on her wrist.

"Well, you better get back to Fiona Firestone," she says. "Maybe I'll see you inside?"

"Okay, yeah," I say. "I'll definitely be ... looking for you."

"Okay," Haley says, smiling. "Good luck this week!" She walks up to one of the red doors, opens it, and disappears inside.

"What did you just say?" I whisper under my breath. "I'll definitely be looking for you? What am I, a creepy detective in a bad movie?" I shake my head and roll my eyes at myself.

Suddenly I realize there are two kids about ten feet away staring at me like I'm talking to myself, which, I guess I am. I put my earbuds back in and return my focus to the screen.

"Welcome back, Lake. Now then, there are one hundred competitors here at the school this week for The Fires, of which you are one. Eliminations will begin tomorrow morning, so again, I urge you to

pay close attention to all of my instructions and do your best to advance as far as you can. Is all that clear?"

I stand in silence for a few seconds until I realize that the video of Fiona is actually waiting for me to respond. I'm not really used to talking back to a screen.

"Umm ... yup, all clear?"

"Good," she continues. *"The last thing you'll need before I send you inside is your ID Band. Please place your left wrist on the green circle."*

I slowly pick up my arm and place my hand on the green circle. Before it even touches the surface a shiny thin band pops out and clasps itself tightly to my wrist. I pull my arm back instantly, mostly just as a reflex, and check it out. It looks just like the bracelet Haley was wearing.

"That is your ID Band. It will be your companion throughout The Fires. It will help with directions, it will update your status in the competition, and sometimes it will even be the key you need to move on. You can take it off when you sleep, but otherwise you should have it on at all times."

I run my finger and thumb around the circumference of it. It's smooth to the touch, and somehow the perfect fit. It's too snug to slide around on my arm, but not so tight to be uncomfortable. There's a small button the size of a tic-tac mint on the underside of the bracelet that I'm assuming is the release to take it off.

"Speaking of being the key," Fiona continues, *"now that you're wearing your band, the red doors of The Great Room will unlock as you grab the door handle. There are so many interesting people here, I strongly suggest you introduce yourself to as many fellow competitors as you can before tomorrow's eliminations. Now then, please proceed into the Great Room."*

The screen goes dark and I remove my earbuds. At the other Stations, the two kids who were staring at me a few minutes ago are now staring at their fingers, wondering if their blood had really just been sampled. Three other kids are headed our way down the hall, ready to start their check-in.

"Alright, let's do this, Lake," I say to myself and step up to the red doors. I reach out and grab the door handle, but it won't turn. I jiggle it and try a little harder, but still, nothing. The door won't budge.

I look over at Dr. V to see if she can help me, maybe she's supposed to unlock the doors or something? She's got her head down torturing her keyboard again, but just as I'm about to say something I remember what Fiona had hinted at just a minute ago.

The ID Band unlocks the door. I was using the wrong hand.

With my left hand I grab the door handle, and it easily unlatches.

I open the door and step inside the Great Room.

14

The first thing that every great secret agent does when they enter a new place is to "case the room," so that's what I'm doing from the moment I walk into the Great Room.

Why they call it "casing," I have no idea, but I know you've got to examine everything in and around a room as you walk in. You want to eliminate surprises.

After two or three scans of the room I'm pretty sure Fiona Firestone isn't here yet. The room is mostly filled with other seventh graders, plus a few adults in tuxedos scattered around with trays of food and drinks.

There has to be at least seventy-five kids already in here, which means I'm one of the last to arrive. Most of the kids are huddled in groups, talking and laughing with a cup of lemonade or fruit punch in their hands. They all seem more friendly and outgoing than me, but I guess that's nothing new.

There's one group in particular that I keep coming back to as I hang by myself in the corner. A blond kid wearing a white puffy vest and bright white sneakers is talking to four or five others, who are clearly enjoying his storytelling. Everyone's laughing, and they all seem really comfortable around each other. I can't imagine ever feeling like that in a room full of people I just met.

"Hey, dude, what's your name?" a voice behind me says.

Startled, I turn around to see a huge grin on the face of a kid that's a few inches taller than me. He's got glasses on and a tightly faded afro that makes him seem even taller.

"Hey. I'm Lake," I say. "You kinda scared me."

"Sorry, didn't mean to," he says. "I'm Zig Simmons, but you can call me Ziggy. Or Zig, I don't care. Did you say your name was Lake? That's cool."

"Thanks. My parents were going to call me Brooke if I was a girl, but then I came out a boy, so they decided to stick with the water theme."

"No, Lake's a cool name." Zig says. "I like it."

"Yeah, better than Ocean, I guess."

"So, you just get here?"

"Yeah, a few minutes ago. What about you?"

"Been here for a couple hours, but they only let us come into the Great Room about thirty minutes ago," he says. "Kinda getting bored actually. I'm ready for this competition to start."

"Yeah, same," I say.

"So where you from?"

"I'm from Glenville, about two hours from here."

"Oh, nice," Zig says. "Third oldest town in our state! Established in 1897."

"Wait, how did you know that? You're not from Glenville, are you?"

"Nah, I'm from Ash City. I just know stuff. Trivia's kind of my thing. You got a thing?"

"Do I have a thing?"

"Yeah, what are you into?" Zig asks. "Sports? Movies? Trivia? Video games?"

I do have a thing, but I'm not about to tell some kid I just met that I'm going to be a secret agent someday. "I don't know, normal kid stuff, I guess. Sports, video games, messing around with computers."

"How crazy was it to have your name chosen last week?" Zig asks.

"Oh man, so crazy, right?" I smile. "I still can't believe I'm here."

"Well, believe it, dude. You're here and it's about to go down."

A server comes by with a plate of food options: meatballs on toothpicks, crackers with shrimp on them, and orange cubes of cheese.

"The shrimp is so good—you gotta have some," Zig says.

"No thanks," I say. "I hate seafood. Especially shrimp."

"Your loss," Zig says stuffing two into his mouth at the same time. "You know which country the US gets most of its imported shrimp from?"

"No, but I'm guessing you do?" I say.

"India," Zig says.

"Interesting," I say, which is a lie.

"You want to walk around?" Zig asks. "I'll introduce you to some people."

"Nah, I'm good."

"Seriously?" Zig says. "You don't want to meet people?"

"I mean, I'll meet them eventually. I'm just not big on small talk and introductions and all that."

"Ha, dude, you're funny." Zig says. "Don't like to meet people? Hahaha."

I have no idea why Zig thinks this is funny.

"Well, you need to get over that," Zig says, hitting me in the arm with the back of his hand. "Besides, didn't you catch what Fiona said in the orientation video when she strongly suggested that you meet people tonight?"

"Oh, right," I say. "She did say something about introducing yourself to as many people as possible. You think there's gonna be a test or something?"

"I don't know, maybe," Zig says. "Maybe you'll have to match up names and faces or something? But test or not, you gotta meet some people while you're here. Follow me."

Next thing I know I'm following Zig who is walking right toward Blond White Vest and his merry group of friends. "C'mon, let's go meet these kids," he says. "They seem like they're having a good time."

Introducing myself to this circle of kids is the last thing I want to do in this room right now. I'd rather eat shrimp off the floor while Mr. Lincoln and Beardy take blood from both my arms with giant needles.

But like it or not, it looks like Zig isn't going to give me any choice.

15

"Hey guys, I'm Zig," Ziggy says, forcing his way into the small circle of kids we've just approached.

The group suddenly gets silent, and everyone looks at White Vest to know what to do next. This moment of awkwardness is exactly why I don't introduce myself to people.

"Are you gonna tell us your names?" Zig asks, unfazed.

"I'm Hudson," White Vest finally says.

"See, that wasn't that hard!" Zig says. "This is Lake, by the way," Zig says patting me on the shoulder. "Anyone else have a name?"

"This is Meatball," Hudson says, pointing to the kid to his right, who is holding a small plate with a few meatballs on it. This makes the other kids in the circle laugh, including Meatball.

"I kind of had an accident," Meatball says staring at a huge red stain on his shirt that seconds ago was hidden by his hands. It looks like he dropped a meatball on himself and spent ten minutes rubbing it into the fabric as hard as he could. That would suck. "My name's actually Derek," Meatball says.

"Yeah, but we like Meatball better," Hudson says. "Isn't that right, Meatball?"

Meatball shrugs and uses a toothpick to put another meat-ball in his mouth, this time without dropping it.

One by one the other three kids say their names, and I do my best to remember them. Adam is tall with spiked hair, Laura looks like a fish that's about to sneeze, and Erik has a wispy little mustache that he probably should start shaving because it looks terrible.

"I'm from Ash City, and Lake's from Glenville," Zig says.

"Isn't Glenville close to where Fiona Firestone grew up?" Meatball asks.

"Yeah," I say. "I live, like, thirty minutes from the house she grew up in."

"Dude, that's awesome," Meatball says. "I'm the biggest Fiona Firestone fan in the world."

"Oh, that's cool, I'm a big fan too," I say, relieved that there's at least one other person here who appreciates how amazing it is to be at her school.

"Yeah," Meatball continues, "still can't believe I'm actually inside the school built by the most influential creator in the world."

"Um, second most influential creator in the world," the sneezing fish girl says. When we all dart our eyes at her she says, "What? There's nothing wrong with being second."

"Who's your number one?" Meatball asks, no longer smil-ing. "And please don't tell me his initials are R.B."

"Of course it's Rogan Bosch," she says. "He might not get as much publicity as Fiona Firestone, but he's smarter, richer, and will eventually be known as a better inventor."

"Fiona Firestone doesn't care about money," Meatball says, his face starting to match the stain on his shirt. "Her inventions make the world better. Rogan Bosch will never match the posi-tive influence that she has."

"Here we go with the 'positive influence' argument again," Laura says rolling her eyes. "Next you're going to tell me that

Rogan Bosch is only working on a weather device because he heard Fiona Firestone was working on one, too?"

"It's the truth, isn't it?" Meatball says. "He always tries to copy the stuff she invents."

"You Fiona Firestone stans are all the same," Laura sighs.

"Did you know that the word, stan, became a slang synonym for someone who is a big fan of something because of the Eminem song by the same name from the year 2000?" Zig interjects.

"Wait, what weather device?" I ask, not wanting the subject to be changed.

"Rumor has it that both of them are making progress on a device that can control the weather over a very small area," Meatball says. "Like, over a city park or a baseball field."

"Nobody can control the weather," Zig says, echoing what I was thinking.

"Well, technically it's not about controlling weather," Laura says. "It's about rain prevention and temperature control in a micro-climate. Creating a sort of controlled bubble over a small area."

"So, you know, it would be huge for outdoor weddings and sporting events," Meatball says.

"Hm, like the rain delays that affected the World Series in 1925 and 2016," Zig says. How he is able to remember those dates I have no idea.

"Um, sure, if you say so." Meatball says.

"The flip side," Laura says, "is that in the wrong hands the technology could be used as a weapon of mass destruction. Entire communities could be forced into a drought. Neighborhoods could experience severe winter-like conditions in the middle of summer. Plants, animals, and eventually people could die. It's kind of a big deal."

"Right, didn't think of that," Zig says.

"It's huge," Meatball says, looking right at Laura, "and that's why Fiona Firestone needs to figure it out first."

"Listen," Laura says, "I don't hate Fiona Firestone. She's fine —she's just overrated. But I'm happy to be here at her school, and I can't wait to win one of these five scholarships."

"Alright," Hudson says, "enough of Nerd War III. You guys are putting me to sleep."

"Yeah, you clowns are boring," Adam says, just as a loud voice booms over the sound system.

"Competitors, may I please have your attention!" Mr. Lincoln is standing behind the podium near the front of the Great Room. Beardy is a few feet behind him on his right. There's no sign of Fiona Firestone anywhere.

"Most of you came with me about a half an hour ago on the short tour I gave of the school," Mr. Lincoln continues. "But for those of you who missed that, I'm going to give one more. Follow me out these doors for a quick tour and we'll be back here in the Great Room in about ten minutes to finish things up for the evening."

Mr. Lincoln walks off the stage and heads out the west exit of the Great Room. Without saying anything to each other, Ziggy and I follow right behind him.

16

———

There are about twenty-five of us crammed into the hallway as Mr. Lincoln tries to get our attention.

"Please quiet down so everyone can hear," he says. "I just want to give you a quick overview of the school so you can get your bearings."

I notice that the cute blond girl from check-in is in out here too, but I remind myself to stay focused. A good secret agent needs to know his surroundings.

"To my right and your left is the Southwest Wing of the school," Mr. Lincoln says. "There are some offices and classrooms here, as well as the South Patio and South Lawn. Our Computer Science Labs are in that direction as well."

Wait, did he just say "Computer Science Labs"? As in, there are more than one? Crapville Middle doesn't even have a single computer for students to use, and this place has more than one room full of them?

"You are free to check out anything in the Southwest Wing at any time, but for now we'll keep moving."

At any time? I assumed we'd have a curfew, but maybe not?

"Behind me," Mr. Lincoln says, briefly spinning around, "

are the bunk rooms where you'll sleep. Boys are straight ahead, and girls are off to the left."

"I hope the rooms are nice," Zig whispers to me.

"Gotta be, right?"

Mr. Lincoln takes off at a brisk pace and we follow him down the hallway.

"The Rec Wing is through these double doors," he says pointing to his right. "We'll open that up to all of you for free time at some point this week. Tons of games and activities—it's really quite impressive."

I laugh to myself at the thought of Crapville Middle School having a whole wing dedicated to games. They used to have half a gymnasium, but they found traces of black mold in it last year. I've heard it's been closed off to students ever since.

Mr. Lincoln leads us down the long hallway that runs just outside the north wall of the Great Room, calling out rooms one by one as we walk by them. "There are restrooms here, this is the laundry room, and here we have a little observatory," he says as he stops beside a small space with couches and a giant glass wall that looks outside.

"Fiona Firestone is really into birds, so we have a small bird sanctuary set up outside this room with bird baths, feeders, and specific plant life that attracts them," he says. "She even created a species recognition technology that picks up all the visiting birds on camera and displays what kind they are and all sorts of information about them on the monitors there."

"Whoa," Zig says, loud enough that everyone looks at him.

"Yes, it is impressive," Mr. Lincoln says as he starts walking again. "Speaking of impressive, *this* is the kitchen," he says, pausing in front of a set of swinging double doors a few feet further down the hall.

"We have an excellent chef here at The Firestone School," Mr. Lincoln says. "Chef Rachelle left an acclaimed restaurant in New York City just to work with Fiona Firestone. In fact, they've worked together to create a state-of-the-art brick oven that could revolutionize the pizza industry. It uses a proprietary combination of convection, conduction, and radiation to give you bubbly cheese and a perfectly crisp crust in half the time of a traditional brick oven."

"I just realized how hungry I am," I say to Zig.

"Take a peek in the windows as we walk by and you'll see it," Mr. Lincoln says as he starts walking again. "And if you're lucky enough to stick around after The Fires, you might actually get to taste why Chef Rachelle is the best."

As I walk by the kitchen doors I see the oven he was talking about. It's massive, and centered right in the middle of the kitchen. This must be a good gig for a chef to leave a New York City restaurant just to come work at a school.

"Behind me is the Northeast Wing of the school," Mr. Lincoln says, stopping at the end of the hallway. "Strictly off-limits to all of you, not that you could get into it even if you wanted to."

"What's in the Northeast Wing?" a voice behind me asks. I glance over my right shoulder to see that it's Laura, the Rogan Bosch fangirl.

"Some of our offices and other things you don't really need to know about," Mr. Lincoln says, slightly annoyed. "We also have a separate Security Wing off the southeast corner of the school. That is obviously off-limits as well, but none of you will have access to these areas, so you really don't need to worry about that."

I turn to look that way and realize Haley is standing right beside me. She catches me looking at her and she smiles, so I smile back.

"The only other thing down this hall that concerns you," Mr. Lincoln says pointing to his left, "is the nurse's station. Far end of the hallway, on your left. We will have a nurse on call at all times. If any medical issues arise, that's where to go. Other than that, I think that concludes our tour."

With that, he leads us back into the Great Room through

the east doors. As he does, I'm reminded that this isn't a museum or some high-tech office building, but a school that I have an actual chance of attending for the next six years of my life. I have a chance to trade awful cafeteria food, a moldy gym, and a pigeon infestation, for gourmet pizza, an entire game wing, and a high-tech bird observatory.

How can I go to Crattville Middle School after seeing this?

I can't. I won't. I came here to win and that's exactly what I'm going to do.

17

Zig and I file back into the Great Room, and I spot Hudson staring at me from across the room.

"Man, that was awkward earlier," I say.

"What, the tour?" Zig asks, confused.

"No," I say. "That whole conversation with Hudson and Meatball and that Laura girl."

"Yeah, that whole Fiona Firestone vs. Rogan Bosch thing was a bit too much for me," Zig says, "but don't worry about Hudson, he's harmless. Sometimes people try to pretend like they're too cool to make new friends, but it's an act. People need people, man—that's what my mom always says anyway."

"I guess," I say, not really buying it. I spot a row of chairs against the far wall and consider going over there to sit so I can avoid everyone. There's only one other kid over there, a guy with curly brown hair and cowboy boots, and he seems perfectly content not interacting with anyone. I'm sort of jealous.

But then I see her again, the cute blond girl from check-in and from the tour. She's over by the drink table, talking to a girl I haven't met yet.

Zig sees me looking her way. "You want to go meet her?" Zig asks, changing direction to head toward them.

"I already did," I say. "Her name is Haley."

"Look at you!" Zig says. "Mister Outgoing! Did you meet her friend, too?"

"No, not yet."

"Well, let's go," Zig says, and before I can object his arm is around my shoulder leading us right toward them.

"Hey, ladies," Zig says, way smoother than I ever could. "Haley, I think you know my buddy Lake."

Haley smiles. "I guess you weren't lying when you said you'd be looking for me."

"I mean, I wasn't really looking for you," I stammer. "I mean, I wasn't not looking for you, either, but yeah ..." I trail off, not sure how to finish the sentence.

I can feel Zig glaring at me, wondering why I'm so bad at talking.

"Well, I'm glad you came over," Haley says, bailing me out. "You guys want some drinks?"

She grabs two cups of punch off the table and hands them to us. "Oh, by the way, this is Jess."

"You guys are cute," Jess says, totally taking me off guard. "I mean, not you and Haley," she says, correcting my misunderstanding. "Well, you and Haley might be cute together too, but I meant you and Ziggy. You know, the short white, shy kid and the tall, friendly African-American kid. You guys could totally be buddies in a TV show or something."

"Uhh, thanks?" Ziggy says to Jess. "And you girls could have your own show, too. I guess Haley would be the nice quiet one, and you'd be the loud, likable one whose mouth is always getting her into trouble."

"Ouch," Jess says.

"Hey, I said likable," Ziggy clarifies.

"Well, I've been called worse than loud," Jess says. "What

can I say, I just own it at this point. My parents always say that I should have been born with a volume knob."

"My parents used to tell me something similar," Zig laughs. "On car rides they would say that they wished I had a mute button."

"Did your parents stay in town last night or did they drop you off and head home?" Haley asks Zig.

"They drove right back," Zig says.

"Yeah, my mom did too," I say. I guess her and Viv went to the mall first, but that doesn't seem like a detail anyone would care about.

"Did your dad have to work?" Jess asks.

The question catches me off guard, and before I can think, I just blurt out, "No, he passed away."

"Oh my gosh, I'm so sorry," Jess says, the color leaving her face.

"It's okay," I say. "It happened when I was five. It's been a long time."

"Sorry, Lake," Haley says.

"Yeah, that sucks, dude, I'm sorry," Ziggy adds.

"Do you remember much about him?" Jess asks.

"I have some memories, yeah," I say, "but it was a long time ago. I'm good, honestly. It's not something I talk about much."

A few seconds of silence go by, but I'm not sure how to gracefully change the subject.

"Speaking of good," Ziggy finally says, "have you guys tried the shrimp? They are *so* good."

"Hard pass," Haley says. "I'm actually allergic to shellfish."

"Oh, really?" Zig says. "You know what's interesting, 2.3 percent of the population is allergic to shellfish."

"That's not interesting" Jess says.

"I think it's interesting," Haley says. Even her voice is kind of cute.

I finish my punch as Mr. Lincoln's voice comes over the loudspeaker.

"Students, please wrap up your conversations and turn your attention this way. It's been a long day for some of you, and tomorrow will be a big day for all of you. Welcome again to The Firestone School for The Firestone Fires."

As he announces this all the kids in the room clap and holler, and I lean over and whisper to Zig, "I guess Fiona's not making an appearance tonight."

"Guess not," he says to me as I put down my empty cup.

"In a moment," Mr. Lincoln continues, "you'll be dismissed to your bunk rooms. Rooms 1 through 5 are for the ladies, and Rooms 6 through 10 are for the gentlemen. Your ID Band will not only display your room assignment but will also be your entry key for accessing the room."

I glance down at the bracelet on my left hand, but there's nothing about a room assignment on it that I can see.

"Your wake-up call is at 7:15 a.m., and breakfast will be served in the cafeteria at 8:00 a.m. Good night and good luck, everyone."

Right as Mr. Lincoln finishes his sentence, I feel a buzz on my left wrist. I look at my ID Band, which now reads:

ROOM 8

"Okay, Room 8," I say to Zig.

"Room 6," Zig says back.

"That sucks," I say. It would have been nice to be in the same room.

Everyone makes their way out of the Great Room, and we follow the crowd down the hall. "I guess I'm this way," Ziggy says when he sees the sign for Room 6.

"Alright," I say, "see you in the morning."

"Yeah, let's save each other seats for breakfast, depending on who gets there first," Ziggy says.

"Okay, cool," I say.

I see the sign for Room 8 up ahead and, just as I'm starting to feel really good about where I'm at and what's about to go down, I realize what I just did.

I just drank two full cups of punch without thinking—way more than I should have.

If I wake up in a wet bed tomorrow morning, the first morning of The Firestone Fires, I'm going to die.

18

The moment I walk into our bunk room I'm shocked at how nice it is. Way better than any summer camp I've ever been to. I should have known. This is Fiona Firestone's school, after all.

There are ten of us to each room, at least until kids start getting eliminated, I guess—and the moment I walk in I'm so mad at myself for not hustling to get there sooner.

Most of the beds have already been claimed, so I throw my bag on an empty bed near the door. I was hoping to be only a few steps away from the bathroom for my late-night trips to pee, but it's too late for that now.

I already know I'm going to pee two or three times tonight before bed, in hopes of emptying myself out as much as possible. I got so distracted by Haley that I completely forgot one of my most critical missions of this whole experience:

DO NOT WET THE BED.

I was guzzling punch like a thirsty camel out there tonight. Gosh, what an idiot I can be sometimes. A good secret agent never loses sight of the mission.

As I head over to the bathroom, I check out who my roommates are. I recognize a few of them from earlier in the Great Room, but I don't know most of their names. Then I see who has the two beds closest to the bathroom: Hudson on the left and Meatball on the right.

"What's up, Flake," Hudson says.

"Isn't it Lake?" Meatball corrects him.

"Flake, Lake, whatever," Hudson says.

I walk past without saying anything, just a small smile and a little wave. I know Hudson is just trying to poke at me to see what I'll do. I've been around plenty of guys like him before. What makes some kids feel the need to push everyone else around a little to see who will push back? I don't get it.

In the movies the hero usually takes a stand and punches the bully in the nose to save the day, but this isn't the movies. In real life the bully gets back up and beats the living snot out of you. And then a few weeks later when your black eye has healed, he does it again. No thanks.

I use the bathroom and join the rest of my roommates setting up my bed and organizing my clothes for the morning. Mr. Lincoln's sidekick, Beardy, pops his head in our door and lets us know that our lights will automatically shut off in fifteen minutes. He pulls out his phone and swipes a few times and suddenly the huge screen on our wall wakes up and displays a countdown timer that is at 15:00 ... 14:59 ... 14:58 ...

We all finish getting our stuff set up with five minutes left, and Meatball suggests we go around the room and say our names and where we're from. That takes a few minutes, and while I'm sort of paying attention to what everyone is saying, I'm more focused on the countdown timer. With a minute left I head over to the bathroom to pee one more time.

"The Flake Man!" Hudson says as I walk by. I shake my head and roll my eyes, but don't say anything.

The lights go out just as I'm taking my ID Band off and getting into bed. After a few minutes of guys burping and making fake fart noises—I can make some of the best, by the way—things eventually get quiet in the room.

Before I fall asleep, I go over everything that happened today, something I do almost every night. I think every secret agent does something similar to this, where you process the day's events and think ahead to what your mission will look like for tomorrow.

As I go through the last twelve hours, I realize it was probably one of the craziest days of my life. Waking up at home, the nervous drive to the school, my mom making a scene at registration, Fiona Firestone's check-in video, getting my ID Band, and meeting Zig, Haley, and Jess. So much happened, and The Firestone Fires haven't even actually started yet.

Speaking of The Fires, what's my plan for tomorrow? I'm going to meet up with Ziggy for breakfast, make sure I eat enough to have energy for the day, and after that I have no idea. I don't know when the events will start or what they will be like, I just know I have to be ready.

I still can't believe that my name was pulled in the drawing and that I am here, at The Firestone School, with a shot at earning a scholarship. I can't blow this chance. I can't get distracted by Hudson and his antics or by Haley and her cute smile. I have to stay focused so I can win one of these five spots. Man, Haley's smile is really cute, though.

But first, I need a good night's sleep. And more importantly, I need to wake up dry in the morning.

I decide to get out of bed and pee one last time. I know there's probably nothing in there anymore, but even if it's just a few drops, it's worth it.

I quietly tiptoe into the bathroom, do my thing, and then head back to my bed. But as I walk past Hudson's bed my knee cracks.

I pause for a second. Maybe he didn't hear it.

I start walking back to my bed, and I hear Hudson rustling in his sheets.

"Peeing again, Flake?" he whispers loudly, sounding half-asleep. "What is wrong with you?"

I make a face at him that he can't see in the dark and get back into bed.

I drift off to sleep, praying that in the morning my sheets will be dry.

19

"Lake, wake up dude!"

"I'm up, I'm up," I say, which is only half true. It takes me a few seconds to remember I'm not at home, which explains why there's a goofy-looking kid standing over my bed.

"You got ten minutes until breakfast," Meatball says. "This is the third time I've tried to wake you up."

"Sorry," I say. "I sleep really hard."

At this point, I'm about seventy-five percent awake, which is usually the moment I realize that I either survived the night without taking a leak in my bed or I am soaking wet with pee.

I think I'm dry, and touching the leg of my pajama pants confirms it. Phew! First night was a success, and suddenly I'm filled with excitement about the day ahead.

I pop out of bed and quickly get ready, joining the rest of my roommates a few minutes later as we head down the hall to the Great Room for breakfast.

"Thanks for making sure I got up, Meatball," I say, before realizing I used the nickname Hudson gave him.

"I mean, Derek, right?" I correct myself.

"Oh, I don't care, you can call me Meatball," he says. "Derek is kind of a boring name. And no problem on the wake-up call. Hudson wanted us all to leave you alone so you overslept, but that would have sucked."

"Yeah, seriously," I say, annoyed that Hudson actually wanted me to miss breakfast. What if I got eliminated from the competition for missing a meal? I need to be better at waking up, and I need to keep an eye on Hudson.

"Well, thanks for looking out for me," I say. "I guess I owe you one."

We enter the Great Hall and I immediately see Ziggy sitting next to a few empty seats. He waves me over.

"Morning man, how'd you sleep?" Ziggy asks.

"So good I almost slept through breakfast," I say. "Meatball here kinda saved my butt."

"It took me three tries to get him out of dreamland," Meatball says.

"Where'd you get your food?" I ask Zig. He's got a heap of scrambled eggs, four strips of bacon, and three small pancakes all crowded onto his plate.

"Once you sit down a server will bring it over to you," he says, his mouth full of eggs. "It's so good. Do you know that an egg has about seventy-five calories and six grams of protein?"

"Ooh, tell me more, Wikipedia," Hudson says as he sits down across from us with his buddy Adam. "So, who's ready to go home today?" Hudson says, smiling.

"Not me," Ziggy says. "How'd you sleep last night, Hudson?"

Hudson makes a face like he just smelled a fart. "How did I sleep?" he says. "What kind of question is that? What are you, my dad?"

"Yeah, what a clown question," Adam says.

This doesn't faze Ziggy, who takes a huge bite out of a pancake.

"Well, I slept good," Meatball says. "Pretty sure I fell asleep in about ten seconds."

"Meatball, you know you were talking in your sleep last night?" Hudson says.

"Oh was I?" Meatball says, laughing. "My mom says I do that sometimes. I've never heard it—I'm usually sleeping."

"Yeah, I heard it too," Adam says. "It was weird, bro. You were saying all sorts of crazy things." Hearing the word "bro" makes me think of T.J., which makes me think of Nick. Man, I wish Nick was here for all of this.

"Do you remember what I was saying?" Meatball asks.

"Yeah," Adam says, "first you said something like 'The next dog is the real dog, then comes the ice cream dog.'"

This cracks everyone up, even Meatball. Well, most of us are laughing. Hudson still has that fart smell look on his face.

"What else did I say?" Meatball asks.

"I wish I could remember," Adam says. "Oh wait, right at the end you said something like, 'Bring me all of the shiny forks for battle' or something like that."

We bust out laughing again, just as a few servers show up and put plates in front of us. The smell of the food reminds me of how hungry I am.

"I got you, Meatball," I say, stabbing my eggs, "you can have my shiny fork for the battle once I'm done eating."

"By the way, Flake," Hudson says, "How many times did you get up to go to the bathroom last night? Was it seventeen or eighteen?"

"Eighteen times to pee!" Adam laughs. "What a clown!"

"It was at least eighteen," I say, going along with the joke in hopes that Hudson will let it go. "Tonight I'm gonna try for twenty."

"Hey, there's Haley and Jess," Zig says.

"Oh, are those their names," Meatball says. "Which one is the one on the right in the blue shirt?"

"That's Jess," Zig says. "Want me to introduce you to her?"

"Nah, I'm good," Meatball says. "I'm not great at talking to girls."

"Join the club," I say.

"Whatever," Zig says. "I think Haley thinks you're cute, Lake. She was being super nice to you last night."

"You guys have no idea how girls work, do you?" Hudson says, taking a big swig of milk and letting out a burp under his breath. "They don't fall in love with you in five minutes."

"Oh, you're an expert on girls, huh?" Zig snaps at him.

"Compared to you guys, yeah," Hudson says.

"Yeah, compared to you clowns," Adam chimes in for no reason. I think that's the third time he's used the word "clown" in the last five minutes.

Just then Haley and Jess walk right by our table holding glasses of orange juice. "Hey guys," Jess says.

"Jess, come here!" Ziggy says, getting them to stop. "Did you meet Derek yet? We call him Meatball. Meatball, this is Jess, and that's Haley."

"Nice to meet you, Meatball," Jess says with a smile.

"You too," Meatball says without looking up at her. I guess he wasn't kidding about not being great at talking around girls. Makes me feel a little better about my awkward interaction with Haley last night.

I look over at her to see if she's looking my way, and she is. We make eye contact for a second, but then we're both startled by the loud sound of someone tapping a microphone.

TAP TAP TAP. "Is this on? Okay, it is. Good morning competitors!" Mr. Lincoln says.

"As you finish your breakfast, I want to give you a brief rundown of what will be happening today. In a few minutes you'll all head back to your bunk rooms where we have some paperwork for you to fill out."

A few audible groans go up across the Great Room.

"I know, I know," Mr. Lincoln says, "no one likes paperwork, but it's something we must do. We'll get it all out of the way and then meet back here in the Great Room at 11:00 a.m., where we'll be joined by a very special individual."

The groans across the room are replaced by excited whispers.

"And then following this morning's event, you'll head back to your bunk rooms for lunch, followed by some afternoon lectures."

"Lectures?" I whisper to Zig. "Gross."

"Shut up, Flake," Hudson says, causing Adam to laugh. After a few cackles he whispers, "You're a clown," to me, which almost makes me laugh. This guy is obsessed with clowns, apparently.

"We'll see you back here, shortly," Mr. Lincoln says as he collects his papers and walks away from the microphone. He takes a few steps, but then he stops and heads back to the podium.

"Oh, one more thing," he says.

"Twenty of you will be going home before lunch."

20

W e had over two hours in our bunk room to fill out forms, but all anyone wanted to do was talk about the fact that twenty people are going home today.

The forms themselves weren't too bad. Lots of legal stuff that I just skimmed and signed. And even though Mr. Lincoln called it paperwork, there wasn't actually any paper. It was all on tablets that were sitting on our beds for us when we got back to our room.

Just before 11:00 a.m. we all filed back into the Great Room, where Mr. Lincoln was waiting to address us all.

"Welcome again to the Firestone Fires," Mr. Lincoln says. "I would like to finally introduce you to your host. She is widely recognized as one of the most brilliant minds on the planet, and she is the founder and creator of many things, including this school. And for those of you lucky enough to survive The Firestone Fires, she will be your headmaster during the upcoming school year."

"That's gonna be us," Ziggy whispers to me.

"Yup," I nod back.

"Ladies and gentlemen, please welcome Fiona Firestone!"

The sound of one hundred kids clapping and hollering fills

the Great Room as Fiona Firestone emerges and makes her way to the stage.

As the applause slowly dies down, the click clack of her high heels on the hardwood floor grows louder with each step. She's dressed in a scarlet red skirt and a white blouse, with red lipstick to match. The waves in her dark brown hair are bouncing on her shoulders as she ascends the platform.

She's always looked pretty on TV, but in person she's beautiful, even from fifty feet away.

"You see the birds?" Zig asks, just as I notice them. There, on a small perch behind her, are the two birds I saw on television during the drawing for The Fires.

"Finches, I think," Zig says. Of course he would know what kind of birds they are.

"Good morning, competitors," Fiona Firestone says, adjusting the microphone to the perfect position. "I hope you all slept well and enjoyed your breakfast earlier. For some of you, that will be the last meal you have here at The Firestone School."

We all kind of knew this was happening, but hearing it come out of her mouth gives it a heavier weight than I expected.

"The word 'proficient'," she continues, "is rarely used these days, and I find that sad. It's one of my favorite words because it sums up what we want in our students here at the school. To be proficient is to be accomplished and advanced, to be skillful at something to the point of mastery."

"Lake's proficient at peeing," Hudson says, just loud enough to get a few laughs.

"Take the Gentoo penguin," she continues. "They are one of my favorite bird species because they do one thing really well: they swim fast. Olympic swimmers top out around five miles per hour in the water, but a Gentoo penguin—despite being the third largest species of penguin—can reach speeds of up to twenty-two miles per hour. *That* is proficiency."

"Fascinating," Zig whispers. I'm not sure I agree.

"Unfortunately, some of you," Fiona Firestone says, "are not proficient but *deficient* in the art of listening, as was evidenced during last night's elimination event."

With that last sentence, my eyes get wider than I even thought was possible. Everyone else is equally stunned; suddenly the whole Great Room is buzzing.

"What does she mean by last night's event?" Meatball says.

"I don't know," Ziggy says, slightly panicked. "Did any of you guys leave your bunks for an event?"

Everyone at the table says no, as the sound of confused voices grows louder.

"Okay, quiet down everyone. Please, give me your silence and attention," she says trying to regain control of the room. "If you will all just quiet down I will explain."

It takes about fifteen seconds, but eventually the room gets as close to silent as it's going to get.

"As you will learn this week, The Firestone Fires have nothing to do with fire at all. If you were expecting torches or a fire walk, you're going to be disappointed. But just as fire refines things, this competition weeds out those of you who don't belong here. In the end, only those of you who deserve a scholarship to The Firestone School will be awarded one."

I shift uncomfortably in my seat, wondering where this is going.

"During your check-in yesterday evening, before you all entered the Great Room, I strongly suggested you meet as many fellow competitors as possible. And while some of you heeded my instructions, others completely ignored them. For twenty of you, that choice is why you will be going home this morning. Burned up in the first elimination of The Fires."

Oh crap, it sounds like we're about to be quizzed on who people are. I'm trying to think of how many names and faces I can remember. There was Hudson and his buddies, I think I can remember all of them. I know most of the guys from my room last night, and then there's Haley and Jess.

But wait, why does it even matter how many names I know right now if the event was last night? I'm so confused.

"On the screens beside me," she continues, "will be your ranking from last night's event—an event that you all participated in without even knowing it." Fiona is smiling now—clearly, she's enjoying this.

"Last night's meet and greet here in the Great Room was a little bit more than just a meet and greet. It was a chance for you to show me that you take my words seriously, and that you value the importance of connecting with other people."

I look around at the rest of the kids at our table and everyone has the same blank gaze on their face. Well, everyone except Hudson, who seems to be enjoying the tension of the moment. No one wants to be sent home on the first morning of The Firestone Fires. Imagine having that conversation with kids at school next month.

"How long did I last? Well, ummm, about twelve hours." Ugh. The thought of having to go to Crapville Middle School to tell everyone that I didn't even last a day in The Fires puts a huge lump in my throat.

"You see," she continues, "one of the features of your ID Band is advanced GPS and proximity technology. I know exactly how much time you spent in the Great Room last night, and I know how much of that time you spent by yourself instead of interacting with other students like I told you to do."

Oh no. Fiona Firestone emphasized two things in that orientation video: meet as many people as possible, and don't ignore my advice.

I think I failed at both of them—and I think I'm about to be sent home.

21

I woke up this morning thinking The Firestone Fires
hadn't started yet, but little did I know the first challenge
was already finished before I fell asleep.

I run my finger over the shiny band on my left wrist and it's
no longer a cool accessory. I'm kind of mad at it, because the
information it gave to Fiona Firestone last night might be my
downfall.

She clears her throat and continues.

"If you did what I suggested in the orientation video," she
says, "you have nothing to worry about. But if you were off on
your own or didn't feel like meeting anyone, you have no one to
blame but yourself. The first rule of this school is that we're
better together than we are on our own."

I'm sweating more and more with each sentence, trying to
think about how many people I actually interacted with last
night in the Great Room. Ziggy was the first person I talked to,
and after that maybe seven or eight other people? Is that it? Did
I not interact with ninety other kids last night? I can't believe
how dumb that was.

"Now I know what some of you are thinking," she says, "that
this isn't fair, because some of you were only in the Great Room

for thirty minutes, but others of you were there for a full hour. But rest assured, Dr. V and I have developed an algorithm that takes all of the data into account and gives me a true picture of who was interacting with others and who wasn't, all prorated based on the actual time you spent in the Great Room."

"We started with one hundred competitors last night," she continues, "in a moment we'll be down to eighty. Twenty of you have been eliminated because of your self-absorbed, Lone Ranger, I-can-do-this on my own attitude."

"Wow, that's a harsh way to put it," Zig says to me, but I'm too nervous to even respond.

"In thirty seconds the full rankings for last night's event will appear on the screens beside me," Fiona Firestone says, "and your ID Bands will display your ranking."

I nervously tap my ID Band, as if giving it some attention might change the results that it's about to show me.

"If you see a number between eighty-one and one hundred, you've been eliminated. Please see Mr. Lincoln in the back of the room to arrange your departure. The rest of you can head back to your bunk rooms for lunch, followed by afternoon lectures. Good luck."

She steps away from the mic and heads off the stage, her two finches flying right behind her. On the screens, a giant counter appears, counting down 0:30 ... 0:29 ...

"I'm out, dude." I say to Zig. "The bottom twenty going home? I don't think I'm gonna to make it."

"Nah man, I think we're good," Zig says. "We talked to a bunch of people."

"You did, maybe," I say, my voice jumping up an octave. "But I didn't talk to anyone when I first got there. You were the first person I talked to!"

0:20 ... 0:19 ...

"Yeah, but I introduced you to Hudson, Meatball, Adam, Laura. Then we talked to Haley and Jess, too!" Zig says.

"Yeah, but that's *it* for me," I say. "How many people did you meet before I got there?" I ask Zig.

0:11 ... 0:10 ...

Zig cringes. "A lot, dude."

He's not gonna say it, but I think he knows he's safe and I'm not.

0:06 ... 0:05 ...

"Well," I say, "I think I'm done. First day and I'm going home."

0:02 ... 0:01 ...

The countdown hits zero and I close my eyes, both hands clenched into fists.

I feel the buzz on my wrist, but I still can't look. I don't want to see it. I don't want to see the number.

"42!" Meatball says, "Yes!"

"Whooooo," Zig exhales loudly. "71!"

Okay, now I know I'm going home. If Zig came in seventy-first, I've got to be in the bottom three. Maybe even dead last.

"Dude, seventy-one!" Zig says again, only louder.

"I know," I say, finally opening my eyes. "I heard you the first time. Good job, man."

"No, *you*, you idiot," Zig says, punching me in the chest. "*You* got 71. You're safe! Check your wrist!"

I look down and sure enough, the ID Band says 71. I let out a huge breath of air and my mouth stays open. I can't believe I'm still in it. I can't believe I'm not going home.

"Ziggy," I finally say, "you saved me, man."

"What are you talking about?" he says.

"I would have been dead last if it wasn't for you coming up to say hi to me and dragging me around to meet people last night."

"Whatever, man, it's cool," Ziggy laughs. "I'm just glad you're still in it."

"What did you get, anyway?" I ask. "What was your rank?"

Ziggy holds up his ID Band which is displaying a single digit, the number 5.

"Fifth!" I say, "that's amazing!"

"My mom was right, man," Ziggy says.

"About what?"

"Remember what I told you last night when we were walking around?"Ziggy says.

"She was right, man, people need people."

22

The twenty eliminated kids say their goodbyes and slouch out of the Great Room. Most of them are keeping it together, but a few are in tears.

None of my new friends are going home, so that's cool, but two of the kids in our bunk room finished in the bottom twenty, so they're gone. I also see the curly-haired kid in cowboy boots walking out with Mr Lincoln toward the exit. Last night I was jealous of him because he was sitting by himself. This morning, not so much.

We head back to our rooms where lunch is waiting for us, and then it's on to our lectures for the afternoon. The last thing I thought we'd be doing at The Firestone Fires was sitting in lectures, but at this point I've learned I can throw all my expectations out the window.

The first lecture we have to sit through is all about Fiona Firestone's life. Where she grew up, where she went to school, when she fell in love with birds, and how she became the world-famous inventor we know today. I'm not gonna lie, it's a little weird.

Beardy is the one presenting, and by "presenting," I mean,

he is just reading off his notes the entire time. He apologized for not knowing the material better, but he said that this was his first time teaching the lecture because Mr. Lincoln decided last week that he didn't want to teach them anymore.

The worst part of this lecture is Beardy's voice, which sounds like a cross between a dying mouse and the high-pitched squeal of someone getting kicked in the privates. He's a big guy, but he's got a tiny voice.

I'm sitting between Jess and Meatball, and I'm not too happy about it. As we filed into the lecture hall I tried to stay as close to Haley as possible so we would sit next to each other, but at the last second Meatball butted in between the two of us, so now she's on his other side. The funny thing is, Meatball probably wants to trade seats with me as much as I do, so he could be sitting next to Jess. But switching now would be way too obvious.

Beardy wraps up the Fiona presentation and lets us know that our second lecture will begin in ten minutes. We're dismissed into the foyer, where we find the largest selection of candy bars, chips, and soda I've ever seen. I laugh to myself as I grab a Twix and a Coke because this would never happen at Crapville. I could get used to this.

"What did you guys think of that?" Zig asks, taking a bite of a Snickers.

"So good," Meatball says. "I mean, I already knew most of it, but I love hearing Fiona Firestone's backstory."

"Oh, please," Laura says. "The true stuff was interesting, but Fiona Firestone is no saint like that lecture made her out to be."

"Oh, like Rogan Bosch is," Meatball says.

"I thought it was booo-riiiing," Jess says. "I almost died in there from boredom. I can't believe they're making us sit in lectures during the Fires."

I'm kind of with Jess on this one. As much as I love Fiona Firestone, that was brutal. I'm already dreading the fact that we have to go back in for another one, unless I can somehow get a seat next to Haley this time.

"Hey, you guys all want to hang out after dinner tonight?" Zig asks.

"You think they're gonna give us free time?" Haley asks.

"Dinner is at 6:00 p.m.," I say, "so unless they send us to bed at 7:00 p.m., they have to give us some free time, right?"

"Okay," Jess says. "Let's all meet up in the back of the Great Room after dinner and figure out something fun to do."

"Love it," Meatball says. "The Super Six."

"What are you talking about?" Zig asks.

"That's us," Meatball says, pointing around the circle. "We're the Super Six! I just came up with that!"

"Worst nickname ever," Jess says. "Please don't ever call us that again."

"You know what's interesting," Zig says, "The Super Six was also a cartoon series in the 1960s created by Friz Freleng who went on to create *The Pink Panther*."

"That's not interesting," Laura says so bluntly that it makes us all laugh.

"Well, I don't care if you don't like it," Meatball says, "we're the Super Six, and we're gonna win this competition."

"Yeah," I say, "except for the fact that there are only five scholarships available."

"Technically only four," Laura says. "One of them is already mine."

"Wow, cocky much?" Haley says.

"Just stating facts," Laura says, with enough attitude to make me do a double-take. Between her dislike for Fiona Firestone and this little display of sass toward Haley, I'm starting to wonder if we should be a Fab Five, not a Super Six.

"Alright everyone, back into the lecture hall," Beardy yells, "time for the second half of Fiona Firestone's story!"

We head back inside, and this time I'm able to make sure

I'm sitting next to Haley. Although, it almost seemed like maybe she wanted to sit next to me, too?

Beardy starts lecture number two, this time squeaking about the history of public education and how Fiona's ideas on schooling are changing the world. He mentions that it had been his dream to work for Fiona Firestone since the school opened, and how grateful he was to get hired the previous summer.

Surprisingly, he also mentions Rogan Bosch a few times, but in a way that makes Fiona Firestone seem way more important and influential. I can't see Laura's face, but she must be fuming.

I don't know if it's because I'm bored or if I ate too much for lunch, but halfway through Beardy's presentation I can feel myself starting to drift off to sleep. I adjust myself in my seat and take a deep breath, convinced that I'm fully awake again, but the next thing I know, Haley is elbowing my arm.

"Lake, you're falling asleep," she whispers.

"I know," I say, "how are you not?"

"You have to pay attention," she says. "You never know if we're going to get tested on this stuff."

"Shoot, you're right," I say.

I hadn't even thought about that, but it makes sense. Why else would we be sitting in lectures in the middle of a competition? There must be a test coming later on this stuff.

That's when it hits me that I've been doing a terrible job of staying focused on my goal. That's the kind of stuff that can get a secret agent killed on a dangerous mission. I keep forgetting I'm not here to make friends or sit next to a cute girl in a lecture —though she really is cute.

Forget the Super Six. I mean, I'm happy that there are some nice kids here to hang out with, but I'm not here for them—I'm here for me. And at least one of them is going to have to go home before me if I want to accomplish this mission. I hope it's Laura, but if it's not, oh well.

The Firestone Fires are a chance of a lifetime. If I don't stay focused every second this week on winning, I'm going to regret it for the rest of my life.

Six years at Crapville Middle and High School or six years at The Firestone School. That's what's on the line this week.

I'm not letting anyone get in my way.

23

————

Well, our plans to hang out as the Super Six after dinner last night never happened.

While we were eating Chef Rachelle's amazing Fettuccini Alfredo, Mr. Lincoln hurried into the Great Room and told us we were all being immediately dismissed back to our bunk rooms. He promised us that dessert would be sent to us, and about an hour later, it was.

The only explanation we got was a brief message on our television from Fiona Firestone right before bed, saying the school was dealing with "a minor issue until further notice."

Meatball said he bet it had something to do with school security. Hudson called it "high level mind games," whatever that means. All I know is that it was a major letdown because I was excited to hang with everyone, especially Zig and Haley.

"Until further notice," ended up lasting all the way through breakfast and almost until lunch, which was an incredibly long sixteen hours. Everyone had a theory about what was going on, but no one knew.

They brought breakfast to our rooms around 9:00 a.m., which helped us kill forty-five minutes, but the last hour has been brutal. Hudson keeps picking fights with everyone, but no one is biting. The only thing keeping me from going insane was the great feeling I had when I woke up in a dry bed for the second night in a row.

But just now a new message appeared on our TV:

PROCEED TO THE SOUTH LAWN FOR THE NEXT ELIMINATION EVENT.

Moments later, the door to our room unlocks and everyone spills out into the hallway at once, so happy to finally be free. We make our way down the Southwest wing and onto the patio overlooking the South Lawn. The grass is so incredibly lush and green, but I'm not sure if that's because it really is, or because I've been locked in a bedroom for half a day. Just last week Nick, T.J., and I were talking about this, and now I'm here. Man, I wish Nick could be here right now.

As I'm making my way to the stairs leading down to the lawn, I notice a large shed off to the left. Through the open doors I think I can see Haley inside it. I change direction to head that way, and sure enough, as I get closer, I see Beardy and Haley inside.

"What's going on over here?" I ask.

"Hey, Lake," Haley says, seeming happy to see me. "Check this out!"

"What is this?" I ask.

"The drone shed," Beardy says. "If it flies, you can be sure Fiona Firestone collects it—birds, planes, helicopters, and especially drones."

"Is that an HLX-2500?" Haley asks.

"Sure is," Beardy squeaks. "Have you flown one before?"

"No," Haley says. "But I have an HLX-1000 and a 2000 at home."

"I didn't know you were into drones," I say.

"Yeah, I work on them and race them at home," she says. "Kind of a nerdy hobby, but I love it."

"Not nerdy at all," I say. "Do you do official races and stuff?"

"Yeah, I've won a few local races and have placed in a few

state competitions," she says. "I qualified for Nationals last year, but I didn't do that great in them."

"Nationals?" I say, surprised. "I didn't know I was in the presence of a legendary drone pilot."

"I finished bottom five in Nationals for my age group," she says. "Not so legendary."

"Check this out," Beardy says, pulling a sheet off something big in the corner of the shed.

"Whoa!" Haley exclaims, clearly more impressed by what she's seeing than I am. "Is that what I think it is?"

"Yup," Beardy says, "the HLX-5000."

The drone is massive. Its body is the size of a push lawn-mower, and the propellers are even bigger. It must weigh a hundred pounds.

"I didn't even think those were on the market yet," Haley gawks.

"They're not," Beardy says, "but Fiona Firestone has connections, so they just sent her this beta unit to test. Apparently it doesn't fly well, so they've asked us to keep it in the shed until they can do more testing on the prototype."

"It's bigger than I thought," Haley says. "I bet Zig would love to see this!"

"No, you can't say anything about this," Beardy says, his tone suddenly serious. "Honestly, I shouldn't have even showed it to you guys. Promise me you won't say a word to anyone that this drone is in here."

"What's the big deal?" I ask, genuinely curious.

"I just —" Beardy starts, before collecting his thoughts. "Things are on high alert around here and the last thing I need is to be getting in trouble for showing the wrong thing to the wrong people."

"We're not the *wrong people*," Haley says.

"I'm sorry, that came out wrong," Beardy says. "You guys are fine, I'm sure—but it looks like things are about to get started down on the lawn. You guys should head down there."

Haley and I take his squeaky advice and join up with the rest of the Super Six. As I walk through the lush grass I notice my sneakers are getting soaked, which is kind of weird. There's not a cloud in the sky today and there wasn't one yesterday, either.

"Hey, Haley," Zig says as we approach. "Enjoy being locked up all night?"

"Not really my idea of fun," Haley says.

"Yeah, that was one of the worst nights of my life," Jess says. "Caged up like zoo animals—I literally almost went crazy."

"Has anyone heard what that was all about?" Haley asks.

"They didn't tell us anything," I say, "but the way they rushed us out of the Great Room last night makes me think something's up at the school."

"I think it has to do with the Climate Bubble," Meatball says. "You guys notice how soaked the grass is?"

"Meatball's right," Zig says. "This is more than just dew, and the forecast for this entire week called for zero rain. I checked it before we came here so I knew not to bring a raincoat."

"You think they were testing it or something?" Haley asks.

"Maybe," Meatball says.

"I doubt it," Laura says. "I think she was just keeping us locked up as part of the competition. She's trying to test our patience to see who can handle it."

"That's what Hudson was saying," I chime in.

"Pshhh, if that's the case, then I'm not gonna last long," Jess says. "Seriously, that was the worst. They better give us *double* free time tonight."

"Who says we're gonna get *any* free time tonight?" Meatball say. "What if they're doing more testing today? They might stick us back in our rooms after this event!"

"I will literally sneak out," Jess says. "I'm not getting stuck in that room again."

"We should sneak out anyway," Meatball says. "Let's explore this place a little bit. We've been here almost two whole days now and we haven't seen any of it except what Mr. Lincoln showed us on that tour!"

"I'd be up for that," Ziggy says, which kind of surprises me. I figured he'd have some statistic about how seventy-two percent of all kids who sneak out end up getting caught or something.

"Seriously? What are you guys, eight years old?" Laura says. "If you get caught sneaking around this place, they'll probably send you home. Actually, now that I think about it, go for it—it will make it that much easier for me to win The Fires with you gone."

"You only get sent home if you get caught," Jess says. "Besides, we're not sneaking around to cause trouble, we just want to do some exploring. They're not gonna send us home for that. What do you think, Haley? You in?"

"I guess, as long as we're not causing trouble," Haley says, which surprises me even more than Ziggy. I did not think she'd be the "sneak around after hours" type.

The thing is, I don't mind sneaking around in certain situations. I'm actually pretty good at it. Back at home I'm always completing the missions I give myself around the house. Last week, I snuck a fake entry into Viv's diary while she was in the shower. I picked the lock on her bedroom door with a paperclip, then picked the lock on her diary, too. The last entry was about some guy at school that might like her, and I added one little sentence to the end of the paragraph:

He's so dreamy, I bet his diarrhea smells like cinnamon and laughter.

I really hope she goes back and reads that, just so I can enjoy how mad she'll be.

Anyway, the thought of getting busted and sent home from The Firestone Fires just because we wanted to walk around the school in the middle of the night sounds like the worst idea I've ever heard. There's no way I would ever do that.

"What do you think, Lake?" Haley asks. "You want to come explore with us tonight?"

Every fiber of my body is telling me to say no, but my eyes are locked on Haley's and her smile scrambles my brain for just long enough to get me to say the opposite.

"Definitely," I say. "Sounds like fun."

24

Having just agreed to do something that I think is a terrible idea, I now have a pit in my stomach the size of a softball. When it comes down to it, I'm probably gonna chicken out. I don't care how much fun I'd miss out on, it's just not worth it to me to do anything that might get me kicked out of The Fires.

My train of thought is suddenly broken by the sound of a helicopter headed our way. A few seconds later the noise is so deafening that everyone stops talking and covers their ears. That's when we realize the helicopter is landing on the lawn, about a football field away from us.

The propellers finally stop, and Fiona Firestone steps out onto the grass and into a golf cart with Mr. Lincoln. They start heading our way.

"Must be nice to have your own driver," Jess says.

"Must be nice to have your own helicopter," Haley says.

I've seen plenty of helicopters in my life, but almost all of them were about 10,000 feet over my head. Watching one land a couple hundred feet away was pretty cool.

"Did you know that about fifteen percent of helicopter crashes are fatal?" Zig says to the group.

"Yeah, I did know that, actually," Jess says.

"Really?" Zig asks.

"No, of course not," she says.

Mr. Lincoln pulls the golf cart up to the eighty of us assembled on the lawn, and Fiona Firestone, dressed in a pair of designer jeans and a leather bomber jacket, steps out.

"Sorry I'm late," she says, taking off her sunglasses. "More minor issues."

"She probably had to take a big dump," Meatball whispers, which makes the handful of kids around us chuckle.

"Yeah, a big clown dump," Adam adds.

My eyes are fixed on Fiona Firestone and her commanding presence. Her eyes are on us—slowly moving left to right and back again like she's sizing us up. She raises her right hand above her head and snaps her fingers twice. "Wilbur! Orville!" she says, and suddenly the two small birds I had only previously seen in the Great Room land on her shoulders.

"Now then," she continues, "it's time for the next event of The Fires: the Puzzle Race." I look around at the other seventy-nine kids on the lawn with me, sizing them up. While I can't tell at a glance how smart they are, I do notice that most of them seem pretty physically fit. If this was just a foot race, I'd have to push myself to make sure I placed high enough, but apparently, it's more than that.

"The Puzzle Race consists of three laps around the school," she says. "After each of the first two laps, you will have to complete a puzzle before setting out again. Just grab whatever tablet is in front of you for the challenge—it will sync up with your ID Band."

To my left, Hudson is cracking his knuckles with a smirk on his face. I can tell he's trying to give off that "this is going to be so easy" vibe, and honestly, it's working. I suddenly feel a little intimidated about this whole thing.

"Okay everyone, make your way over to the starting gate."

Fiona says. "The Puzzle Race will begin in a few minutes. First fifty to finish move on, the last thirty are gone."

"You ready for this?" I ask Haley.

"Ready to beat you," she says, smiling.

"Oh, you think so? Just promise you won't be mad when you get to the finish line and I'm already there."

"No need to promise when it's not gonna happen," she says, her smiling widening.

She puts up her fist for a fist bump right as I'm put up my open hand for a high five. But then we both switch when we see what's about to happen, and the end result is that I fist bump her high five.

"Awwwwkwarrrrd!" a voice says from behind us. "Oh, I'm sorry," Hudson says, "did I ruin your cute, little moment?"

"Good luck, Hudson," Haley says to him, taking the high road.

"Good luck to you, Haley, and worst of luck to you, Flake," he says, as he forces his way past us toward the starting line.

Could this guy be any worse?

My goal is still to win this whole thing, but I'm starting to think about what it would be like if I stay and Haley gets eliminated. I think I'd actually be sad, which is not good. What's happening to me? Am I forgetting the whole point of this week? A great secret agent would never lose sight of the goal of his mission, especially not because of some cute girl he just met. I mean, even if she does like me, it's not like we're gonna date or anything. We're only twelve. Wait, why I am thinking about this stuff seconds before an event? *Focus, Lake!*

I step up to the starting line beside Haley. I can see Hudson a few spots to her left. Ziggy, Jess, Laura, and Meatball are on my right.

Fiona Firestone is now up on the back patio that overlooks the lawn, sitting in something that is half chair, half throne. "Competitors, please space yourselves out along the starting line. Again, first fifty to finish will remain in the competition, the remaining thirty will be headed home tonight. Good luck."

She nods at Mr. Lincoln, who raises a bright red flare gun.

"On your marks, get set ... "

BANG!

25

———

The flare gun goes off and I'm immediately passed by almost all the other kids, who are sprinting as fast as they can.

That's okay, though. That's part of my plan and here's why.

One loop around the school is probably just a little bigger than the typical track around a high school football field. I'm guessing it's less than a half a mile, but close. That means that by the end of this race, when we've circled the school three times, we'll have run about a mile and a half.

I don't know about these other kids, but I'm not sure I can sprint for that long. That's why I'm not sprinting to start. Even if they can sprint the entire first loop, they're going to be out of gas near the end of the race.

I cross over the front driveway and turn the corner onto the North Lawn, peering back over my shoulder to see about ten kids behind me. I'm tempted to pick up my pace from a run to a sprint, but I brush off the idea. A great secret agent is always open to deviating from the plan when he absolutely has to, but I still trust mine.

As I make the final turn back onto the South Lawn I can see that most of the kids in front of me are already holding their tablets, working on their first puzzle. I run through the checkpoint into the puzzle area and my ID Band buzzes and glows red.

I grab a tablet while trying to catch my breath and the screen lights up:

LAP 1 COMPLETE

THIS IS YOUR FIRST PUZZLE

(SWIPE LEFT)

I swipe away the welcome screen and I'm presented with some brief instructions:

SOLVE THE 3-DIGIT CODE AND YOU CAN BEGIN LAP 2.

(AN INCORRECT GUESS FREEZES YOUR TABLET FOR 30 SECONDS)

I swipe left again.

DIGIT 1

$(1 + 2 + 3 + 4 + 5 + 6 + 7 + 8 + 9) / (9)$

Okay, I'm gonna have to do some quick math in my head, but I got this. It takes me a few seconds, but I think this first digit is a 5. I enter it into the answer box and swipe left.

DIGIT 2

$(1 \times 2) \times (3 \times 4) \times (5 \times 6) \times (7 \times 8) \times (9 \times 0)$

Okay, this one is a little more complicated: 2 times 12 is 24 times 30 is ... shoot what is it ... ummm, 720, I think. Okay, 720 times 56? Crap, I don't think I can do 720 x 56 in my head.

I swipe left to skip to the next digit and notice that at least half of the kids are already gone and have started Lap 2!

DIGIT 3

(Fiona Firestone's Age When She Graduated High School - Your Rank in the First Event + 65)

Shoot, I knew I should have been paying more attention during lectures. Beardy threw out so many ages as he was going through her story. Was she fifteen when she graduated high school or was that college? Or was that how old she was when she applied for her first patent?

At least I remember that my rank in the first event was 71. I'll never forget seeing that on my ID Band and the smile on Ziggy's face. So if Fiona Firestone graduated at fifteen, that's 15 minus 71 plus 65 ... which is ... ummm ... 9. I enter it into my answer box and swipe right to go back to digit 2.

DIGIT 2

$$(1 \times 2) \times (3 \times 4) \times (5 \times 6) \times (7 \times 8) \times (9 \times 0)$$

Oh yeah, I was stuck at 720 times 56. I'm about to start figuring that out in my head when I see it, and I kick myself for not having noticed it the first time. A good secret agent always takes in the whole problem before diving into the details.

There's a zero in this multiplication problem. Anything times zero is zero!

I enter 0 into the answer box and swipe left twice.

YOUR GUESS IS
5 - 0 - 9
[SUBMIT]

I hit the submit button and instantly my ID Band buzzes and changes from red to green. I drop my tablet on the table and start my second lap, glancing behind me as I do to see how many kids are still working on their first problem in the puzzle area.

My jaw drops as I realize there are only five kids there. Everyone else is already on Lap 2 and, in the distance, I can see a few kids, including Hudson and Ziggy, rounding the last turn about to start on the last puzzle.

I'm in seventy-seventh place and only fifty move on?

Forget pacing myself, it's time to sprint.

26

Lap 2 is an all-out sprint.

I suddenly don't care about whether or not Haley makes it, or any of my other friends for that matter. This is the same feeling I had about twenty-four hours ago when I thought I was going home to six years of Crapville schools. The thought of it makes me speed up even more.

Maybe trying to pace myself was a bad idea? Then again, maybe the only reason I'm running so fast right now is because I saved some energy on the first lap.

As I cross over the driveway and head for the west side of the school I feel a sudden chill in the air. I look up to see that dark clouds have appeared over the school from out of nowhere. I wipe the sweat from my forehead without breaking stride and wonder if I'm getting sick or something. It feels like the temperature has dropped forty degrees.

Bolting as fast as I can, I catch up to the group in front of me, who have all slowed down from a sprint to a run. They're all breathing heavily and a couple of them have even slowed down to the point of jogging.

I'm not worried about saving energy at this point, so I run past them and take the final turn. I pass four or five more kids as I sprint into the puzzle area and grab a tablet again. There has to be at least fifteen kids behind me now, which would put me in 65th place. Still not good enough.

My ID Band once again changes to red, letting me know I can't start the final lap until this puzzle is finished. I'm breathing so heavily and my hands are shaking so violently that I can barely hold the tablet still as the screen lights up.

LAP 2 COMPLETE
THIS IS YOUR FINAL PUZZLE
(SWIPE LEFT)

I swipe.

SOLVE THE PUZZLE
(A NEW LETTER WILL APPEAR EVERY 30 SECONDS)

I swipe left again.

20—21—01—19—21 *** 14—01—17 *** 21—11—19—02—02

HINT: ONCE YOU SOLVE IT YOU CAN DO IT.

I read the hint out loud a couple times, but the more I do the more confused I am. "Once you solve it you can do it." What does that mean?

I'm guessing there's a code for the letters, but I don't even know where to start to try to figure it out. Every word has to have a vowel, so one of those three letters in the middle word is a vowel, right? Or maybe the middle word is "the"? I don't know.

I notice the last two letters of the last word are the same, so that's either going to be something like LL or TT or FF, I think?

I look up and see that most everyone is still working on this puzzle, so that's good. There might be eighty of us still here?

The only problem is, the kids who got here a minute or two ago already have a few letters given to them because you get a new letter every thirty seconds.

I also notice the goose bumps covering both of my arms. This has nothing to do with me getting sick; it is definitely cold outside. Like, middle of February cold. Suddenly, the number 21 at the end of the first word starts blinking, and then it changes to a T.

$$\underline{20}\text{---}\underline{21}\text{---}\underline{01}\text{---}\underline{19}\text{---}\underline{T}\text{ *** }\underline{14}\text{---}\underline{01}\text{---}\underline{17}\text{ *** }\underline{21}\text{---}\underline{11}\text{---}\underline{19}\text{---}\underline{02}\text{---}\underline{02}$$

HINT: ONCE YOU SOLVE IT YOU CAN DO IT.

Okay, that doesn't help me much.

Oh, wait, yes it does! There are two other 21s in the solution that didn't automatically fill in. I use the keypad to fill them in myself.

$$\underline{20}\text{---}\underline{T}\text{---}\underline{01}\text{---}\underline{19}\text{---}\underline{T}\text{ *** }\underline{14}\text{---}\underline{01}\text{---}\underline{17}\text{ *** }\underline{T}\text{---}\underline{11}\text{---}\underline{19}\text{---}\underline{02}\text{---}\underline{02}$$

HINT: ONCE YOU SOLVE IT YOU CAN DO IT.

Still not enough information.

"Got it!" I hear Hudson yell as he races away from the table with a green-glowing ID Band. He's not even ten feet into his last lap when Ziggy jumps up and tosses his tablet on the table and takes off after him.

"Once you solve it you can do it." What do I want to do? I want to run. I want to finish. I want to stay in this competition. I want to win. I want to avoid going to Crapville. I want to flush Hudson's face in the toilet. I want Haley to like hanging out with me. I want to know what's really happening behind the scenes at Gary's Sandwiches. Those things are all true, but none of them fit the solution, and the solution is what I need right now if I'm going to complete this mission.

Another letter appears. The 01 in the middle word is replaced by an A.

20—T—01—19—T *** 14—A—17 *** T—11—19—02—02

HINT: ONCE YOU SOLVE IT YOU CAN DO IT.

I was right, that middle letter is a vowel. And there's another 01 in the first word as well. The puzzle area is getting louder now as every few seconds another kid solves the puzzle and takes off.

20—T—A—19—T *** 14—A—17 *** T—11—19—02—02

HINT: ONCE YOU SOLVE IT YOU CAN DO IT.

After a few seconds of staring at it, it hits me. The first word is probably "START." Start ... start what?

Start Eat Tacos? Start Fat Truck? Start Gas Troll?

No, none of those work, and wait—there's a 19 in the last word, too, and I almost missed it. If the first word is "START," there's an R in the last word, too. I fill it in, along with my guess of START.

S—T—A—R—T *** 14—A—17 *** T—11—R—02—02

HINT: ONCE YOU SOLVE IT YOU CAN DO IT.

Start Bad Tires? Start Hay Turbo? Start Wax Tarps?

I'm not coming up with anything, but then I remember that the last two letters have to be the same. And wait: if A is 1, and T is 21, does that mean the code is so simple that I missed it? Is T the 21st letter of the alphabet?

I count it out using my fingers and it is! R is 19, S is 20, and T is 21.

I just assumed the code was complicated, but it seems like it was the simplest solution the whole time? I can't believe that such a careless mistake might be what sends me home.

But what's more unbelievable is what I just saw land on the screen of my tablet.

A snowflake.

27

I look up and see a thousand more snowflakes falling, following right behind the first one.

It's snowing in July? And not just a light snow, either. In the span of a minute it's gone from clear to snowstorm.

It has to be that weather-controlling invention that I've been hearing about, but I don't have time to think about that now. At least half of all the kids have started Lap 3. If I can start my last lap in the next thirty seconds, I should have this! I quickly figure out the other letters based on the code where A is 1, B is 2, C is 3 and so on, and I fill in the solution.

S—T—A—R—T *** N—A—Q *** T—K—R—B—B

HINT: ONCE YOU SOLVE IT YOU CAN DO IT.

Wait, that can't be right. Start Naq Tkrbb?

I say it again out loud as if the second time it will make sense.

Start Naq Tkrbb?

I count out the letters again, and the numbers all line up.

Maybe the solution to this puzzle is made-up words? I guess Fiona Firestone never said it had to make sense.

I swipe left and hit the ENTER button; my ID Band blinks red and buzzes. That's not right. Of course it's not. Start Naq Tkrbb doesn't mean anything, Lake. Sometimes I am the world's biggest idiot.

The screen resets to the letters that have been revealed and I fill in the few guesses I think are right.

S—T—A—R—T *** 14—A—17 *** T—11—R—02—02

HINT: ONCE YOU SOLVE IT YOU CAN DO IT.

There are probably only twenty-five or thirty kids left here now and most of us are going home. Out of the corner of my eye another kid pops up and starts running. It's Haley! She might make it to the next stage after all.

I focus back on my screen, brushing the fallen snow off of it, and then it hits me. If those last two letters after the R are the same, they have to be vowels. No consonant would work in that spot. And not just any vowels, I think the only ones that would work there would be Es. I type it in to see what it looks like.

S—T—A—R—T *** 14—A—17 *** T—11—R—E—E

HINT: ONCE YOU SOLVE IT YOU CAN DO IT.

No sooner do I type in the last E than it comes to me.
Of course!
START LAP THREE!
The hint makes perfect sense! Once you solve "Start Lap Three," then you can start Lap 3!

I type it in, swipe right, and submit. Though it's coated with snow, my ID Band buzzes green as I take off in a full sprint toward the east side of the building.

I'm pretty sure there were less than thirty of us in the puzzle area, which means I've got to pass some kids on suddenly slippery terrain if I want to make the cut. Only the Top 50 move on, and I'm probably in fifty-fifth place.

As I'm sprinting across the lawn I hear, "Go Lake, you got this!" behind me, and I turn to see Ziggy crossing the finish line with Hudson.

I round the northeast corner of the school and see two kids in front of me that I should be able to pass. By the time we take the second turn I'm right on their backs and already looking ahead to see who else I can catch. That's when I notice Haley about twenty feet in front of me. She's gaining ground on two other kids, and as they hit the snow-coated driveway, she passes them.

I'm not sure I've ever run faster in my life than I am right now. You ever have one of those dreams where you try to run fast but your legs don't want to move? Well, this feels like the exact opposite. I keep pushing myself to run faster, and it keeps happening.

The scary part is that I know I could slip and fall at any moment. There's already a one-inch-thick coating of snow on the lawn and I've seen a few kids lose their footing and fall hard onto the ground, sliding at least ten feet before they can get back up onto their feet.

As I take the corner onto the West Lawn, I see that I've made up a bunch of ground. The two kids Haley just passed are only ten feet in front of me, and Haley is just in front of them.

I'm not sure I have much left, but I've got to find something more. I round the final corner and the finish line comes into view through the heavy snow, about one hundred feet away. For a second I wonder if it even matters. What if the first fifty have already crossed and my fate is sealed? Then I focus back on Haley and decide that, whether or not I go home, I'm going to at least beat her.

The last stretch of lawn toward the finish line is just slightly downhill, and as I hit the final fifty feet it feels like I'm out of control. I pass the two kids that were between Haley and me, and as we approach the finish line Haley is only a couple of feet in front of me, almost close enough that I could reach out and tug on her shirt.

The cheers of the other kids are deafening at this point, and my heart feels like it's about to explode, but in those last fifteen feet I find one extra burst of energy that pulls me beside Haley. We cross the finish line at the same time.

I don't even try to stop myself without falling, I just dive headfirst into the snow and slide at least fifteen feet like I'm on a Slip 'N Slide. Once I come to a stop, I brush myself off and get to my feet and try to catch my breath. I'm doubled over with my hands on my knees, feeling like I'm about to puke.

"Dude, amazing finish," Zig says.

"Where did you come from?" Haley says, also out of breath. "You almost beat me!"

"Almost!" I say, barely finding enough breath to speak. "I totally beat you."

I take my hands off my knees and stand up to see Haley smiling, holding up her wrist. "Think again, slowpoke," she says, her ID Band showing a green 48.

I look down at mine.

A green 49.

"49! Wait, we did it," I say. "We made it!"

"Yeah, we did!" Haley says, brushing the snow out of her eyes and holding up her hand for a high five. I slap her hand, this time not screwing it up, and honestly I don't even care that she beat me.

We made it. I made it.

Top 50.

28

S till out of breath but amped from adrenaline, we file back into the Great Room while the thirty eliminated kids follow Beardy into the lobby to hand in their ID Bands and collect their bags. I noticed a couple of my bunk mates in that group, and I'm looking around the Great Room now to see if I notice anyone else who's not here.

Ziggy and Meatball are still here, sitting beside me at my table, and a few tables away I see Haley and a few other girls that I recognize but couldn't name. Laura is at the far end of their table sitting by herself. She's another one I wouldn't mind seeing eliminated at this point.

"Close call, Flake," Hudson says to me as he walks by.

"Made it through, that's all that matters," I say back with a smile. I'm seriously so pumped right now, even Hudson's needling isn't going to get to me.

"Sucks that thirty kids are gone," Meatball says. "But man, how about that snow?"

"I know, right?" I say. "Had to be that weather thing you guys have been talking about, right?"

"Yeah, I guess it went a little haywire," Meatball says. "Never seen a snowstorm in July before."

"Or maybe it was supposed to be part of the challenge?" I say with a shrug. "Where did you finish in the race?"

"Twenty-eighth," Meatball says.

"I finished nineteenth," Adam says even though no one asked him. "Hudson finished first. He totally clowned all you clowns."

"Yeah, we saw," I say. "Oh, and what on earth was going on with that code? I never actually cracked it."

"It was vowels, then consonants," Haley says.

"Yeah, it took me a minute, too," Zig says. "Numbers 1 through 5 were all the vowels in order: A, E, I, O, and U. Then B was 6, C was 7, D was 8, F was 9, and so on, all the way to Z being 26."

"Oh, wow," I start to say, but I'm interrupted by a woman's voice breaking in over the loudspeaker.

"Listen up, my dears, I have a couple of announcements before you are dismissed for the day. Please grab your seats and I'll share them shortly."

The voice is not Fiona Firestone's, but I don't need to look to know that it's Dr. V, her head of security. She's one of those adults who calls everyone "dear" or "honey" or "sweetie". I usually don't trust those people because it feels like they're using nice nicknames to cover up that they have a little bit of mean and nasty in them. I'm not sure yet if this is the case with Dr. V. She's adjusting her glasses and typing something into her laptop as she waits for us to quiet down.

I look around for Jess for a few seconds before noticing that she's in the corner with Hudson. They give each other a congratulatory high five, which catches me a little off guard. This is the second or third time I've seen them talking, and each time they seem more and more comfortable with each other. It's so weird to me, because Jess is really nice and Hudson is kind of the worst.

"Find your seats," Dr. V says from the stage. "And while you do, try not to make too big of a mess with the melting snow. That certainly was an interesting twist on the Puzzle Race."

The way she says this makes me wonder if maybe the freak snowstorm wasn't supposed to happen. Maybe the climate invention isn't as close to ready as some people think.

"Now then," she continues, "I guess congratulations are in order to all of you for making it this far. You, my loves, have made the Top 50."

As she says this most of the kids in the room start clapping and hollering to celebrate this achievement, which I can tell, even from across the room, sort of annoys Dr. V. "Settle down please, I wouldn't get too excited," she says. "You've made it past the easy part, but remember, this story is not going to have a happy ending for most of you."

"She seems like a lot of fun," Ziggy whispers, making me laugh.

"A few reminders for the rest of the week," Dr. V says. "First, you must *never* leave the designated areas you're supposed to be in. If you are supposed to be here in the Great Room, you need to be in the Great Room. If you are supposed to be in your bunk room, you need to be in your bunk room. Failure to follow these rules will lead to immediate elimination."

Dr. V starts typing again. I'm not sure if she's actually writing something, or if this is just something she does when she's not talking. Like some kind of weird typing addiction.

"Obviously, there are certain areas of the school that we will open up for elimination events, like we just did with the South Lawn. And during free time, which you will have later today, you will be allowed in the Rec Wing. But again, do *not* wander around the school, my dears. If we find you where you don't belong, you're gone."

It strikes me as weird that she's lecturing us about sneaking out, considering we were just talking about that earlier. There's no way she could have heard us planning that. We were in the middle of a huge lawn with no one else around us. Regardless, there's no way I want to sneak out now.

After a few seconds of silence, her face crinkles into a much more serious look, like someone just stole her lunch, ate it in front of her, and burped it into her face.

"It is a privilege to be on these grounds," she says pointing at us as her voice rises. "If you don't realize that, if you don't understand how lucky you are to even be here for this week, then you don't belong here."

The whole Great Room is completely silent at this point, everyone frozen by Dr. V's tone. She looks from side to side, scanning the room as if she's searching for someone that she can't find. After a brief pause, her scowl recedes back into a smile.

"You are here for the chance to earn a scholarship to The Firestone School," she finally says, breaking the silence. "And my dears, if any of you are not here for that reason, I will find out who you are and there will be grave consequences."

"And trust me," she says, as she slams her laptop shut.

"...I *always* find out."

29

———

"**W**hat was *that* about?" Meatball says as Dr. V walks off the stage.

"I don't know," Ziggy responds, "that was weird. Seemed like she was looking for someone."

"You think they have information they're not telling us?" I ask.

"Of course they do," Zig says.

Hudson is smirking at us. "You guys are so dumb," he says, shaking his head. "She's obviously just trying to scare everyone into following the rules. Adults do that all the time. Classic scare tactics and you guys are buying right into it."

"Yeah, right into it like a bunch of clowns," Adam says.

"I don't know, dude," Zig says, "she seemed like she was talking to someone about something specific. That whole thing was weird."

Just then Jess and Haley walk up to our table. "Let's go check out the Recreation Wing—supposedly they just gave us access," Jess says.

That sounds good to us, so Zig, Meatball, and I follow the two of them out the north exit of the Great Room. Only instead of heading straight toward our bunks like usual, we take a right and approach a closed set of double doors.

"Let's see if this works," Jess says, grabbing the handle with her left hand. She turns it and it opens, her ID Band flashing green as she does.

We step through the double doors and find ourselves in a giant space with tables, TVs, and arcade games. It's like a huge coffee shop, only instead of coffee and boring adult conversations about mortgages and personality tests there's candy, ice cream, and kids playing arcade games.

"Whoa, dude, this is dope," Zig says.

"Oh man, free brownies?" Meatball says, grabbing one from a nearby dessert counter. "Am I in heaven?"

Laura sees us from across the room and runs over. "You guys, this place is amazing," she says. I don't think I've ever seen her this excited unless she's talking about Rogan Bosch.

"This is just a tiny part of it," she says, referring to the huge room we're in.

"What, really?" I ask.

"Yeah, this is just, like, the arcade room, or something. The rest of the Rec Wing is through those doors."

"Let's check it out," Haley says, walking over to the large wall fridge to grab a soda. "Want something, Lake?"

"I'm good for now, thanks," I say. While I am a little thirsty from the race earlier, I'm trying to do a better job of pacing myself with drinks this afternoon and evening. I drank too much again last night, but thankfully it didn't lead to an accident.

Everyone else grabs drinks, and we follow Laura across the room and out into huge hallway. "There's so much stuff out here," she says. "Check it out, there's two basketball courts over there, ping pong and air hockey in these rooms over here, and then further down there are rooms with board games and video game consoles I've never even seen before."

The space is massive, and now it makes sense why this

section of the building seemed so big from the outside. The Rec Wing alone feels like half the size of Crapville Middle School, with way more technology than they'll probably even have twenty years from now. I'm blown away by how cool it all is and how this could be where I go to school next year.

"What's at the end of the hall?" Jess asks Laura.

"I think those are tennis and racquetball courts all the way down at the end, and right before that are the movie theaters."

"Movie theaters?" Haley says. "Plural?"

"Yeah," Laura says, "two full-sized theaters, buttered popcorn, reclining seats, all of it. I'm telling you, this whole wing is ridiculous."

"What do you think of Fiona Firestone now?" Meatball asks her with a smile.

"I mean, I'm impressed," Laura says. "I figured this school would be all about classrooms and labs, but she clearly wants her students to have fun, too."

"That's why she's the best," Meatball says, to which Laura just rolls her eyes.

"Well, I don't know about you guys," Zig says, "but I'm gonna go see what these video game consoles are all about."

"Same," Meatball says. "You coming, Lake?"

"I actually might go check out what movies they're showing," I say. If it was just us guys, I'd probably rather go play video games, but it seemed like Haley was pretty excited that there were movie theaters. I'm totally taking a risk here, but if she was about to check out the movies, too, we might get to go together, and it won't seem like I'm following her. Of course if I'm wrong, it might just be me sitting by myself drowning my loneliness in a large bucket of buttered popcorn.

"Yeah, I want to go watch a movie too," Haley says.

Yes! Thankfully no one is looking at me right this second because I'm trying to hold back a smile and it's not working. I can't believe how perfectly I played that one. Now, not to screw it up.

"Okay, cool," I say.

"I think I'm gonna go shoot some hoops," Laura says to Jess. "You want to come?"

"Ugh, I hate basketball," Jess says. "I was thinking about checking out racquetball—I've never played it before."

"Oh, it's fun!," Laura says. "I'll come play with you!"

"Interesting thing about racquetball," Zig says. "It was invented in the 1950s by Joseph Sobek and initially called Paddle Racquet."

"Zig, you really need to learn what the word 'interesting' means," Jess says.

"Well, it's interesting to me," Zig says to Jess, before smacking Meatball in the stomach. "Let's go, dude. If they have any kind of fighting game you're going down."

Zig and Meatball take off down the hall while Jess whispers something to Haley that I can't hear. Whatever she says, it makes Haley laugh and playfully shove her. I think they're talking about me, but you never know with girls. Jess and Laura start walking toward the racquetball courts, and suddenly I'm standing there alone with Haley.

You know that weird feeling you get sometimes when you realize there's only one other person in the room with you? This feels like that, only times a hundred because that other person is this cute girl I just met who may actually kind of like hanging out with me.

"Hey, you two!" Jess shouts from ten feet down the hall, "have fun on your movie date!"

"Not funny!" Haley says, turning to me. "Sorry, I knew she was gonna say something like that."

"It's fine," I say. I want to follow it up with something funny or clever, but nothing comes to my mind quick enough. Why does that always happen around girls? But then I do think of a joke, and I just blurt out, "Anyway, this isn't a date," I say. "I never go on dates with girls two days after I meet them."

"Oh yeah?" Haley says, laughing. "So how long do you typically wait?"

"Eh, usually until day three," I say, and she laughs even harder. Funny thing is, I've never even been close to being on a date before.

"Actually, I've never been on a date before," I say, "have you?"

"Of course not," she says. "My dad says I'm not allowed to ask until I'm sixteen, but he won't say yes until I'm eighteen. Come on, let's go see what movie is playing."

She walks ahead of me and I am finally able to relax for a second. As I do, the biggest smile ever stretches out on my face.

30

"Okay," Haley says pointing at the giant framed posters on the wall, "looks like the next two movies playing are *Curse of the Cloak* or *The Seven Balloons.* You pick."

"I don't care at all," I say. "*Curse of the Cloak* looks pretty good, but I heard it's scary. *The Seven Balloons* is like a love story I think, but I really don't care—whichever one you want to see."

"I'd rather watch *The Seven Balloons,*" Haley says, "but it's probably super cheesy. I'm just not really into scary movies. Are you sure you don't care?"

"No, it's fine," I say. "*Seven Balloons* it is."

The funny thing is, last week when I was hanging with Nick a commercial for *The Seven Balloons* came on and we were both making fun of it so bad. Nick said he'd rather eat seven balloons filled with T.J.'s taco breath than watch it.

It really does look like the most boring movie of all time, but what do I care? I'm about to sit next to Haley for two hours. Nick would lose his mind if he knew I was about to watch a movie with a cute girl. Neither of us have ever been on a date before because we're only twelve, but whatever you'd call this, I'm pretty excited.

We grab a large popcorn to share and head into the dark theater, which only has three other kids in it as far as I tell. I almost grab myself a soda, but at the last second decide not to. The popcorn is going to make me thirsty, but I'll let myself have one glass of water with dinner and that's it. If I can limit it to that, there's no way I'll wet the bed tonight.

"Well," I say, looking around the mostly empty theater, "we can pretty much sit anywhere we want."

"I like being in the fourth or fifth row," Haley says, "is that too close?"

"No," I say, "I like to sit close too! My buddy Nick always likes to sit near the back of the theater, and it drives me crazy."

"Yeah, same with my friends," she says.

We settle into our seats in the fourth row and recline them all the way back.

"Imagine going to a school with movie theaters in it," Haley says.

"I know right?" I say. "I still can't believe we're here. Were you watching the drawing live last week when they pulled all the names?"

"Yeah, of course," she says. "I was actually home by myself so I was just jumping around the room like a maniac. I scared my dog so bad he peed in the kitchen."

"Yeah, I was watching with Nick and another buddy and we were all going crazy," I say, before remembering how it really played out. "Actually, that's not true. I think I kind of sat there speechless for a while as Nick and T.J. went crazy. I've been dreaming about entering The Firestone Fires for so long, I couldn't believe it. It's pretty much the best thing that's ever happened to me."

"So you didn't think about declining the invitation?" she asks.

"Are you kidding me? Of course not!" I say. "Did you?"

"I mean, not really," she says, "but I did kind of go back and forth for a day or two. It was a tough choice."

"Are you serious?" I can't believe she genuinely was waffling on the decision. "This school is basically the hardest in the country to get into. They barely let anyone in, and it's so expensive only rich people can afford it. It's like ten times harder than getting into Harvard."

"I know, I know," she says, "that's why I eventually said yes. But honestly, I love my school and my friends. The thought of not going to the same school as them for the next six years makes me want to cry, you know?"

"Not really," I say. "I mean, I'd miss Nick for sure, but that's pretty much it. The other kids at my school suck. They're only into their little cliques and laughing about other people with their inside jokes. I honestly can't wait to get away from that."

Haley takes a sip of soda and lets out a little burp under her breath. "Oops, excuse me," she says laughing, "that one snuck out."

"I'm so offended," I say, and then force out a burp of my own.

"Eww, gross!" she says, and for a split second I wonder if I took the joke too far. "I can't believe you would burp in front of a girl you just met two days ago. You just ruined your chances of ever dating me."

"Well, I've got six years for you to forget about it," I say, and we both laugh about it for a few seconds. "But honestly," she says, "I get what you're saying about kids being mean and stuff. But you do realize every school is like that, right?"

"I guess," I say, "but I'm just tired of the kids in my school." Even as I'm saying it, I realize how dumb it sounds.

"Yeah, but The Firestone School is going to be like that, too. Maybe worse!" she says. "Let me ask you this, do you ever try to make new friends or do stuff with some of the kids at your school that you don't really know?"

"No," I say, realizing how bad that sounds.

"Well, that's probably part of your problem," she says. "You don't like the kids at your school because they're not friendly to you, but you're never friendly to them? That's not really fair."

"Yeah, but it's different at my school," I say.

"I don't think so," she says, which catches me a little off guard. "I think you just need to stop assuming everybody doesn't like you and start trying to be more friendly. Kind of like you're being with me right now."

I'm not really sure how to respond to that, so I grab a handful of popcorn and shove it in my mouth.

"LADIES AND GENTLEMAN THE SHOW WILL START IN TWO MINUTES," a voice says over the loudspeaker.

I lean over to Haley and whisper, "I'm really excited to learn about what happens to all seven of these balloons."

"Stop it!" she says, laughing. "You said you didn't care if we watched this!"

"I'm kidding, I'm kidding," I say.

"Seriously," she says, "if you want to go watch The Dumb Curse of the Dumb Cloak, go for it. I promise I won't be mad at you for totally lying to me and saying you didn't care and abandoning me in this theater."

"No," I say, "that movie looks bad too—they both look equally terrible."

"Oh my word!" she says, pretending I hurt her feelings. "You're so mean!"

"Mean to what? To the movie?" I say. "I don't think the movie has feelings."

"Well," she says, "you can get up and leave at any point if you've had enough of the balloons. I don't care as long as you leave the popcorn."

Truth is, all the money in the world couldn't get me out of this theater right now. I know we just met and she's probably just being kind to me because she's a nice person, but sitting here next to Haley is the only place I want to be.

31

It's 9:00 p.m. now, but I'm so tired and exhausted that it feels like it's after midnight.

The lights just went out in our room and I'm lying here thinking about what would have happened if I had tried to hold Haley's hand during the movie. At one point my left arm might have been touching her right arm on the armrest and the thought crossed my mind, but there was a zero percent chance I was actually going to do it. Kids in the movies do stuff like hold hands or lean in for a kiss. In the real world, none of my friends ever do that stuff.

I toss and turn for another forty-five minutes, going over the other events of the day and I remember that earlier everyone was talking about sneaking out. Thankfully, no one brought it up again the rest of the day. That's a major relief because after Dr. V's stern warning, I have no interest in getting kicked out of The Fires for sneaking into off-limit areas.

Just as I'm feeling like I might doze off, I decide to use the bathroom one last time. I peed right before getting into bed but that was a while ago, and if one more trip is the difference between waking up dry or wet, I'll do it.

Of course Hudson gave me a hard time earlier, throwing

brilliant nicknames at me like "Lord of the Pee" and "The Urinator," but it's been quiet in the room now for almost half an hour. I think they're all asleep.

I tiptoe across the room and into the bathroom, careful to do my business as quietly as possible. Turns out I probably didn't even need to go one last time, as there was almost nothing in me. Do I wash my hands? I don't want to make any noise, but I imagine Hudson lying awake in the other room, ready to tell everyone how I peed a bunch of times, and that I didn't wash my hands, either. "The Lord of the Pee Hands"—I can hear it now. I decide to risk it.

I carefully turn the faucet until the steady trickle of drops becomes a flow, noting that the faucet weirdly seems louder when it's dripping than when it's flowing. I skip the soap this time, opting instead just for a rinse, and dry my hands on my pajama pants.

A thought occurs to me that almost makes me laugh out loud. How funny would it be if after pulling off the perfect stealth bathroom trip I momentarily forgot where I was and used the high-powered hand dryer? The entire room would wake up. "Not funny," I whisper to myself under my breath.

I'm almost back in my bed when I nearly fall on my face. Somebody left their shoes in the middle of the room. Even though I catch myself before falling, I have to take a couple of quick, hard steps to regain my balance. They are way louder than I want them to be.

I freeze.

I can hear the rustling of bed sheets. There's at least one person tossing and turning, maybe more. There's just a little bit of light coming in under the door from the hallway, so if anyone wakes up enough to open their eyes and look around, they might see me.

Do I stay here for as long as it takes for the movement to stop, or do I shuffle over to my bed and climb in?

I hear more rustling, and decide to stay frozen, but a few

seconds later I regret that decision. What if someone does wake up and sees me standing like a statue in the middle of the room? How am I going to explain that? I try to convince myself that I can still make a break for my bed, but it doesn't work. I stay frozen.

"Don't forget to feed the raisin wizard," a voice mumbles behind me. It's Meatball talking in his sleep, and it takes everything in my power not to bust out laughing. I slow my breathing and stay under control.

"Why does the falcon want to kill the wizard?" Meatball says, and again I almost lose it. What on earth is he dreaming about?

The next three minutes feel like an hour, but Meatball doesn't say anything else and eventually the rustling stops. When I'm finally convinced everyone is sleeping soundly again, I shuffle toward my bed. Just as I'm about to climb in, it hits me. That feeling that I've had so many times before and never want to feel again. The faint feeling that a migraine headache is coming on.

"Crap, I think I'm getting a headache," I whisper to myself, followed by the immediate realization that I never grabbed the Advil from the kitchen before I left home. I tell myself that maybe it's not a headache, maybe I'm just overtired, but I know better. And I know that if I don't take something before I go to sleep, I'm going to wake up with a headache that will only get worse all day. That's how these things work for me.

What was I thinking only drinking one glass of water since lunch? I was so worried about not wetting the bed that I probably dehydrated myself. Mom has warned me about doing that before.

I think it over for a few minutes, but I know I have no choice. I have to go to the nurse's station to get some medicine. If I don't, I'll be trying to stay alive in The Fires tomorrow with a splitting headache. I can't believe I forgot to pack medicine!

Dr. V warned us about wandering around the school, but

this is different, right? This isn't sneaking around to explore, this is getting medicine I need to function. But still, is there a chance I'm going to get in trouble for this? I'm not going to be able to prove that I have a headache, they're just going to have to take my word for it.

My other option is to go drink a bunch of water in the bathroom now, and hope that it hydrates me enough, but that usually doesn't work for me. Plus, it could lead to me wetting the bed, so I'm not gonna go that route. I need some medicine, or I'm gonna be useless tomorrow.

I consider waking up Meatball to ask if he has any medicine, but I doubt he does. Besides, that will probably wake half the room up, and that sounds worse to me than getting stopped by someone on staff in the halls. I just need to go see the nurse and not worry about getting in trouble. I'm not doing anything wrong.

I put my ID Band back on so I can get back into the room and tiptoe over to the door. Carefully, I twist the knob and pull it open about sixteen inches. I slowly peak my head outside and look up and down the hallway. It's empty.

Ugh, am I doing this or not? Maybe it's too risky. Maybe dealing with the headache is the smart move?

I start to close the door, but just as it's almost shut, I stop.

No, I have to do this. I'm not causing trouble—I'm feeling a little sick and I'm getting medicine. Besides, I've done missions like this at home countless times. I'll be back in the room before anyone knows I'm gone.

I open the door back up just enough to slowly slide my body into the hallway and let the door silently close behind me.

32

———

I walk quickly toward the Great Room and then turn left, my bare feet silently moving across the cold floor.

I retrace the steps Mr. Lincoln took when he gave us a quick tour the other night. He didn't actually take us to the Nurse's office, he just showed us what direction it was in. I walk down the long hallway past the kitchen, the bird observatory, and the laundry room, and turn right.

My head is starting to throb a little harder, which confirms this was a good idea. I head into the Southeast Wing, where Mr. Lincoln said the nurse's station is, stepping as lightly as I can. The first set of rooms are dark inside, but neither seem like the nurse's station. The one on the left looks like a classroom and the one on the right seems to be a small storage space.

I tiptoe further down the hall and the next set of rooms is where I find it. The room on the left has a laminated sign on the door that reads:

THE NURSE IS NOT IN.
USE THE PHONE INSIDE AND DIAL *42.

I gently push the door open and the lights automatically

come on, illuminating a state-of-the-art nurse's office. I can't say I've ever really noticed the difference between nurse's offices before, but I bet you this one is way nicer than the one at Crapville Middle.

I grab the phone, but as I'm about to dial I see what I came for. A few feet away is a large glass jar filled with small paper two-packs of ibuprofen. I put the phone back on the cradle and grab a handful of the pill packs, one for now and a bunch for later should I need them. I rip open one of the packs and swallow both pills, thankful once again for my secret agent training that allows me to do it without any water.

I step back out into the hall and breathe a sigh of relief. If nothing else, I won't wake up with this headache tomorrow. I gently pull the door closed behind me, but as I do, I hear something. I freeze, listening as intently as I can. What sound I can hear—if it's a sound at all—is coming from further down this hallway. I close my eyes to focus, and it becomes clear that the sound I'm hearing is two people talking.

My first instinct is to head back to my room, but I stay frozen for a few seconds, growing more and more curious about what I'm hearing. I know I should go back, but if I can just get a little closer, I can maybe hear who it is.

I move toward the sound, one light step at a time. For a few steps the voices don't seem to get louder at all, but after I pass another set of dark, empty rooms things start to get clearer. It sounds like two women talking, and it seems to be coming from behind the wall on the right. They must be in the room behind this wall.

I put my ear to the wall, but the sounds are too muffled to make anything out. I can't understand a word, but it does seem like they're excited or they're arguing. I move just a little further up the hallway, and I can see the doorway to the room about ten feet ahead of me. The light is on in the room, casting a faint shadow into the hallway that reveals that the door is half open.

I take one final step to get just a little bit closer, and as I do, the voices get much clearer. I immediately realize who I'm listening to. It's Fiona Firestone and Dr. V.

An intense surge of adrenaline rushes through me. If either of them walk out this door, I've got a lot of explaining to do. I reach into my pocket and run my fingers along the paper packet to make sure I still have it. I don't plan on sticking around long enough to get caught out here, but if I do, this is my hall pass. I've got a true story about needing medicine, and the empty pill packet to prove it.

I close my eyes, trying to make out any words in the conversation.

"I understand what you're saying, Fiona," I hear Dr. V say, "but these scholarships aren't nearly as important as the MCD. You do realize what happens if it gets into the wrong hands?"

"Of course I realize," Fiona says. "We've been over every scenario countless times. But we've never had a high-level security breach in over five years. Why are you so worried that the first one is going to happen this week?"

"All the details are in my reports, which you said you read," Dr. V says.

"I *did* read them," Fiona says.

"Well, then you already know," Dr. V says. "The red flags are all there. Increased attacks on our servers, double the normal chatter on the dark web, and the broken window in the Northeast Wing a few days ago. Occam's razor says that something nefarious is going on here, and we both know who is likely behind it."

"Do we know for sure that it's Rogan?" Fiona asks.

"No, we don't know anything for sure, but I can tell you that this is the most sophisticated attack I've ever seen. So while I have no proof that it's Rogan Bosch behind this, I'd bet my life that it is."

"Well," Fiona sighs, "the stakes are too high to take unnecessary risks. The Microclimate Dome is the most important project I've ever worked on, and we're so close.

"If it's so close, how do you explain that freak snowstorm this afternoon?" Dr. V asks.

"That was unfortunate," Fiona says, "but I told you already, that was one line of code that had a mistake in it. It's been identified and fixed, and I think it's ready now."

"You *think* it's ready or you *know* it's ready?"

"I know it will be ready," Fiona says. "But until we're across the finish line, we can't take any chances. We have to do whatever it takes to protect it."

"Are you just saying that, or are you really willing to do whatever it takes?" Dr. V asks.

"Why, are you suggesting what I think you are?" Fiona asks.

"I'm afraid so," Dr. V says. "I know it's the last thing you want to do, but my official recommendation as your head of security is that you cancel The Firestone Fires and send all the students home immediately."

33

Hearing Dr. V suggest canceling The Fires causes me to audibly gasp, and I instinctively cover my mouth, even though I'm too far away for them to hear me.

Every second I'm out of my room increases my chances of getting caught, but I need to hear the rest of this conversation.

"If we cancel The Firestone Fires this week there won't be enough time to restart them," Fiona says. "The school year starts in a few weeks. It's now or never."

"I know, " Dr. V says. "It's a last resort, I get that." She pauses. "But as important as these scholarships are to you, the Microclimate Dome is on another level. If we can safely deliver it to market without it getting leaked, the MCD will be the best thing we've ever done as a company. It could be the thing you are remembered for."

"Well, I'm not worried about how people remember me," Fiona says, "but I am worried about this technology falling into the wrong hands. If that happens, entire climates could be wiped out, and *that's* what people will remember me for."

There's silence for a few seconds, and I think it's probably time for me to go.

"There's one more thing that I didn't put in my reports this morning." Dr. V says.

"What is it?" Fiona asks.

"I have nothing concrete to go on right now, but I have some suspicions about the ones who are left," Dr. V says.

"The students?" Fiona asks, her voice reaching a new level of worry. "Who?"

"I don't have names yet," Dr. V says, "but with all of the external interference getting flagged by our security protocols, I'm starting to wonder if it's a diversion created for someone else."

"A diversion for what?" Fiona asks. "I'm not sure I'm following."

"Whoever is trying to hack our system is clearly not worried about being seen, but yet they don't seem to be worried about getting caught, either. To me this means one of two things. Either they're so good they know we won't catch them, or they're purposely trying to get our attention so we're focused on the wrong thing," Dr. V says.

"So you think one of these students is in on this?" Fiona asks.

"Maybe," Dr. V says, "or maybe someone on staff here? I know it seems crazy to say with no proof, but this is too important to not listen to my gut on this."

"I trust your gut," Fiona says. "It's never wrong."

"I know. That's why I left this out of the report and I'm telling this to you face to face, so there's no record of it that can be intercepted," Dr. V says. "And that's also why I moved the MCD files without telling anyone."

"You moved them?" Fiona says, startled.

"Yes, I don't think they are safe on our servers anymore, so I moved copies of the plans onto three flash drives and completely removed them from our servers. This flash drive I'm giving you right now is for you to keep on your person at all times. I have a copy that I will keep as well, and I've hidden the third one in your office."

"My office?" Fiona says in a loud whisper. "Why can't you find somewhere to hide them in the Security Wing? I spent thirty million dollars making it the most secure storage facility on earth."

"I know that," Dr. V says, "and so does everyone else. If someone is trying to physically steal the plans, that is the first place they are going to look."

"So where in my office are you hiding the plans?" Fiona asks.

"Well, technically they're not *in* your office," Dr. V says. " I carved a small notch out of your office door, along the very top edge that no one ever sees. The flash drive is sitting securely in there."

"Are you serious? That does not seem like a good spot for the plans to a billion-dollar technology." Fiona says.

"That's exactly what I'm counting on," Dr. V replies. "Who would ever think to look there? Besides, the whole Northeast Wing is off limits to all the students and most of the staff. For now, it will work."

"If it is someone on the inside, like you think," Fiona says, "then maybe we really should send everyone home. Maybe we should evacuate the whole school until next month, if that's the only way to be safe. Do you really have no idea?"

"Well, there are two people we are monitoring very closely —" Dr. V starts to say, but that's the last word I hear because a door slams at the very far end of the hallway. I look up and see the backside of a janitor pushing a mop about thirty feet away. He's walking backwards as he mops, bopping his head to whatever he's listening to on his headphones.

I start walking backwards, slowly at first but picking up speed with each step. I'm keeping my eyes on him the whole time to make sure he doesn't turn around and see me. When I finally hit the end of the hallway, I turn the corner and make a beeline back for my room.

My heart is racing as I get to the door, and after a few deep breaths I hold up my ID Band to unlock it. I open it slowly, sneak inside, and close it behind me. My bed is only a few feet away, but I stand there perfectly still in the darkness so I can catch my breath and see if my entrance has woken anyone up. After a few minutes of silence I'm convinced no one is awake, so I crawl into my bed. Only, as I'm getting under my blanket, I bump my head on the wall as I'm getting under my blanket and a few guys rustle in their beds. I wait for someone to ask what the noise was, but no one says anything.

As my heartbeat slows down, my mind starts racing. Fiona Firestone is seriously thinking about canceling The Firestone Fires? There's no way this adventure can end like that! I get chosen in the drawing, I make it into the Top 50, and then I get sent home because of some dumb feud between her and Rogan Bosch?

I don't know what this Microclimate Dome is, other than the fact that it covered me with snow in the middle of July, but at this exact moment I hate it. It might be responsible for me missing out on an education at The Firestone School. If Dr. V thinks someone on the inside is trying to steal the plans, no wonder she yelled at us after the race earlier today. Hudson laughed it off and said she was trying to scare us for no reason, but there was a reason after all.

There's gotta be a way I can help, and I'm going to stay up all night if that's what it takes to make sure this competition doesn't get canceled. At least that's my plan.

Three minutes later, I'm sound asleep.

34

———

"**Y**ou snuck out last night?!" Zig says, his eyes wider than I've ever seen them.

I just finished giving him and Meatball a thirty-second rundown of what happened the night before. We're standing by ourselves in the corner of the Great Room while everyone is waiting for breakfast to be served.

"I didn't sneak out," I tell him again. "I needed medicine and I had to get it from the nurse."

"I can't believe you snuck out," Zig laughs, shaking his head. "Do you at least feel better?"

"Yeah, thankfully," I say.

"So wait," Meatball says, "Fiona Firestone is actually thinking about canceling The Fires?"

"I mean, that's what she said," I say, looking around to make sure no one is close enough to hear us, "but it sounds like she doesn't want to. I guess it's a last resort if there's no other way."

"Can we do anything?" Meatball asks.

"Like what?" I ask.

"I don't know," Meatball says, "like, help figure out what's going on. I don't want to go home."

"Well, she's got a whole security team already working on it," Zig says. "I'm not sure how much we can help."

"Let's think about what we know at this point," I say, drifting into secret agent mode. "We know there were one hundred students here for a scholarship competition, and now fifty are left. We know Fiona and the staff are concerned about someone stealing her latest technology—"

"The MCD," Zig says. "That's what you said she called it, right?"

"Yeah, the Microclimate Dome," I say, pointing at Meatball. "That was the thing you and Laura were talking about the first night we were here, right?"

"Yup. The thing that made it snow yesterday on a summer day," Meatball says.

"We also know that they have never had a breach of security at the school before," I say, "but they're so worried that they moved the data files around and they might even cancel The Firestone Fires."

"Wait, what do you mean 'they moved the data files around?'" Meatball says.

"Yeah," I say, "apparently Dr. V is so worried about the servers getting hacked that she took the plans offline."

"That sounds risky," Zig says.

"I know, right? I think they're hiding them," I say, careful not to share every detail I know.

"Like somewhere here at the school or off campus?" Zig asks, and again I lie. "I don't know, I think somewhere in the school, but she didn't say where."

"And you said they think Rogan Bosch has something to do with this?" Meatball asks.

"It sounds like it," I say.

"Dude, this is crazy," Meatball says, "are you sure you weren't sleepwalking?"

"Positive."

"Hey, there are the girls," Zig says, noticing that Haley, Jess, and Laura are headed our way. "Should we tell them?"

"I don't know," I say, "maybe let's wait until we know more before we say anything?"

"You don't trust them?" Zig asks, surprised.

"It's not that I don't trust them," I say, "I just don't know them. What if one of them isn't here for the right reason?"

"So, you don't trust them," Zig repeats himself.

"I guess not," I say, sort of surprised that I don't.

"Hey boys," Jess says.

"Hey Jess," Meatball says awkwardly without making eye contact.

"You guys ready to make it into the Top 25 today?" Haley says, smiling.

"Wait, are twenty-five people going home today?" Zig asks.

"Fifty people might be going home today," Meatball says under his breath, but a little too loud.

"What does that mean?" Jess says. I try to change the subject back to The Fires.

"Haley's right, probably," I say. "I could see us getting down to the Top 25 today and then maybe the Top 10 tomorrow."

"Did you rebels sneak out and go exploring last night?" Laura asks.

"Nope," Zig says glancing at me for a second, "did you girls?"

"Nah," Jess says.

"I knew you wouldn't," Laura scowls.

"I knew you wouldn't," Jess repeats in a mocking voice.

"Oh, that's real mature, Jess," Laura says.

"About as mature as you cheating in racquetball yesterday," Jess says.

"Are you still whining about that?" Laura says. "It was your first time playing and I beat you, get over it."

"Seriously, you two," Haley chimes in. "They've been doing this all morning."

"What are you guys arguing about over here?" a voice interrupts us from behind me. It's Hudson, flanked on his right by Adam, like usual. "Am I interrupting some kind of triple date?"

"Nah," Zig says. "We're just talking about how many people might get eliminated today. We're thinking from fifty to twenty-five."

"Good thing it's Top 50, not 45, right Flake?" Hudson says.

"Lucky clown," Adam says. "So close to going home to mommy."

"Still here," I say, trying to pretend like their ribbing isn't bothering me.

"Barely here," Hudson says, "but your time is coming, Pee Boy."

"Okay, dude," Haley says, getting right in Hudson's face, "we get it. You're the cool bully, like in the movies. What's next, you gonna steal our lunch money or stuff us in a locker? Or wait, I know. You're gonna ask Lake why a girl is fighting his battles for him, right?"

"I mean, isn't that what's happening right now?" Hudson smiles.

"Wow, you really are like a cartoon character," Haley says. "You even have a clown sidekick and everything," she says pointing to Adam.

"Hey, you're the clown!" he says to her.

"Why don't you guys go find a table so we can finish our conversation," Laura says, flicking her hand at Hudson and Adam like she's swatting a fly away from her sandwich. "Go on now, get some breakfast."

"Oh don't worry, we're done here," Hudson says, turning to Adam. "Let's go."

"Man, I hope they get eliminated today," Laura says. "Either of those two winning a scholarship would be such a waste."

"Oh, Flake," Hudson says as he walks away, just loud enough so I can hear. "Watch your head when you're climbing into your bunk in the middle of the night. Wouldn't want you to hurt yourself."

35

"Good morning, students," a squeaky voice echoes over the loudspeakers, interrupting our breakfast. "I hope everyone slept well and is ready for today's elimination event. I know you're finishing up your breakfast, but please take a moment to welcome your host, Fiona Firestone."

I'm not sure why Fiona Firestone insists on being introduced whenever she addresses us, but I join in the applause as she takes the stage. Every time I've seen her, she looks like she's ready for a photoshoot. Today is no different. She's wearing a slim black dress, high heels, and her hair is up in some kind of fancy hairdo. On their perch at the back of the stage, her two small birds quietly watch her every move.

"Good morning students," she smiles. "I hope you enjoyed this morning's breakfast!"

Well, this is weird. Not only does she not seem like someone who's about to cancel a scholarship competition, she actually seems ... happy? I can't recall seeing her face this bright since we got here.

"Now that we've gotten rid of the lesser half of the group," she says, "we're down to our final fifty."

When she says this the entire Great Room breaks out into

applause again. Honestly, it feels great to still be here. Whatever today's elimination event is, I need to survive it so I can be here tomorrow morning doing this same thing.

"Some of you won't be cheering for very long," Fiona says, killing the mood. "Breakfast is now officially over, and it's time for our next elimination event—another race of sorts. In a few moments you will be broken up into groups as designated by a number that will appear on your ID Band. Please find your group and await further instructions."

As she finishes her sentence she looks to her right at Dr. V, who is sitting at a table working on her laptop. She presses a key and instantly my ID Band buzzes and displays the number 7 on it in bright green.

"I'm Group 2, what about you guys?" Zig says, holding up his left arm. I can barely hear him from everyone talking and getting out of their chairs.

"Four!" Meatball says.

"I'm in seven," I say, but I'm pretty sure no one hears me. Chaos has broken out in the Great Room as kids are scrambling all over, trying to find their groups.

"Bro, go find your group!" Zig yells at me over the madness. "This could be the elimination event!"

Shoot, he's right. If Fiona sent people home on the first day for not being social, she'd definitely send them home for being too slow to get organized.

"NINES OVER HERE!" a girl screams.

"ONES IN THE CORNER!" a deep voice bellows from behind me.

"WHERE ARE THE SEVENS?" I hear a girl yell to my right.

"I'm a seven!" I say, yelling back in her direction, and suddenly I see a hand reach out from between two people and grab my arm. She yanks me toward her, and I realize it's Laura.

"We're looking for sevens! Where are the sevens?" she yells as she drags me behind her. She's hurting my arm, but I don't care. We need to find our group before we get eliminated.

"Sevens over here, c'mon you guys," says Hudson, who doesn't try to hide the disappointment on his face the moment he realizes it's me. He's standing next to Jess, who also has a seven on her ID Band.

"TWOS ARE ALL HERE!" I hear Zig shout from the other side of the room.

"SO ARE THE TWELVES!" a girl with a raspy voice shouts even louder.

Fifty kids scrambling around a room trying to get in groups, and no one wants to lose the race to find their team. Despite the fact that the groups all seemed to be formed, the room keeps getting louder. I can barely hear Fiona Firestone start yelling into the microphone.

"WHOA, WHOA, WHOA, SETTLE DOWN EVERYONE," her voice booms over the sound system. "This part is not a race. I repeat, this is not a race. Please just stand with your group."

To our left, two groups start arguing about which one finished organizing first, and raised voices turn into screaming as two kids stand nose to nose.

"EVERYONE CALM DOWN!" she finally yells at the top of her lungs, which actually works to quiet the room. "Well then," she says, taking a deep breath. "Now that it appears everyone has found their group and has regained their sanity, please pay close attention. In a few moments you will all head to a designated room that corresponds with your group number. Again, this part is *not* a race. You will be well aware when the elimination event has actually started."

I'm listening to the instructions, but I'm also scanning the room to see if I can find Haley to see what group she's in. So far, no luck.

"Once you are in your room," Fiona says, "you'll receive further instructions from me on the nature of this team competition."

With that statement, the room starts to get loud again.

"That's right, I did say *team* competition, which begs the question—does anyone know what a murmuration is?" The question catches me a little off guard. This is the first time she's asked for any type of feedback from us while at the podium.

"Yes, you," she says, pointing to Zig. He's the only one in the room with his hand raised.

"It's the name for a flock of swallows that are all flying together, synchronously," he says.

"Very good, young man," she says, turning back to the rest of us. "If you've never seen the beauty of a murmuration, make a note to watch it on video sometime; truly captivating. But it's not just beautiful—it's also an incredible example of practical teamwork. It often means a falcon is nearby, and the swallows know that their best chance for survival is working together."

"As you've already heard me say before, we are better together here at this school. The swallows know this, and before this week is over, you'll know it, too. It's imperative that you work well in a team environment to find solutions to problems. My greatest innovations were not achieved by locking myself up alone in a room—they were solved by working with others."

"That's the difference between her and Rogan," Laura whispers to me. "Rogan Bosch doesn't need anyone's help."

I roll my eyes and ignore her.

Fiona continues. "Please proceed—*quietly*—through the yellow doors to my left and your right. There are twelve rooms off of the hallway, one for each of your groups."

The fifty of us head out through the yellow doors in search of our rooms, ignoring Fiona's request that we do so quietly. I see Zig up ahead of me about ten feet or so, but right when I'm about to call his name to get his attention, he disappears into Room 2.

The room numbers don't seem to be in any particular order.

Room 8 was the first one we passed, then Room 4, and Room 2, where Zig had entered.

"There it is!" Jess says, "Room 7!"

I walk in behind Jess, and Hudson and Laura file in behind me. As she closes the door behind her I realize it's just the four of us. There's a large television screen on the wall, like we have in our bunk room, but not much else.

"Okay, what we do now?" Laura asks.

Before any of us can answer a loud voice booms from the television.

"DOOR LOCKS ACTIVATE." The voice is Fiona Firestone's, and it's accompanied by the loud sound of our door latch locking shut.

"Okaaaay," Jess says, "that just got a little creepy."

"LIGHTS OFF," the voice says.

And suddenly the room is pitch black.

From somewhere in the darkness Jess corrects herself, "Make that *a lot* creepy."

36

The darkness is so deep, it feels like the temperature just dropped ten degrees. My teeth are chattering, but I'm not sure if it's from the cold or from how anxious I suddenly feel.

How did I get here? Locked in total darkness at The Firestone School with three people I just met, all trying to stay alive in The Firestone Fires?

"Okay, here's what I think we should—" Laura starts to say, until she's interrupted by Fiona Firestone's face on the television.

"Welcome to the Escape Room Challenge, which will start the moment my lovely face disappears from this screen."

Maybe it's the darkness of the room, or maybe it's the television itself, but I swear I've never seen a picture as bright and clear as this one. We've got an ultra high-definition television at home, but this picture quality is insane.

"The goal is to escape your room and return to the Great Room," she continues. *"The first six teams to do so will move on. The other six teams will be eliminated."*

"Wow, half of us are about to go home!" Jess says.

"Shhh! Obviously," says Laura. I can't see the dirty look Jess is probably giving her right now, but I'm sure it's intense.

"When the lights come back on, you'll see that the door to your room has a touchscreen keyboard. Enter the right password and the door unlocks. Enter the wrong password, and the keyboard is disabled for sixty seconds. Each room has a unique password, and that password is the only way to escape."

Fiona Firestone's bright face continues, *"When the challenge starts, you'll see some vital information on this television screen: two clues, two timers, and one list. You will be given two clues to solve this puzzle. These clues will be the same for every group."*

"Is anyone good at clues?" Jess asks.

"Shhh! Listen up!" Laura says again through gritted teeth.

"Don't shush me, Laura," Jess fires back.

"Both of you shut up!" Hudson says.

"In the top left corner of this screen will be your first clue. In the top right corner will be a clue you receive gradually. One new letter every five minutes until eventually the entire clue is revealed."

"In the bottom left-hand corner will be a list of all of the teams who have completed the challenge. And finally, in the bottom right corner will be two timers. The one counting up from zero represents the overall competition time and the other will count down from sixty seconds every time you enter an incorrect password."

"I suppose I am feeling a little bit generous so here's a free hint. Each of your passwords are longer than two letters but shorter than ten. And with that, we begin."

Just like that, her face vanishes and the lights in the room come on, temporarily blinding all of us. As my eyes slowly adjust, I see a screen full of information, exactly like she described.

The clue in the top left says:

WHAT BROUGHT YOU HERE TOGETHER
WILL GET YOU OUT TOGETHER

In the top right, there's an unrevealed clue: ten blanks with a space in the middle.

— — — — — *** — — — — —

In the bottom left, twelve small, gray circles, each with the numbers one through twelve, representing the groups.

And in the bottom right, a timer counting up from zero.

00:07 ... 00:08 ... 00:09 ...

"Okay," Laura says, the first thing we need to do is—"

BEEP! BEEP! BEEP!

"What the heck?" I say covering my ears to block the noise from the blaring sound.

"Okay," Jess says, standing at the door's keyboard. "At least we know the password isn't PASSWORD."

"Are you serious right now," Hudson growls.

"Jess, you can't just do that," Laura barks. "You just locked the door for a whole minute."

"It's only a minute," Jess says. "Look, it's already down to fifty-five seconds anyway. Not gonna hurt to try out a few common passwords."

"Only a moron would use PASSWORD for a password," Hudson says. "You really think Fiona Firestone is a moron?"

"Well, she's no Rogan Bosch," Laura says. "But Hudson's right, it's not gonna be something obvious."

"Plenty of people use PASSWORD for a password because no one expects it," Jess says.

"Please tell me you don't use PASSWORD for your pass-words," Hudson laughs.

"I actually just changed all my passwords to BUSTER123," Jess says, her face frowning a bit as she says it. "That's the name of the puppy my parents got me for my birthday two weeks ago. He's so cute—I miss him so much." She says this last part in an embarrassing baby talk voice.

"You might want to keep that to yourself, there, champ,"

Hudson says to Jess. "The baby talk *and* the telling people what your passwords are." The two of them are giving each other a hard time, but there's a hint of flirting in there that sort of grosses me out.

"Okay, how about this," I say. "No more putting in passwords unless we agree as a team to put one in. All in favor?"

"What do you think this is, Flake, student government?" Hudson says.

"No, Lake's right," Laura says, "we all should agree."

"Okay, so what about this clue?" Jess says. "WHAT BROUGHT YOU HERE TOGETHER WILL GET YOU OUT TOGETHER. What does that mean?"

"Could mean anything," Hudson says.

"I came here in a car?" Jess says.

"Well, I came here in a truck," Laura says sarcastically, "so that's obviously not it."

"Guys, listen," I say. "Let's stop snapping at each other and get back to brainstorming."

"Hey, an M!" Jess says.

In the top right corner, a letter in the second clue has been revealed.

"Okay, well, I guess we get a new letter every few minutes," I say. "The 'M' only narrows it down to about seven million possibilities."

"What if the password is HALLWAY?" Jess says. "It's what brought all of us here, and it's what would get us all out of here right?"

"Hey, that's actually a good guess!" Laura says. "Go try it."

Jess turns back to the door and types it in. BEEP! BEEP! BEEP!

"Shoot. I thought that was it," Jess says.

"It couldn't have been it," I say.

"Oh really," Hudson says, "and how would you know that?"

"Because," I say, "Fiona Firestone said that each room has a unique password. The clues are all the same, but the passwords are different. And since all twelve groups got to their rooms through the same hallway, that couldn't have been the password."

Hudson makes a face because he knows I'm right, and he doesn't like it.

DING!

This new sound coming from the television—much more pleasant than the annoying triple BEEP!—gets our attention immediately.

That's when we see it.

The circle with the number four in it has changed from light grey to bright green.

Group 4 just escaped.

37

"Alright," Laura says, "there are only five spots left. We've got to figure this out."

Okay," I say, "let's go back to our clue. What brought us together other than the vehicles we came here in? I mean, the competition brought us here, but that doesn't make any sense because, again, the password has to be different for each group. That's the part I can't figure out."

"T!" Jess shouts, pointing to the screen. We all try to process the partial clue.

$$\underline{\quad}\ \underline{\quad}\ \underline{\quad}\ \underline{T}\ \underline{\quad}\ ^{***}\underline{M}\ \underline{\quad}\ \underline{\quad}\ \underline{\quad}\ \underline{\quad}$$

I've always been great at word puzzles, but there's just not enough information yet on this clue. I start guessing out loud to see if I can get lucky.

"White Mazes? Party Mulch? Zitty Meats?"

"What are you doing, moron?" Hudson asks.

"I'm brainstorming about what the second clue might be," I say.

"So stupid," Hudson says, shaking his head.

"Hey," Jess snaps at him, "you have any better ideas, blondie? If not, then shut it."

DING!

"Group 11 just got out," Laura shouts. "That's two teams already! What are we missing here?"

Just then a thought comes to me. "Wait a minute! Maybe it's not about what brought us all to the competition, maybe it's about what brought us into this room."

"Yeah, but we know it's not the hallway," Jess says.

"Right, but I'm not talking about what physically got us here," I say. "I'm talking about why the four of us are together."

"Ooh, right, this is good," Laura says. "I think you're onto something. How did they figure out how to break us all into groups of four?"

"Well, that's the thing," I say. "We're not all in groups of four."

"How do you know that?" Hudson asks.

"Well, two reasons," I say. "I saw Ziggy go into Room 2 with four other people. That was definitely a group of five."

"And?" Jess says.

"Well, think about it," I say. "There are fifty of us left, and there are twelve groups, right? There have to be some groups with more than four people. Four times twelve is forty-eight."

"How did I not think of that?" Laura says. "So do you think there's a reason some groups are bigger than others, or was it just random?"

"I don't know," I say, "but it must be the key to solving this."

DING!

"Looks like Zig's group just got out," Jess says pointing to a now-green circle with a two in it on the screen.

"That's half the teams!" Laura says. "C'mon guys, how can we not figure this out?"

"Another T!" Jess says, as another letter is revealed.

"We should at least be trying some different passwords that make sense," Hudson says in a strangely calm voice. He's the only one of us who doesn't seem worried that there are only three spots left.

"No! No random guesses," Laura snaps. "Don't lock the keyboard for no reason."

At this point I'm not sure if I agree with her. Guessing the password is sort of impossible, but it still seems like a better idea than just sitting here watching our chances of staying in the competition disappear.

"The good news is we're probably just one or two letters away from figuring out this second clue," I say. "But the bad news is, so is everyone else."

If three teams already figured out their passwords, we should be able to, as well. What am I missing here?

"Okay," I say, "even though we know the teams are different sizes, I think the key is figuring out why the four of us are together."

BEEP! BEEP! BEEP!

We all turn to see Jess back at the door. "Well, it's not BEAUTIFUL," she says.

"Beautiful?" Laura asks, confused.

"Yeah, we're all kind of good-looking people. I thought maybe that was the connection." Jess is smiling, and I have to admit, even though I'm on the verge of being eliminated from The Firestone Fires, that was kind of funny.

"I guarantee no one has ever called Flake beautiful in his life," Hudson says. For once, I agree with him.

Just then I notice a fourth revealed letter in the hidden clue.

$$\underline{}\,\underline{I}\,\underline{}\,\underline{T}\,\underline{}\,{}^{***}\underline{M}\,\underline{}\,\underline{}\,\underline{T}\,\underline{}$$

"Okay, they just gave us an I," I say, mumbling out loud.

"Fifty Malts? Witty Manta? Dirty Mutts?"

"Idiot idiot," Hudson says, mocking me.

DING! DING!

"WHAT!" Laura shouts. "Groups 12 *and* 1! There's only one spot left."

"Next group out is the last group to move on," Jess says.

"OBVIOUSLY!!!" Laura snaps.

I try to block out the bickering, but I just can't focus. There's no way my journey is gonna end here. To be chosen out of tens of thousands of students to make it here, and to get halfway through the competition, only to go home now? No way.

"Guys, give me some passwords to try," Hudson says, for the first time seeming a little panicked.

"We don't have anything to try, Hudson," Laura says. "It's been twenty minutes, and we haven't figured anything out."

"WHAT BROUGHT YOU HERE TOGETHER WILL GET YOU OUT TOGETHER?" Jess says, repeating the clue for the thousandth time. "Thanks, Fiona Firestone, for the worst clue ever."

"Fine, I guess we just give up then," Laura says, sitting down in the corner. "This literally just went from the best birthday to the worst birthday ever."

"Oh, you didn't say it was your birthday," Jess says. "Happy birthday!"

"Yeah, a real happy birthday," Laura frowns. "Welcome to being twelve years old, here's your suitcase, see you later."

And that's when it hits me.

"That's it!" I shout.

"What's it?" Jess asks.

"The password!" I say.

"What, SUITCASE?" Hudson asks.

"No," I say, jumping out of my chair pointing toward Laura. "It's your birthday today."

"Yeah, so what," Laura says.

"And two weeks ago it was Jess's birthday—that's when she said she got her new dog."

"Yeah, and ... " Jess says.

"Let me guess," I say, running to the door, "Hudson, your birthday is this month too, right?"

"Yeah, next week," he says. "July 30th."

"That's what brought us together!" I say. "My birthday is July 9th. That's what the second clue is!"

$$\_\_ \underline{I} \_\_ \underline{T} \_\_ ^{***} \underline{M} \_\_ \_\_ \underline{T} \_\_$$

"It's BIRTH MONTH!" Laura says.

"Exactly," I say. "That's how every group could have the same clues but a different password! We were grouped together based on our birthdays."

WHAT BROUGHT YOU HERE TOGETHER
WILL GET YOU OUT TOGETHER

"Oh, duh," Jess says, "and the name of every month has more than two letters and less than ten letters."

I'm at the door now, punching J-U-L-Y into the keypad.

The door unlocks and I fling it open.

"Let's go!"

38

I lead the way as our team races down the hall to the Great Room. As we're approaching the closed double doors, I hear another team fill the hallway behind us.

"Open it up!" Hudson yells.

I pull on the handle and, as we burst through the doors, we're instantly met with cheers from the other kids inside. The four of us run into the middle of the room, where Mr. Lincoln and Beardy are stationed.

"Congratulations, Group 7!" Mr. Lincoln says, as the cheers from the other students reach a crescendo. It's only as they start to die down that we hear the banging on the Great Room doors from the team that was just behind us in the hallway.

"Unlock the doors!" someone is saying from the hallway.

"It appears Group 9 is not aware that they are no longer in the competition," Mr. Lincoln says, motioning to Beardy that he should take care of the problem.

"I'm on it," Beardy squeaks, making his way out of the side door.

"Everyone find a seat," Mr. Lincoln says. "I'll have a few announcements for you before you are dismissed."

I'm still trying to catch my breath when it dawns on me that

I don't even know if Haley is still here. I know Zig and Meatball made it through because they were in Groups 2 and 4 , but I never saw which team Haley was on.

I scan the room to try to find her and, right when my heart is about to sink, I spot her standing with Meatball and Zig. She gives me a little wave when she sees me heading in their direction.

"Super Six!" Meatball says, "somehow we all made it to Top 25!"

"Actually, Top 24," Zig says. "I counted twice."

"Even better!" I say.

"Yeah, well if it wasn't for this guy," Jess says pointing at me, "we'd be going home. How did you guys solve your password so fast?"

"I don't know," Zig says, "we just kind of stumbled into it. I figured it had to do with teamwork, so I made everyone say a few things about themselves and it turns out two of us were born on Valentine's Day. Do you what the odds of that are?"

"No, but I bet you do," Laura says.

".27 percent!" Zig says.

"Yeah," Haley says, "we kind of did the same thing! But we weren't even first. Meatball's team was already in here when we escaped."

"Hey, people born in April are naturally smarter than everyone else," Meatball says. "Isn't that right, Zig?"

"Well, actually," Zig starts to say, but he's interrupted by Mr. Lincoln, who is now on the Great Room stage holding a microphone.

"Would the six of you care to join the rest of us?" He scowls. "Or would you prefer to join the students currently packing their belongings?"

"Sorry, sir!" Zig yells out, as we all walk across the room and find a seat with the other eighteen students.

"Now then," Mr. Lincoln says, "congratulations on making it into the Top 24 of The Firestone Fires. I would love to tell you that you're going to have the rest of the day to enjoy this feat, but I'm afraid we've had a change of plans in the competition."

Just like that, the room goes from sort of quiet to dead silent.

"The Firestone Fires usually take a week to complete," Mr. Lincoln says, "but this year that will not be the case."

"Is he about to send us all home?" Meatball whispers to me. I'm wondering the same thing.

"Unfortunately this year," he continues, "we are putting the competition on an accelerated track."

"What does that mean?" Jess whispers, and right on cue Laura shushes her.

"The next elimination event will be this evening," Mr. Lincoln says, "and more than half of you will be going home." A chill runs up my spine as he says this, because this means that when I go to sleep tonight I'm either going to be in the Top 10 or headed home to Glenville.

"This change has one other major effect on our schedule." Mr. Lincoln continues. "Every year we honor the Top 10 of The Firestone Fires with a small party to celebrate their achievement. We like to keep it a surprise, but thanks to the current circumstances I'm ruining that surprise for you now. If you make it past this evening's event you can look forward to that celebration tomorrow. Are there any questions?"

Laura shoots her hand up and shouts out her question before she's even called on. "Why has the competition been 'accelerated,' as you put it? Is there something going on here we need to know about?"

Mr. Lincoln looks over to this right, and for the first time I notice that Dr. V is standing off to the side in the shadows. She gives Mr. Lincoln a small nod, almost like she's giving him permission, and he nods back.

"I can only share a few details," Mr. Lincoln says, "so these will have to suffice. The moment we feel like this school is a dangerous place for you, we are going to send you home. Since we are not sending you home at the moment, we believe you are safe—for now"

Mr. Lincoln glances back over at Dr. V and then continues. "Likewise, the moment we feel like the technology and intellectual property here at the school are not safe, we will take actions necessary to ensure they remain safe. Again, we are continuing The Firestone Fires for now, albeit on an accelerated timeline, so as far as you're concerned there is nothing further you need to know."

Mr. Lincoln pauses to take a sip of water and, as he does, I realize I've never heard it this quiet in the Great Room. It's partly because there are only twenty-four of us now, but also because we're all so locked in to what we're being told.

"I know what some of you are probably thinking," Mr. Lincoln says. "I've heard the whispers and rumors, and I also saw what was falling from the sky during the Puzzle Race. However, I'm not going to confirm or deny the existence of any top secret project or plans that might be causing this situation. Fiona Firestone always has many projects ongoing at once and all of them are valuable to her. We never comment on those specifics, and we certainly won't start now."

He pauses to collect himself, clearly thinking through the wording of whatever sentence he's about to say.

"But ... I will say this," he adds. "If any of you hear anything or see anything here at the school that seems suspicious, please relay that to one of us here on the staff."

Jess raises her hand and starts waving it back and forth at Mr. Lincoln.

"Yes, you with the annoying, bubbling energy," he says as he points to her.

"Mr. Lincoln, how are we going to see or hear anything suspicious?" Jess asks. "It's not like we're roaming all over the school. You guys even had us on lockdown for half a day, which I'm assuming had something to do with this. I don't see how we can help when we're only ever with each other?"

"Well, that's exactly the point," Mr. Lincoln says, making eye contact with Dr. V for a third time. Again she nods at him.

"When I say we are looking at every possibility, I mean *every* possibility. Everyone is under suspicion ... "

He pauses again and takes a sip of water.

"... everyone including the twenty-four of you."

39

I check the clock.

It's 6:05 p.m., which means only seven minutes have passed since I last checked it. Feels more like seven hundred.

I adjust my head on my pillow, close my eyes, and breathe deeply. Tonight's elimination event should be starting any minute now, so I'm just killing time and trying to stay relaxed. There are only three of us left in this room. All our other roommates are gone from The Fires; it's just me, Hudson, and Meatball.

They gave us a bunch of free time this afternoon, but it was kind of hard to enjoy it. My mind hasn't stopped racing since Mr. Lincoln's address to us this morning. And only now in the quiet of our bunk room am I able to start processing it.

The more I think about it, the more I can't believe we are still here. If the school's at risk, why not just send us home? Why keep two dozen students here if you feel like one of them is trying to steal from you?

I try to get into secret agent mode, to really break it down in my head, but I just can't stay there. All week I've had trouble staying focused. It feels like I've spent ninety percent of my time this week either trying to win a challenge, or trying to get Haley to laugh at something I said.

To me, this is what separates a secret agent from a spy. Maybe some people think they're the same thing, but I've always thought they were different.

Spies just steal things—that's their job. They go undercover, they pretend to be someone they're not, and they steal things.

Secret agents, though, do a lot more than just steal. They gather intelligence, they put together strategies, and they protect the people and things that need protecting. Most importantly, they are able to use the fragments of information they collect to see the bigger picture. That's what I need to do now.

Focus, Lake. Focus.

Based on what I know, what is happening here? What are the three most likely possibilities?

Possibility number one is that the scholarship competition is more important to Fiona than protecting these top secret files, and that's why we're still here. That doesn't really make sense, though. I know what I heard last night. She told Dr. V she would cancel the competition if she had to, so that scenario is out.

Possibility number two is that there really isn't a significant threat to the school, and they're lying to us. But that doesn't make sense either, because Dr. V and Fiona had no idea I was listening to them last night. They were genuinely concerned.

So this leaves possibility number three as the only option. There is a real threat to the school, but Fiona thinks keeping us here makes more sense than sending us home. But why? What benefit does she get from having students here during this threat, especially if one of them might be in on it?

C'mon, Lake, the answer is right there. Keep digging.

What if Fiona doesn't just want to stop this robbery attempt from happening—what if she wants it to happen so she can catch the thief in the act? And ... what if she wants us here because she wants our help? She knows that to get this far in the Fires, we have to be smart and clever.

Lucky for her, one of the twenty-four students still here has been training his whole life for this moment.

That would be me, Lake Mason.

"Lake Mason."

"LAKE MASON ... HELLO, EARTH TO LAKE MASON!"

I snap out of my deep thoughts to realize that Meatball is standing beside my bed, and probably has been for the last thirty seconds.

"Dude, were you in a trance or something?" Meatball asks.

"I told you we should have just let him sleep," Hudson says from across the room.

"I wasn't sleeping," I say, sitting up. "I was just thinking."

"Daydreaming about making out with Haley, probably," Hudson says.

"Eww, no," I say, probably a little too defensively.

"Well," Meatball says, "if you want to get more time with Haley, you're gonna need to make Top Ten. Let's do this."

"I gotta say, Flake," Hudson says as we head out into the hallway to the Great Room, "I don't really like your odds of moving on."

"It's ten spots, dude," I say. "I have just as good a chance as you."

"Flake, I'm getting through this event," Hudson says. "That leaves nine spots for the rest of you scrubs."

It's not just the the fact that he says it that bothers me—it's the way that he says it. He's always so stinking cocky about surviving these events, and then he always does.

It makes me wonder if he's really that confident in himself, or if he knows something the rest of us don't. It also makes me want to grab him by his dumb blond head and flush his face in a toilet bowl, but that's probably not a good idea.

I know one thing, though. On my list of possible suspects for who the student mole might be, Hudson is suspect number one. But for now the detective work will have to wait. If I don't finish Top 10, none of this matters.

We walk into the Great Room and immediately notice that the chairs and tables have been changed around in a way we've never seen before. The center of the room is empty, but all around it there are twenty-four small tables spread out, each with a single chair beside it.

Beardy greets us as we walk in and gives us our instructions.

"Tonight's elimination event is a test," he says in his high-pitched voice. "Please find an empty table and sit quietly. We're almost ready to start."

A test? Okay, wow. I have no idea what we're going to be tested on, but I'm usually pretty good with tests.

I pick out an empty table and scan the room. I see Haley a few tables away, and she smiles at me when she sees me. I smile back, but behind my smile is a little bit of fear, too. Is this the last time I'm going to be in the same room with her? I wonder what the odds are of both of us finishing Top 10 out of twenty-four students. I bet Zig would know.

I take my seat, which is one table over from Zig, and he gives me a thumbs up sign while mouthing the words, "Let's go!"

I take a deep breath and close my eyes, feeling the weight of the moment more than I have all week.

Ace this test and I have a fifty percent chance at a six-year scholarship to The Firestone School.

Bomb it and I have a one hundred percent chance of six years of the Crapville Education System.

No pressure, Lake.

40

_____

"Listen up!" Mr. Lincoln says from the front of the room, while Beardy walks around handing tablets, pencils, and paper to every student.

"This evening's event is simple. You've got one hundred multiple choice questions and one hundred minutes to answer them. Every correct answer is worth five points, meaning a perfect score is five hundred. Every incorrect answer will cost you two points. Any questions that you leave blank will be worth zero points. Are there any questions?"

To my right I see Jess raise her hand.

"So we shouldn't guess if we don't know the answer?" she asks.

"That is up to you," Mr. Lincoln says, slightly annoyed. "If you can narrow it down to two possible answers, you've got a fifty-fifty shot of earning five points. But yes, if you're wrong, you'll lose two points."

"Sorry for asking a question when you asked us if we had any questions," Jess says with some sass, which causes a few of us to chuckle.

"Okay, everyone has their iPads and scratch paper," Beardy squeaks from the back of the room.

"This test is unlike anything you've ever taken before," Mr. Lincoln says, ignoring Jess. "We call it the FACT," he says, spelling it out. "F-A-C-T. It stands for the Focus And Concentration Test, and it will cover everything from math to grammar to history to science and everything in between, even common sense."

Did he just say common sense? How do you test for common sense?

"To this point," Mr. Lincoln continues, "we've tested your social skills, physical skills, and teamwork skills. This evening we'll be testing you in other areas. How well do you take tests? How intelligent are you? And how do you handle distractions? We're about to find out."

Handling distractions? That's a weird thing to say before a test in a quiet room on an empty campus.

"Let's put one hundred minutes on the clock. You may begin *now*."

I swipe to unlock my tablet and am instantly presented with Question 1. On the right side of the screen is a sidebar that lets you scroll through all one hundred questions if you want to skip around. The first few are fairly easy, and I feel good about my answers. Question 6 is a really complicated algebra problem, and I spend a minute trying to solve it with my pencil and paper before deciding to skip it. I'll come back to it if I have time later.

After answering a few more questions I notice eighty-five minutes are left on the clock. I'm fifteen minutes in and I'm on Question 19. That's a good pace, I think.

By the time I get to Question 30, I'm feeling pretty good. I've skipped seven so far that I either didn't know, or didn't want to take the time to figure out. That means I've got over twenty answers I feel confident about.

I find my place back at Question 30 and just as I do a piercing beep—so loud it actually hurts my ears—fills the room. I cover my ears and look up from my test to see that every else is doing the same thing.

"ARE YOU GONNA FIX THAT?" Laura yells over the sound of the beep.

"OH, IT'S NOT BROKEN," Mr. Lincoln screams back, putting in ear plugs. "WE'RE JUST TESTING THE FIRE ALARMS. SEEING HOW LOUD WE CAN MAKE THEM. LIKE I SAID WHEN WE STARTED, WE WANT TO KNOW HOW YOU HANDLE DISTRACTIONS!"

"WHAT KIND OF CLOWN TEST IS THIS," a kid yells from my right. I don't even have to turn around to know it's Adam.

"I'M SORRY, I CAN'T HEAR YOU," Mr. Lincoln yells back pointing to his ear plugs, but clearly he's not sorry—he's enjoying this. "DON'T WORRY, IT SHOULD BE OVER IN ABOUT FIVE MINUTES."

I take my hands off of my ears and try my best to work through more questions despite the painful beeping. After a few minutes it does seem to become a bit more bearable. I wonder if it's getting softer or if I'm literally losing my hearing by the minute. A few kids have chosen to wait out the five minutes by putting down their tablets, covering their ears, and closing their eyes.

The beeping finally stops. The clock says one hour left and I'm on Question 49, but I've skipped a bunch.

The questions really do cover anything and everything.

Q17: What is the chemical name for salt?
A) Sodium Carbonate
B) Sodium Chloride
C) Potassium Chloride
D) Potassium Carbonate

(I think it's B, Sodium Chloride.)

Q23: Which of these flowers is not a perennial?
A) Daffodil
B) Rose
C) Pansy
D) Magnolia

(I have no idea what a perennial even is.)

Q47: If a human hand has 14 knuckles, how many knuckles are there in a baseball team's starting batting lineup?
A) 126
B) 140
C) 252
D) 280

(Are there nine or ten in a lineup? I think it's nine so I choose 252 over 280.)

I have a good rhythm going when I look up at the clock and see that somehow there are only thirty-five minutes left. I'm all the way to Question 87, but at this point I've definitely skipped at least twenty questions that I'll need to go back to.

Five minutes later, Beardy walks into the center of the room and starts putting up a small circular fence, like the kind they use to keep crawling babies in the middle of a room. I try to ignore him, even though he's whistling loudly in an attempt to distract us.

Moments later the purpose of the fence becomes clear. "Who loves puppies?" Beardy squeaks, holding one in each arm. Mr. Lincoln is holding two as well, which they both release into the fenced-in area.

"Awww, look how cute!" Jess says, putting her tablet down and going over to pet them.

"We've got a whole twenty-six minutes left," Mr. Lincoln says. "Feel free to give your brain a break and come pet the puppies. It might actually clear your mind!"

Jess is joined by two other girls and Meatball in the playpen, where the puppies are chasing tennis balls and gnawing on bones. They do look super cute, but I'm not tempted in the slightest to get out of my seat. I'm not sure why Jess and Meatball are taking the bait, even if just for a minute.

After a few minutes, everyone is back in their seats, so Beardy takes the puppies away. But not before one of them leaves a little brown surprise on the floor that Mr. Lincoln makes Beardy clean up. I finish Question 100 with nineteen minutes left, so now it's time to go back and work on the ones I skipped. If I think I can narrow it down to two answers, I'll probably guess, but for the ones I have no idea on, my plan is to leave them blank.

With ten minutes on the timer, I scroll to the final screen of my test that provides an overview of my answer sheet. I've now made choices on eighty-five of the questions. I've got fifteen that I'm not sure about, and I'm going to take these last ten minutes to see if I can make an educated guess on any of them.

That's when the band comes in.

No, literally; an eight-piece, high school marching band just walks in and starts playing in the center of the room where the puppies just were twenty minutes ago. They weren't kidding about working through distractions.

There are four minutes left on the clock now, and I'm having trouble focusing. This FACT is no joke. I've gone over these remaining questions a dozen times each. I feel like I just need one or two more solid guesses.

When a few of the other kids start laughing, I realize juggling clowns have now joined the marching band in the center of the room. I start laughing too—it's quite a sight.

I look over at Adam, wondering if he'll call the clowns "a bunch of clowns," but his head is down as he's frantically trying to ignore the madness and come up with an answer for one of the test questions.

There's one last question I feel like I should be able to make a good guess on, but I just can't nail down an answer I feel super confident in.

Q42: How many states in the US border Mexico?
A) 4
B) 3
C) 5
D) 2

I think it's either four or five, but I don't know if I feel confident enough to guess. A right answer and I get five points that might keep me in the Top 10. But a wrong answer and I could lose two points that keep me out of the Top 10.

"One minute left on the clock," Mr. Lincoln says.

"Puppies!" Beardy squeaks, putting the four cute dogs back on the floor. With no fence to keep them contained, they run wild around the tables while the band plays and the clowns juggle.

I look back at Question 42, and suddenly I feel good about guessing A. I'm pretty sure it's Texas, California, and two states in between them. Arizona and New Mexico, I think? Twenty seconds left.

Wait, what state is to the right of Texas on the map? Louisiana? Does Louisiana border Mexico, too? I don't think so. But it might? Ugh. Maybe I shouldn't guess. Is it really worth the risk?

"Ten seconds until your tablets lock!" Mr. Lincoln yells over the marching band (and clowns and puppies).

I put my tablet down, I don't think I want to guess. Then I pick it back up tap answer A.

The clock hits zero and my tablet screen locks.

The FACT is over. And so are The Firestone Fires for all but ten of us.

41

M r. Lincoln collects our tablets while Beardy ushers the marching band and the clowns and the puppies out of the room.

I'm completely exhausted, and don't even bother to go find my friends. I just want to sit here for a few minutes and let my brain rest. While I'm nervous about how I did, I also have a sense of peace that there's nothing more I can do at this point.

My answers are submitted. I'm either in the Top 10 or I'm not.

I assume we'll learn the results pretty quickly, and that assumption turns out to be accurate when Mr. Lincoln clears his throat to make an announcement. "Listen up, everyone. The results are already tallied, so let's get right to it."

Wow, this is going down right now.

"The scores are in and the Top 10 is set. It's time to reveal who is moving on in The Firestone Fires," Mr. Lincoln announces. There's no need to ask us all to quiet down at this point, as everyone is in their seat, nervously silent.

"Our top FACT scorer this year, and our first student to make it into the Top Ten with an impressive score of 408 points out of 500: Zig Simmons."

Everyone claps for Zig, and I even let out a little holler for him. Man, that dude is smart.

"Our second Top 10 finalist is the only other student to break 400 points with a score of 402: Laura Dickson."

The applause for Laura is a lot less enthusiastic, but just about everyone gives her a courtesy clap. I know she rubs Meatball the wrong way, but I don't mind her, I guess. She was super annoying the first night, but it seems like over the past few days she's come around a little on Fiona Firestone.

"Our third Top 10 finalist for The Firestone Fires, with a score of 391, Hudson Frost."

Ugh. This guy runs his mouth before every event, but then he backs it up with good results. If I make Top 10, I'm gonna have to deal with his crap for at least another day.

"Our fourth Top 10 finalist, with a score of 388: Ryan Willjonk."

The kid to my left pumps his fist, and now I have a name to put with his face. I think I've said "hi" to him once or twice this week, but that's been the extent of our interactions. He seems like a normal kid who I could be friends with. Apparently he's smart, too.

"Our fifth finalist, rounding out the first half of the Top 10, with a score of 385: Haley Jenson."

Yes! I'm so stoked for Haley! We share a smile, but when she turns away a pit starts growing in my stomach. There are still nineteen of us sitting here who haven't heard our names, and only five spots left. If Haley moves on and I don't, I'm gonna be devastated.

"Our sixth finalist, with a score of 380: Derek Rantelo."

I search the room to see which one of the kids I don't know is Derek, and then it dawns on me. That's Meatball! He's waving his hand at us with a goofy smile on his face, pretending like he just won a beauty pageant or something. I keep forgetting his real name isn't Meatball. That makes four of the Super 6 in the Top 10. Only Jess and I are left.

I look over at her and we exchange forced smiles. Jess would be the first person to tell you she's not the greatest student, and I wonder if she's thinking there's no way she made it into the Top 10. I'm still feeling sort of confident, or at least I was a few minutes ago.

"Our seventh finalist, with a score of 379: Erik Pelz."

"Oh Yeah!" Erik yells, jumping out of his seat with his hands in the air. I don't think I've talked to that kid once since the first night when he was in the same circle as Hudson, Meatball, and Laura. His wispy attempt at a mustache looks just as bad now as it did then, but in this moment I'd gladly wear that mustache to trade places with him and be secure in the Top 10.

"Our eighth finalist, with a score of 370: Britney Leephong."

Uh oh. Just two spots left.

Did I really get that many wrong on this stupid quiz? I can't believe I got this far in The Fires only to go home because I couldn't concentrate hard enough to answer a few questions while clowns juggled to a marching band.

At this point I have a two in sixteen chance of hearing my name.

Those are terrible odds.

"Our ninth finalist, with a score of 365: Lake Mason."

Yeeeeesssssss! I made it. I made it. I made it. Okay, just smile while they clap for you and pretend like it's not a big deal. But it is a big deal! Oh my gosh! I made Top 10! I'm still here. I have a fifty-fifty shot at a Firestone School scholarship!

I try to stop smiling but it doesn't work. And then I see Jess and remember that she's not in yet and there's only one spot left.

"Okay, students, we're down to our last finalist," Mr. Lincoln says. "For those of you who did not make the Top 10, thank you so much for being here. You did well to get this far, but your journey is over."

Jess has this look on her face like she knows what's coming.

She smiles at me, then shakes her head and scrunches her nose. It's her way of silently saying, "It's not happening."

"Top Ten, please stay here in the Great Room. Everyone else can head back to your rooms to grab your bags," Mr. Lincoln says.

"Okay, I won't make you wait any longer," he continues. "Our tenth and final student in the Top 10, with a score of 359, is ...

... Jess Clarkson."

Half the room busts out in applause and the other half lets out loud sighs. Jess is dumbstruck; her mouth is wide open, her eyes fill with tears.

She did it.

We did it.

The Super Six made the Top 10 of The Firestone Fires.

42

It's just before noon and I'm lying in bed, waiting for word that we can head down to the Great Room for the Top 10 party.

In some ways it feels like I've packed an entire summer's worth of stuff into the last four days, but it also feels like this week has gone by in about four seconds. And yet here I am, one of ten kids left in The Firestone Fires, and somehow the five friends I've made this week are all still here, too.

Yesterday we said goodbye to the fourteen kids who didn't make Top 10, which was rough, even for me. I can't imagine what it feels like to get that close and then get sent home. You could just see it on their faces.

Other than the crying, most of the eliminated kids handled it well. Adam was the only one who made a scene. He apparently thought his test wasn't graded properly and demanded to see the answer key to know which questions he got wrong. After exchanging some heated words with Mr. Lincoln, he let us all know that we were clowns, the test was a clown test, and that this was a clown school he didn't want to go to anyway.

We all decided to celebrate by watching a movie together last night—even Hudson, believe it or not. Haley and I sat next to each other, and while I can't be positive, I'm pretty sure it's because she wanted to sit next to me.

I was so excited about making Top 10 that I drank way too much soda during the movie. I made sure to pee three times before falling sleep and thankfully woke up dry again. That's four mornings in a row without wetting the bed, which doesn't happen too often at home. Maybe The Firestone Fires is just what I needed to grow out of this phase?

As for what's next in the competition, no one really knows. Does this "accelerated timeline" mean there's going to be an elimination event tonight after the party? Will the next cut be to seven people or to the final five? They haven't told us anything about what to expect with the next event or if there are any updates with the security threat to the school. I'm trying not to get derailed by any of that. Even if my secret agent skills might be able to help Fiona Firestone, I need to stay focused on the real goal here: redirecting my future from Crapville to Firestone.

A knock on the door interrupts my train of thought, and Beardy sticks his head in. "The guests have arrived," he squeaks. "You guys can come down to the Great Room now."

Meatball and I start to leave the room when we notice that Hudson is still lying on his bed, his feet propped up against the wall.

"You coming, Hudson?" Meatball asks him.

"Eventually," he says. "You scrubs can go, don't wait for me."

Meatball shrugs at me, and we head down the hall.

When we walk into the Great Room I'm greeted by the best surprise ever. There are over two dozen people I've never seen before standing around, but in the middle of them is my mom, and right beside her is Nick! I sprint over and give my mom a huge hug.

"Lake!" she says. "Oh my gosh, I missed you."

"Missed you too, Mom," I say. "How was the drive here?"

"Kind of a nightmare, actually," my mom says. "It poured

the whole way until we got here. Now that I think of it, as soon as we turned onto the driveway the rained stopped."

"Not surprising," I mutter to myself under my breath. They must be using the MCD. Or maybe they're still testing it.

"Dude, Top 10!" Nick says. "Mr. No-Smile over there just told us there's only ten of you left."

"Oh yeah, that's Mr. Lincoln," I say. "Yeah, I've survived four events so far and some of them just barely. But, I'm still here."

"What kind of events?" Nick asks, as a server comes over and offers us sparkling grape juice and mini meatballs on toothpicks.

"All kinds," I say, taking a small sip of my juice. "Actually, the first night was all about interacting with each other. *That* was the whole competition! They monitored how many people you talked to, and I would have been gone if it wasn't for my friend Zig dragging me around to meet people. I'll introduce you to him when I see him—you'll like him."

"Which one is he?" Nick asks. I scan the room and point him out, but Zig is too busy talking to his parents to notice me waving.

"We also had a puzzle race to make the Top 50, where you had to race around the school and solve puzzles in between each lap. I barely got through; came in 49th. You should have seen me, dude, I was flying at the end."

I pause for a second to decide if I should mention that a freak snowstorm broke out in the middle of July. I don't think I'm supposed to say anything about the MCD, so I move past it.

"Then we had this Escape Room team competition that I totally solved for our team. Then yesterday they gave us this test while they distracted us with puppies and clowns and a band right in this room. It was ridiculous."

"Wow, sounds like a crazy week," Nick says.

"Yeah," I say. "You don't even know. I just have to figure out how to stick around for a few more days."

"What's this?" Mom asks, pointing to my wrist.

"My ID Band," I say. "It's pretty cool. It's like a key that lets us into places but then also it has a little screen and can give us information about the events, too. Actually, this is what they used for the first event to know how much we were talking to people."

"That's cool," Nick says. "Did you meet Fiona Firestone?"

"Kind of," I say. "She actually hasn't been around much because she's had stuff to deal with related to the school, I guess."

"What kind of stuff?" Nick asks.

"Uh, long story," I say. "But I guess it's the reason this party is happening a few days earlier than normal."

"Are you making friends?" my mom asks.

"Yeah, I actually am," I say. "Crazy thing is there are six of us who are kind of like, together, and we all made it to the Top 10. Me, Zig, Meatball—"

"Meatball?" my mom asks laughing.

"Yeah, that's what we call him. He's over there by the door," I say pointing to him.

"That blond kid?" Nick asks.

"Oh no, that's Hudson," I say. Apparently, Hudson has finally decided to join the rest of the group. "Yeah, he's not my favorite. He's kind of a jerk, actually."

"Lake, that's not nice," my mom says, tilting her head at me and giving me her "you know better than that" eyes.

"Yeah, well, neither is he," I say. "No, Meatball is the kid to the right of him in the red shirt. Then there's Jess, Laura, and Haley. That's our six. Meatball calls us the Super Six, which is kinda dumb, but whatever."

"Well, I'm glad you're making friends," Mom says, then she lowers her voice. "Do you know if that was a restroom we walked by on the way in? That drive was a little longer than I remembered."

"Yeah, I think so," I say.

"Okay, I'll be back in a minute," Mom says, heading that way.

"So, uh, three girls in the Super Six, huh?" Nicks says. "You like any of them?"

"Kind of ... " I say, which makes Nick nearly spit out his grape juice.

"Wait, which one?"

"Haley," I say, searching the room for her. I eventually spot her in the corner with two people I assume are her parents. "Don't look right now, but she's the blond one over there in the corner."

Nick does look right now, and of course she sees us. She waves and smiles.

"Wow, Lake!" Nick says, whacking my arm and sending my grape juice all over my shirt.

"Dude! What the heck," I say, pulling my sticky, stained shirt away from my chest.

"Oh crap, sorry," he says. "I got a little excited there. Dude, I noticed her earlier. She's cute! And did you see the way she waved at you?"

"Yeah, I think she actually might like me," I say, dabbing at the stain on my shirt with a napkin. "I gotta go change my shirt."

"I'll come with you," he says.

"I don't think guests are supposed to leave this room," I tell him, but then I see how engaged everyone is talking to their families, and I don't think anyone is really gonna notice. "Actually, it's fine. I'll show you our bunk room real quick."

Nick and I sneak out the side entrance of the Great Room, and I assume that no one sees us leave.

43

"So, the Super Six, huh?" Nick asks me as we make our way toward the bunk rooms.

"Yeah, sort of a dumb name," I say.

"Gonna be kind of awkward if five of you get the five scholarships and one doesn't," he says.

"I know, I'm trying not to think about it," I say as we get to the door of our room. "This is us."

Nick grabs the handle, but it doesn't budge. "It's locked."

"Not for me," I say. I push him out of the way and easily open the door with my left hand.

"Oh, the ID Band?" Nick says.

"Yup."

"So, which one is your bed?" Nicks asks as we step inside.

"This one here," I say, reaching underneath it to grab my bag and find a new shirt. "They're pretty nice rooms, but nothing special. Honestly, the bedrooms are probably the least cool part of the school."

I switch shirts and pop into the bathroom.

"Pretty comfortable beds," Nick says from the other room.

"Yeah, not bad," I say. I give myself a quick look over in the mirror and then come out, only to find Nick lying in Hudson's bed.

"Dude, what are you doing?" I say. "That's Hudson's bed!"

"Ooh, Hudson's bed!" Nick says, mocking me. "What, are you afraid of him?"

"No," I say, "you just shouldn't be in someone else's bed."

"Technically I'm not *in* his bed, I'm *on* it," Nick says.

"Whatever, dude," I say. "Anyway, let's go—we need to get back to the party." I grab his arm to pull him off the bed, but he slips out of my grasp. "Nice try," he says, laughing.

I pretend like I'm gonna smack in the face to catch him off guard, and when he puts his arms up I grab his legs and yank as hard as I can. "Off you go!" I say, pulling him right off the bed onto the floor, taking Hudson's pillow and blanket with him.

"Ow, that hurt, you jerk," Nick says, laughing and rubbing the back of his head. He gets up and grabs Hudson's pillow, and as he's putting it back on the bed something catches his attention. "Feels like there's something in here," he says.

"In where, the pillow?" I ask.

"Yeah," Nick says, reaching into the pillowcase. He fishes around for a second and pulls out a folded piece of paper.

"Umm, you probably shouldn't—" I start to say, but he already has it open.

"That's weird," Nick says.

"What?" I ask.

"Looks like your boy Hudson has a date tonight," Nick says, turning the note around so I can read it.

NORTHEAST WING (USUAL SPOT)
2:00 A.M.

"Wait, are you sure that was in Hudson's pillow?"

"Lake, you literally just saw me pull it out," Nick says. "Why would he be meeting someone at 2:00 a.m.?"

"And why would he be meeting someone in the Northeast Wing?"

"Why, what's the Northeast Wing?"

"I mean, I don't even know, to be honest," I say. "It's off-limits to everyone."

"Not to Hudson, apparently," Nick says, glancing down at the note again before looking back at me. "Lake, you're getting that look."

"What look?"

"That look you get when you think you're about to unlock some big conspiracy. It's that 'I'm a secret agent with a mission' look."

I pause for a second to decide how much I should share with Nick. I told myself I wasn't going to tell him any more details, but this kind of changes things.

"Okay, there's something I need to tell you," I say. "Remember when I said in the Great Room that Fiona Firestone has been dealing with some stuff?"

"Yeah ... " Nick says.

"Well, I think this has to do with that stuff," I say.

I explain to Nick everything I know. I tell him about the Microclimate Dome and how Rogan Bosch and Fiona Firestone have been racing to complete it. I tell him about the worried conversation I overheard two nights ago between her and Dr. V. I tell him how Mr. Lincoln even warned us to keep an eye on each other because everyone was under suspicion.

"So you think this note has something to do with that MCD thing?" Nick asks.

"I mean, it has to, right?" I say. "You saw how the rain stopped when you guys got here today. You really think that was a coincidence?"

"Rain stops all the time, Lake," Nick says. "But, even if that was the MCD—that could have nothing to do with this note."

"Or *everything* to do with it."

"I don't know, dude," Nick says, "but you've gotten yourself in trouble with stuff like this before. I mean it could be literally anything. Maybe one of the girls here left it so they could meet up and make out tonight?"

"I doubt it," I say, though the thought occurs to me that Jess has been getting very friendly with Hudson the last day or so. The thought of them kissing crosses my mind and instantly grosses me out.

"Well, just don't be stupid about this like you are sometimes," Nick says.

"What does that mean?" I ask, getting annoyed.

"You know," Nick says, "trying to connect two things that might not be related but somehow you convince yourself they are. Like the time you thought our teacher Mrs. Davis was making counterfeit money out of the back of her science lab. Or the time you thought my neighbor Maurice was working for the FBI."

"This is different," I say. "Although you still never proved to me that Maurice doesn't work for the FBI, but whatever. All I know is that the staff here thinks that one of the students might be up to no good and now there's a hidden note in someone's pillow requesting a meeting in the middle of the night in an off-limits area of the school. Is that really that much of a stretch?"

"I mean, it does seem suspicious, I guess," Nick says.

"Exactly," I say.

"So what are you gonna do? Are you gonna tell that Mr. Lincoln guy?" Nick asks.

"I don't know yet," I say, "but we gotta get back to the party. Put the note back in the pillow and let's get out of here before someone comes looking for us."

"Okay," Nick says, stuffing the folded note back into Hudson's pillowcase. "You sure you remember what was on it?"

"Northeast Wing, 2:00 a.m.," I say. "I got it."

44

We head back into the Great Room, and when we walk in I see something I did not expect: my mom and Haley talking to each other.

"There you are!" my mom says. "Where did you go?"

"Sorry," I say, pointing to Nick. "This doofus knocked my drink all over my shirt, so I had to change."

"Well," she smiles, "while you were gone I met one of your friends."

"Lake, why didn't you tell me your mom was so nice?" Haley says.

"Umm, because she's not and she's faking it right now," I joke.

"Stop it!" Mom laughs. "Haley was just telling me about the Rec Wing and that you guys caught a movie together."

"A date?" Nick chimes in.

"No," I say. "We were just the only two who wanted to see a movie."

Haley's still smiling, but I wonder if I was a little too forceful about the fact that our movie date wasn't a date? I have no idea how to handle this situation right now, and it's starting to feel a little hot in here.

"Well, the movie was good, and we had a good time," Haley says.

"What did you see?" Nick asks.

"*The Seven Balloons*," Haley says, which instantly makes Nick burst out in laughter.

"Oooh, I want to see that," my mom says, but I can barely hear her because Nick is cackling so loudly.

"Dude, tell me you did not watch *The Seven Balloons*?"

"What?" Haley says to Nick. "It was so good!"

"Okay," Nick says, "if you got Lake to sit down for two hours and watch that terrible disaster of a movie, then it was *one hundred percent* a date. Be honest Lake, how bad was it?"

"I mean ... " I stumble, not sure what to say.

"C'mon, tell Haley how terrible it was," Nick says.

"I mean, it was pretty much what I expected," I say.

"So, it was terrible." Nick laughs.

"Hey," Haley says to me, "you said you had fun!"

"I did have fun!" I say. "But not really because of the movie." I realize as I'm saying it how sappy it sounds, but all the words are out before I can stop them.

"Awww," my mom says, "that's sweet, Lake."

"Oh, here come my parents," Haley says. "I want you to meet them."

I turn around to see Haley's parents a few feet away with big smiles on their faces. They seem nice enough, but I couldn't be more sweaty right now.

"Mom, Dad, this is Lake—I was telling you about him earlier. And this is his mom, Julie, and his friend Nick."

"Julie Mason, nice to meet you," Mom says, extending her hand to them. Wait, did Haley just say that she was telling her parents about me earlier? What was she saying? Was it something like, "There's this cute boy I think I like" or "Wait until you meet this ugly creeper who won't leave me alone and probably wets the bed"?

"Hey, I'm Brad Jensen, and this is my wife Michelle," Haley's dad says. "Lake, it's good to meet you. Haley was just telling us that she's made a few good friends here already this week."

"Oh yeah, we're having fun," I say awkwardly. "She's a super nice girl."

Super nice girl? What was that? I don't think I've ever said those three words together before in my life.

On the positive side of things, this is one more sign that Haley likes hanging out with me. It still seems a little too good to be true that a girl this pretty and nice would maybe like me, but clues are clues. As a secret agent, I've got to follow them wherever they lead, even if the conclusion they're pointing to doesn't make a ton of sense.

"Hey, there's Fiona Firestone!" my mom says, pointing to the stage.

"Oh my gosh," Nick says, "I'm in the same room as Fiona Firestone!"

"Ladies and gentlemen," Beardy squeaks from the stage, "can I have your attention, please."

"Ooh, I don't like that man," Mom says, which makes me laugh. "What's his name? Mr. Hilton?"

"I think it's Mr. Hillit," I say. "But I like Beardy better."

"Would you please give an over-the-top welcome," Beardy says, "to our host, Fiona Firestone!"

Fiona Firestone ascends the stage and grabs the microphone as the room applauds her.

"Welcome, everyone, to The Firestone School, and thank you for the kind applause," she says. "As everyone moves in a little bit closer to the stage, can we get an even bigger round of applause for the students who have made it this far in The Firestone Fires and for the friends and family here with them today?"

Everyone claps and cheers as they step closer to the stage.

Seconds later the crowd is completely silent, waiting for her to speak.

"I just want to say a couple of quick words before I get to an announcement," Fiona continues. "I launched The Firestone School five years ago because I wanted to see if I could create a better way for bright, young students to become brilliant, resourceful young adults. I've modeled much of curriculum after the way mama birds teach their young fledglings to fly. The experience here is about leaving the nest, being challenged to grow, failing in a safe environment, and ultimately, spreading your wings and flying. Not everything has worked, but I feel like each year we get closer and closer to achieving my vision."

I feel a brush against my shoulder and realize that Haley is now standing right beside me. I try my best not to smile like an idiot.

"Enrollment here at the school is incredibly exclusive by design, but I've held The Firestone Fires each year because I love the idea of giving students from here in my home state a chance at this unique form of education."

Out of the corner of my eye I see a flash of blond hair. It's Hudson, standing about ten feet from me, all by himself. Everyone else has parents or friends with them; I wonder where Hudson's are? I also wonder who left that note for Hudson, and whether or not he'll actually try to sneak out tonight.

"As you may have heard from your students," Fiona continues, "the competition this year has been a little different, as we've been dealing with some outside issues. I'm sad to say that those issues have continued to persist, and we are going to have to once again modify the competition to ensure the safety of not only my work here at the school, but also the safety of your students as well."

The sound of nervous chatter escalates with this announcement.

"Our competition usually lasts about ten days," Fiona says, "but we are going to have to cut it short this year. In fact, tomorrow will be the last day of The Firestone Fires."

Audible gasps go up all over the room as we realize that we're twenty-four hours away from the end of The Fires. My head is buzzing as I try to process the news. Half of us are about to go back to normal life, and half of us are going to realize a dream and get into The Firestone School. And it's all happening tomorrow.

"There is, unfortunately, one other change as well," Fiona says. "It's something my leadership team and I have gone back and forth on for the past month. We've weighed all the evidence and run every scenario. And just this morning we made a final decision."

Haley and I exchange a worried glance, not sure where Fiona Firestone is going with this.

"While we've never officially come out and said it, I think most of you assumed that there would be five scholarships this year because that's what we've done in the past. Technically, if you look back at all the material we sent, we never actually specified an exact number of scholarships because we just weren't sure."

Wait, what is happening here and why am I having trouble remembering how to breathe?

"Well now, we are sure ..." she says, and a small wave of panic comes over me as I process what it would mean if she is about to announce they are taking away one of the five available scholarships.

Four scholarships not only lessens my chances of winning, but it also means at least one more of my friends is not going to get one. I really hope that's not what she's about to say. This feels like an incredibly cruel gut punch at a time where we're supposed to be celebrating.

"This year," she continues, "there will not be five scholarships to The Firestone School."

She pauses, as if she knows what she's about to say is not going to go over well.

"There will only be three."

45

"**W**HAT?!" was all that came out of my mouth when Fiona Firestone informed us that there were only three scholarships up for grabs, not five. My jaw dropped and my heart sank. That was an hour ago and I'm still not over it.

A few of the kids and even some of the parents were yelling at her about how unfair it was. Britney's dad was the most out of control, screaming words that would be bleeped on most television shows. He threatened to pull his daughter out of The Fires, but once Mr. Lincoln calmed him down, Britney talked him out of it.

The second half of the party wasn't nearly as fun as the first. My mom and Nick tried to cheer me up and keep me positive, but it didn't really work. I just said goodbye to them and now I'm standing on the front step of the school trying to regain my composure and get my head back in the game. The Firestone Fires are still happening and I'm still in it. You'd think that would be enough to have me excited, but I'm still shell-shocked by the news.

I head back into the Great Room where I see the rest of the Super Six sitting at a table at the far end of the room. I walk over and take a seat between Jess and Laura, who are apparently in the middle of another argument.

"I don't care if it was never stated," Laura says, "she knew that we were all thinking there would be five scholarships. She should have given us a heads up."

"But she said they didn't even make the final decision until today," Jess says. "If that's true then she did the right thing. Why get us worried about fewer scholarships if there was a chance they were going to keep it at five?"

"I'm with Jess," Meatball says. "I don't think Fiona Firestone did anything wrong."

"Yeah, of course you don't," Laura says. "Fiona Firestone could cut off one of your fingers and you'd thank her for getting rid of your hangnail."

"Well, if it was a really bad hangnail maybe I would," Meatball says. He's clearly enjoying getting Laura riled up.

"Do you know what the technical term is for being born with less than ten fingers or toes?" Zig chimes in, trying to change the subject.

"Awesome?" Meatball guesses.

"Well, it's actually called 'Oligodactyly,' but yeah, it is kind of awesome," Zig says.

"My point is, you *never* think Fiona Firestone does anything wrong," Laura says to Meatball, "even when she screws us over like she just did."

"Well, you never think Fiona does anything right," Meatball says, "so you're just as bad."

"That's not true," Laura says. "I've been impressed with everything this whole week, and up until about an hour ago, I was starting to warm up to her. But not anymore, not after that stunt."

"I don't think it was a stunt," Haley quietly chimes in. "Look, we all know there's something going on with this climate dome thing. If it's really that important and it's in danger, we're lucky she's still offering any scholarships at all."

"Yeah, but I don't see how a forty percent reduction in scholarships helps save the climate dome," Zig says. "Look, I'm not into this whole Rogan Bosch versus Fiona Firestone feud, but I'm with Laura on this one. That was a crappy thing to do to us with our families right there."

"She didn't *do anything* to you!" Meatball says, his voice rising. For the first time all week it feels like there's real tension and anger in our group, and I don't like it.

"She took away two scholarships!" Laura says.

"She never offered five in the first place," Jess says. "You guys just assumed there was five. Am I right, Lake?"

I've been trying to stay out of this because as much as I want to agree that Fiona Firestone hasn't done anything wrong, I'm still really upset. I'm mad at her for pulling two scholarships she never promised, and I'm mad that my new friends and I are fighting when we should be celebrating.

"I don't know, Meatball," I say, unable to hide how frustrated I am. "Couldn't she have just told us at the beginning of the week that they weren't sure about how many scholarships they were giving out? At least let us know that there was a chance it would be less than five?"

"Thank you!" Laura says, with a real edge to her voice.

"You guys just sound ungrateful," Jess says. "I'm sorry, but there are still three scholarships to the most prestigious school in the country up for grabs."

"Yeah," Meatball says, looking right at me, "you've got a thirty percent chance of winning one of them, and you're all crying like someone just kicked your dog."

"Does it look like I'm crying?" I snap back to Meatball, pointing to my eyes. "I'm not crying, I'm just really ticked off."

"Well, being mad isn't going to help the situation at all," Haley says.

"Well, some of us can't control our emotions like the rest of us, I guess," Jess says, getting up from the table.

"I'm sorry, Jess, I wasn't trying to be mean—" Haley says.

"No, it's fine, I know you weren't," Jess says. "I'm not mad at you guys, I promise. I'm just ... ugh. This whole week has been so crazy. I gotta go ... I'll be back," she says as she walks away.

"She's the worst when she gets like that," Laura says, rolling her eyes at Jess as she walks away.

"No, she's amazing," Haley says, sticking up for Jess. I love that Haley wasn't going to let that slide.

"Look, I get why everyone's worked up," Zig says. "I just don't see the point of getting bent out of shape when we're so close. We've come so far to get here. We're almost to the end."

"I know, Zig. I'll be fine," I say. "I just want to win this so bad, and I liked the thought of winning alongside four of you way more than winning with only two of you."

"Well, either way, we knew all of us couldn't win," Haley says.

"Oh great," Meatball says, pointing to his left. "Look who Jess is going to talk to."

I look over and see Jess wiping away a tear as she talks to Hudson. He puts his hand on her shoulder and from a distance it seems like he really cares about what she's saying. I can't say that I've ever seen him act like that, and I wonder if he actually does have a heart after all or it it's just an act.

For a second, I think about saying something to the others about the note Nick and I found in Hudson's pillow a few hours ago, but it's probably not a good idea. I mean, I think I trust everyone sitting with me, but you never know. Part of me really wants to follow Hudson tonight to see what this meeting is all about, but I've gotten this far in The Fires already. I can't risk getting kicked out for chasing a lead that might not be anything.

Tomorrow is one of the biggest days of my entire life. I need to get a good night's sleep tonight, regardless of what Hudson is up to. As much as I want to rat him out to Fiona Firestone or to follow him and catch him in the act, I know that both of those scenarios could lead to The Firestone Fires being shut down or to me being kicked out of the competition. I'm not willing to take either of those risks at this point.

Jess is laughing now, smiling at whatever Hudson is saying. I'm glad she's not crying anymore, but I don't like that it's Hudson doing the cheering up. In fact, I hate it.

I close my eyes and take a deep breath, refocusing for a second. Don't forget the mission, Lake. Forget about Hudson, forget about Jess, forget about the MCD and whatever else is going on here. You know what, forget about Haley, even just for this last twenty-four hours. Remember why you're here.

Let everyone else get riled up. Let Hudson do whatever he's doing at 2:00 a.m. in the Northeast Wing. Just get a good night's sleep, kick some butt tomorrow, and you're in. You'll be a student at The Firestone School.

It's that close.

46

You know how I said I was going to get a good night's sleep tonight, despite everything going on with the scholarships and The Fires and Hudson and his secret meeting?

I lied.

I mean, not on purpose. I really was planning on getting a full night of sleep. But sometimes, even the best secret agents get sidetracked.

I had trouble falling asleep at first, knowing that Hudson was planning on leaving the room to go meet someone. I wanted to call him out so bad or at least drop a hint to him that I knew he was up to something, but I stayed focused on the mission and kept my mouth shut.

At some point I fell asleep, though I don't remember exactly when. I had a crazy dream, too. Rogan Bosch had snuck into The Firestone School and was watching everything that was happening in The Firestone Fires on a big wall of monitors. He kept whispering into a microphone and giving instructions to someone, but I couldn't hear what he was saying or who he was talking to.

In the dream I kept going from door to door trying to find out what room he was in, but each time I would open a door it would just be a dark, empty room. When I finally got to the last door, which I thought was a bathroom door, I opened it and was immediately sucked off the edge of a cliff and started falling to my death. That's when I woke up.

I turn to look at the clock and it says 1:55 a.m., so if Hudson decided to go through with his meeting, he's probably on his way there now. For all I know it might have been him leaving the room that woke me up.

Still a bit foggy, I quietly roll out of bed, and tiptoe toward the back of the room so I can get close enough to his bed to see if he's in it or not. Maybe he slept through the meeting? If he's in his bed and he wakes up, I'll tell him I was going to the bathroom. I'm sure he'll get a kick out of that.

I take a few more steps and pause to let my eyes finish adjusting, careful that my breathing is as slow and silent as possible. It takes a few seconds, but eventually I can see clearly enough.

His bed is empty.

For a split second I feel the urge to go follow him, to catch him trying to pull off whatever he's up to in the off-limits Northeast Wing. But then I remember why I'm here, and that my only chance of being a student here for the coming school year is if I go back to sleep, wake up rested tomorrow, and win one of those three scholarships.

That's the mission. So long, Crapville. Hello, Firestone.

I tiptoe back over to my bed, careful not to make a sound that might wake up Meatball. I climb back into bed, only as I do, my shorts suddenly feel very cold and very wet. I dart back up and reach down to feel my clothes, and my worst fears are confirmed.

I pat the bed sheets, but I already know what my hands are going to find.

They are soaked.

Everything is soaked.

For the first time all week, and maybe at the worst possible time in my entire life, I just wet the bed.

47

ARE YOU KIDDING ME?

Please tell me this is a nightmare and I'm still sleeping. Of all the times to pee the bed why now? Why here?

I grab another pair of shorts and a shirt from my bag, quietly clean myself up in the bathroom, and change into dry clothes.

I wrap up my wet clothes in the pee-soaked bedsheets and stuff the whole bundle into my backpack. I can't keep this stuff laying around in the room, it's gonna stink so bad. Hudson already gives me a hard time about peeing where I'm supposed to pee, I can't imagine what would happen if he realized I peed in my bed.

Leaving this stuff packed in my backpack for the next day or two isn't ideal, but I don't really have a better solution until it hits me. The tour that Mr. Lincoln gave on that first night—didn't he say there was a laundry room right by the kitchen? If I can ditch this stuff into a dirty laundry bin and find some new sheets, I'm golden.

I check the clock and it's 2:01 a.m. now. I have no idea how long Hudson's meeting will last, but if I go now, I might be able to ditch my wet sheets and put new ones on my bed before he gets back. I don't have time to think about it—I just have to do it.

I put my backpack on and sneak out into the hallway without waking up Meatball. As I head past the Great Room doors, I get a bit of a rush. Pulling off missions like this is something I've been doing for so long, and I'm really good at it. Sneaking around like this kind of makes me wish I had followed Hudson tonight to see what he was up to. I bet I could have done it without getting caught.

Heading down the long hallway north of the Great Room, I walk to the set of doors just past the kitchen and slowly turn the knob. Like I remembered from the tour, it's the laundry room. I slide into the empty room and it only takes a few seconds to figure out where everything is. I pull the bundle of pee-soaked laundry from my bag and bury it in a huge blue bin underneath a pile of dirty sheets, cloth napkins, and towels. Along the wall on the right are stacks of neatly piled clean towels and sheets. I grab what I need, stuff it into my backpack, and head for the door.

I head back down the hallway, past the kitchen again, but this time, as I pass by the window, something catches my eye. The floor is streaky wet, like someone had washed it an hour ago and it's not quite finished drying. And there, along the right side of the room, is a faint set of footprints. Someone has walked through here recently, and I bet I know who that someone was.

The light is too dim in the kitchen to see all the way into the back of the room; if I want to see where the footprints lead, I'm going to have to follow them to find out. I know I should head back, but maybe, if I just see where these prints lead, I can get a little bit of information on Hudson. If I see any sign of trouble, I'll turn around immediately.

I slowly push the kitchen door open and step inside. I move to the right to try and follow the footprints, but I can't see them anymore from this angle. I have to crouch down so the light hits them just right to see them.

I haven't actually been back here into the kitchen before, but up close, seeing the state-of-the-art pizza oven is impressive. It's massive, and, as I walk by it I can still feel a little of the heat from it, even though it probably hasn't been used in hours.

I'm still hugging the right side of the room, and when I get about halfway to the back wall, I have to crouch down to pick up the footprints again. As I do, I realize they only go about five more feet ahead of me and then they stop in front of one of the giant walk-in refrigerators along the right wall. Whoever made these footprints entered the fridge, and by the look of it, they haven't come back out yet.

Is this where Hudson's meeting is? In a walk-in fridge?

I listen closely and I don't hear anything. The kitchen is completely silent, other than the hum of a few quiet fans. If someone was in the walk-in fridge talking, I'm sure I'd be able to hear it. What if these aren't Hudson's prints at all? What if they belong to one of the cooks or cleaners?

If that's the case I think I have a decent enough alibi to cover me. I can tell them I needed clean sheets, show them that they are in my backpack, and tell them I got lost on my way back to my room. It's a dumb story, but it should cover me.

I slowly crack the fridge door open and step inside. It's really dark, but as I take my second step into it an automatic light comes on. There are boxes stacked everywhere, which kind of freaks me out because Hudson could easily be hiding in here. Then again, why would he be hiding? He has no idea I know about his meeting.

I search the room and don't see anything other than what you'd expect to find in a fridge. How could there only be one set of footprints leading in here and none leading out? Is it possible that whoever was in here was in here for so long that their shoes got cold and didn't leave footprint tracks on the way out? I don't think so. Seems to me that you'd leave footprints on a wet floor whether your shoes were cold or not. I bet the best secret agents in the world know the answer to that question. Zig probably does, too.

I keep scanning the room and notice a stack of boxes in the corner that seem a little out of place, as if someone had shoved them a few feet to the right of where they belonged and didn't put them back. When I slide them out of the way, my heart immediately starts racing. There's a faint outline of a small door on the back wall, and while there's no handle or anything, I'm pretty sure if I push on it, it's going to open.

I have no idea what's on the other side of this wall, but if my sense of direction is right, it's the same direction as the Northeast Wing. Is this where Hudson's "usual spot" for meetings is? I push softly on the hidden door and it slowly swings open. As the light from the fridge fills the area behind the door, I realize there's a wall only a few feet behind it, but to the right, it opens up like a small tunnel. At the very end of the passageway, maybe ten feet away, I can see a small ray or two of light coming in from the opposite wall.

I pause for a second. Am I actually going to do this? I can still turn around and get back to the room without anyone knowing I was out here getting clean sheets. I can get back in bed, get some sleep, and be ready for tomorrow.

It seems like the smart thing for me to do, but I just can't do it. Fiona Firestone and her team are on high alert and Hudson is clearly up to something. If I turn around now and find out later that Hudson was helping Rogan Bosch steal the MCD, I'll always wonder if I could have helped stop them.

There's a reason I'm right here, right now. This is the kind of stuff I've been training my whole life for.

I let the fridge door close behind me, crouch down so I can make my way through the tunnel, and head toward the light.

48

The tunnel feels really warm to me as I move through it, probably because I just spent the last few minutes standing in a refrigerator. It also smells like moldy cardboard, to the point where I almost gag a couple times. I try not to think about it as I stay crouched down and take one small step at a time.

I get to the other end of the tunnel and realize that the rays of light were coming through a few small cracks at the bottom of what looks like another door, this one probably leading to a room in the off-limits Northeast Wing.

I move my hand along the wall, feeling for something to grab, and I find a small knob like what you would find on a nightstand drawer. I carefully pull on it and the door opens a few inches. I can barely hear someone talking on the other side. I think it sounds like Hudson, but I can't be sure.

I pull the door open another few inches and I'm finally able to see that it leads to a small closet. There are a few shelves on the wall to my right and left, and straight ahead is a door that leads into a bigger room. That door is cracked open a few inches, and light is flooding in.

I slowly pull the tunnel door toward me enough that I can

slip by it and into the closet. I'm still crouched down like a baseball catcher. As I move into the closet, I let the tunnel door silently close behind me, but not all the way. This would be so much easier if I wasn't wearing a backpack full of bedsheets. I leave enough of my body in the door frame that I can make a quick escape if I need to.

The voice is clearer now, and it's definitely Hudson. But as I listen for a few seconds I realize it's only his voice that I hear. There are breaks in the conversation where someone else is talking, but all I hear is silence. He must be on the phone with somebody. I lean in and close my eyes to focus.

" ... that seems risky," he says. "But if you think that's the best way for us to handle this, I guess I trust you."

There's another pause while Hudson listens to whoever is on the other end.

"I will," he finally says. "They'll be too busy with the scavenger hunt to even notice what I'm up to."

A scavenger hunt? Okay, first thing I'm wondering is how he knows that tomorrow's elimination event is a scavenger hunt. He must be working with someone on the inside, and it sounds like whatever they are up to, it's going down during the event.

"Yeah, you're right," Hudson says, "but between the two of us we can outsmart them. Just make sure you double check all the security clearances in the morning."

Security clearances? Is Hudson talking to someone who has access to Fiona Firestone's security system? If so, Dr. V was right to move the Climate Dome files out of the Security Wing. Hopefully he doesn't know that Dr. V and Fiona are carrying the plans on flash drives, or that there's a third copy hidden in Fiona's office door.

"Alright, I need to get back before anyone notices I'm gone," Hudson says, pushing back the chair he's sitting in.

Hudson says something else, but I don't hear him because it's time for me to beat him back to the room. I slink back into the tunnel, careful that the tunnel door closes silently behind me. I quickly shuffle to the other end and open the door to the cold room. It's dark again but when I step into it, the light comes on. I sprint across the room and slide back into the kitchen.

As I'm headed out toward the hallway I realize that the cold room light is probably going to still be on when Hudson first steps into the room. Hopefully he doesn't realize that it was someone else that triggered the motion light. No time to worry about that now, though.

I race back into the hallway and turn right toward our bunk room. Picking up speed, I take a left and then a right into the hallway that leads to our door and slow down from a run to a fast walk. Hudson is probably walking, not running, behind me, and our door is only a few feet away now.

It shouldn't take me more than a minute to get the bedsheet on, so I should be able to be under the covers by the time he gets here. And even if I'm not, I can lie and tell him I just woke up and was adjusting my bedsheet. He'd be the one who would be trying to cover up for himself, anyway.

I arrive at the door and grab the handle, only it doesn't budge. I try again and nothing. *Nothing?* I look down at my wrist and that's when I realize I don't have my ID Band on. I had taken it off when I got into bed, and forgot to put it back on when I woke up with wet sheets.

The hall is still empty. No sign of Hudson, but he could be rounding that corner any second. I try turning the handle again, hoping it will magically open this time, but nothing happens. I'm a sitting duck out here. There's nowhere to hide. Should I wake Meatball up by knocking on the door? He's the only one in the room, but he's such a sound sleeper that if I knock loud enough to wake him, Hudson might hear it, too.

I could run down to the other end of the hallway and hide in the doorway that connects our bunk rooms to the girls' section, but then what am I going to do? If Hudson gets into the room and the door closes behind him, I'm still locked out.

Then a thought hits me. Maybe I have more time than I think. Maybe Hudson isn't headed back to bed right now, maybe he's headed somewhere else on another mission?

I take a deep breath and turn my head to look back down the hallway and there, standing ten feet from me, is Hudson, with his arms crossed and a big smile on his face.

49

"Well, well, well," Hudson says. "Someone just got busted."

I stay frozen. I don't know what to say.

"What are you doing out here, Flake?" he asks.

"What are *you* doing out here," I fire back, finally snapping out of my fog.

"I wasn't feeling good," he says, rubbing his stomach. "Felt a little nauseous. Went to the nurse's station for some medicine. What about you?"

I know he's lying, but I'm not going to call him out on it. Not yet, anyway.

"I wasn't doing anything," I say. "I'm just trying to get back in the room so I can go to bed."

"Yeah, nice try," Hudson says. "The school is on high alert, and you're outside your room in the middle of the night 'not doing anything?' Seems suspicious to me."

"How do I know you really were at the nurse's station?" I say, trying to take the focus off of me.

"I was getting these, Sherlock," Hudson says, reaching in his pocket and producing a small packet of pills. They look similar to the ones I grabbed the other night, only the packet is pink, not white. "Now tell me what *you* were doing out here or I'm going to go tell security."

It dawns on me that I'm kind of screwed here, but only because I have no idea who Hudson is working with. The person on the other end of that phone call could have been Rogan Bosch, or it could have been someone on staff here. I can't trust anyone right now, which is a problem because I'm out in the hallway in the middle of the night with no alibi other than a backpack full of bedsheets.

If I let him report me, it will be my word against his in front of Fiona Firestone. I could tell her that I overheard her conversation with Dr. V the other night, unless that will get me in even more trouble? I can tell him that I know what he was up to tonight, but he's just going to deny it, right? I don't know—there are no good options.

"That's it, I'm going to get security." Hudson says as he starts heading back down the hall.

"No, wait!" I say. "I know you weren't in the nurse's office!"

"Um, yes, I was," he says, calmly holding up the pill packet.

"No, you weren't," I say. "I can prove it."

"Oh really," Hudson laughs. "I'll tell you what. Let's go wake up Fiona Firestone and Dr. V, and tell them all about it. You tell your story, I'll tell mine, and we'll see how that goes for you. What do you think?"

Man, if he's bluffing, he's good. The last person I want to see right now is Fiona Firestone. I don't want to see her for another twelve hours when she's handing me my scholarship to The Firestone School. That's all that matters right now. I have to get to that moment.

"Flake, you're busted," Hudson says. "Whatever you're up to, it's done. You're done."

"Wait," I sigh, resigned to the one thing that might end this conversation. "I'll tell you the truth, but you have to promise not to tell anyone."

"I'm not promising anything to keep you out of trouble." Hudson says.

"No, this has nothing to do with keeping me out of trouble," I say.

"Then what were you doing out here?" he asks.

I pause for a second because I do not want to say what I'm about to say. But it's the only thing I can think of to keep Hudson from going to Fiona or Dr. V right now. It's the only thing that doesn't jeopardize me winning a scholarship.

"I was in the laundry room getting new bedsheets." I say.

"New sheets?" Hudson laughs. "What did you pee your bed?"

"No!" I say instinctively, but my face can't hide my embarrassment.

"Wait, you *did* pee your bed!" he says, his smile growing wider by the second.

"I didn't pee my bed, I just had a tiny accident," I stammer, thankful that the soaking wet sheets that would prove me a liar are now buried in the laundry room.

"Oh my gosh," Hudson laughs. "Small accident, big accident, whatever. You peed your bed!"

"Please don't tell anyone," I say.

But instead of laughing more, Hudson's face changes. "Wait, you're lying," he says.

"Lying?" I say. "About peeing the bed?"

"Yeah," he says. "You weren't out getting sheets."

"Yes, I was, they're in my backpack."

"Your shorts are dry."

"I washed up and changed."

"So if we go in the room right now, your bed is gonna be wet?" he says.

"I already told you, the dirty sheets are in the laundry room," I say.

"I gotta see this," he says, moving toward the door. "And if there are clean sheets on your bed and you're lying to me, you're so busted."

He opens the door and we step inside. He flicks the light on.

"What are you doing?" I whisper. "You're gonna wake up Meatball!"

"He's not gonna wake up," Hudson says, being loud on purpose. "That kid could sleep through a fireworks show in his backyard."

"Hey, what's the score of the raspberry game?" Meatball mumbles from the other side of the room.

"Oops," Hudson laughs.

Across the room I can hear Meatball rustling in his sheets. "I was wondering why you were running with eggs," he says.

"Meatball, you're talking in your sleep again," Hudson says.

"Shhh," I shush Hudson through clenched teeth. "Don't wake him up."

"You don't usually try to eat fast. I mean run. Run faster," Meatball jabbers.

"Look," I whisper, pointing to my sheet-less bed. "No sheets, because I peed on them a little and needed to change them. Are you happy now?"

"*Oh my word*," Hudson laughs. "Flake Mason wet his wittle bed?"

"Dude, please don't tell anyone," I say, "it was just an accident."

"I mean, I don't know," Hudson says. "This is such a great story, I hate to keep it to myself."

"You don't have to be a jerk about this, you know," I say.

"I know I don't *have* to be a jerk," he says with a big smile on his face. "But it's way more fun than not being a jerk." He heads over to his bed and climbs in, and as he does he says, "I'll sleep on it."

I'm so embarrassed and angry, but I'm strangely relieved at the same time. I guess that wasn't as bad as it could have been? All my life I've feared that the wrong person was gonna find out that I wet the bed. Maybe it's not that big of a deal? At least I kept him from going to Fiona Firestone. I'm still in the competition and that's a win.

I finish making my bed and climb in. But before I fall asleep, I need to rehash what I heard Hudson talking about earlier. Apparently, there is going to be some type of scavenger hunt tomorrow, and that's when he's going to try to pull something off. What he doesn't know is that if he is planning on stealing the MCD files from the Security Wing, he's not gonna find them because they're not there anymore.

After all the craziness of what just went down, I'm back to the same question I was thinking about earlier today. Should I tell Fiona Firestone what I think is going on or should I just worry about my scholarship for now and deal with that later?

The only thing I know is that I'm too tired to figure it out tonight. Maybe I'll wake up with a brilliant plan in the morning, but for now I need to sleep if I want any chance of being sharp enough tomorrow to make the final three and win a scholarship.

"Oh, by the way," Hudson says from his bed across the room, "there are extra sheets and stuff in the bathroom closet. I don't know why you went all the way over to the laundry room, you moron."

"Thanks," I say, hoping he shuts up and falls asleep.

A few minutes later, just as I'm drifting off to sleep, I hear a voice from the other side of the room. "Wait a second," Meatball says, "did I just dream this, or did Lake pee his bed?"

"Go back to sleep," Hudson mumbles. "I'll tell you all about it in the morning."

50

Well, this is it.

The last day of The Firestone Fires.

I was hoping to wake up this morning with a good feeling about how this day would go, but ever since Beardy stuck his head into our room at 7:00 a.m. to get us out of bed, my head has felt cloudier than ever.

As Hudson and Meatball finish getting ready in the bathroom, I sit on the edge of my bed trying to collect my thoughts.

Mission number one today is winning a scholarship. Whether it's a scavenger hunt or it's something else, I have to make the Top 3 today. Nothing else matters. I hope Hudson gets busted for whatever he's up to, but ultimately it doesn't matter. I hope Haley and Zig win the other scholarships, but that really doesn't matter, either. Those would be nice things, but they're pointless if I don't win a scholarship, too.

"I'll see you clowns in the Great Room," Hudson says, leaving the room without us. I guess he's carrying on Adam's "clown" legacy now that he's gone.

I know Hudson hasn't forgotten that I wet the bed last night, but I'm hoping he'll be so focused on whatever he's trying to pull off today that he'll leave it alone and won't say anything. Maybe he'll just tease me about the fact that he knows a secret, but he won't actually tell it. It's my only hope.

There is a small part of me that thinks I should say something to Fiona Firestone or Dr. V about the fact that I know Hudson is planning something for today. I know there are reasons why it might be the right thing to do. The problem is, I'm pretty sure if I say anything, the competition will get canceled. I can't do that to myself and ruin this chance, especially since I don't really have solid proof that Hudson has done anything wrong.

Every time I run the scenario of telling Fiona Firestone what I think I know, it always ends up with me in the nurse's office at Crapville Middle School next year, getting stitches because I didn't let some senior steal my bag of chips. I can't let that happen. Today is my ticket out of spending six years in that lousy excuse for a school.

"You ready to head over for breakfast?" Meatball asks, coming out of the bathroom.

"Let's do it," I say, leading the way.

"Man, it was good seeing my parents yesterday," Meatball says as we walk down the hall.

"Oh, sorry, I don't think I met them," I say. "Actually I only really met Haley's parents, now that I think of it."

"No, it's fine," Meatball says. "You were meeting the future in-laws, I totally get it."

"Shut up," I laugh.

"I did see your mom and your buddy Nick, though," he says. "I should have come over and said hi."

"Yeah, you should have," I say.

"You know what was weird," Meatball says, "you know who didn't have any family there yesterday?"

"Hudson?" I guess.

"No, Laura," Meatball says. "Did Hudson not have parents there, either?"

"I didn't see any," I say. "Maybe they all couldn't make it out on short notice when the schedule changed?"

"Maybe ..." Meatball says as we step inside the Great Room, only to realize we're the last of the final ten students to arrive. They've removed all the tables but one, and everyone is sitting around it, waiting to be served.

"There he is," Hudson says with a smile as we approach the table. "How'd you sleep last night, Flake?"

"Good," I say, not making eye contact with him as I take a seat next to Haley. I hope this is it. Have your fun and make a few little comments, but please, don't blurt out what happened last night.

"So, what is it?" Jess says to Hudson.

I look over at Hudson, who has the biggest, stupidest grin on his face.

"What is what?" I say, afraid to hear the answer.

"Hudson said he had a story for us, but he wanted to wait until everyone was here to tell it," she says. "So, let's go Hud, what is it?"

Ugh, I hate that she calls him Hud. That's the third time I've heard her say it and it's so gross.

"So last night," Hudson starts, "my stomach was a little upset, so I went to the nurse's office to get some medicine ..."

My heart is racing now. I'm trying to think of any way I can interrupt him or distract him without drawing too much attention to myself, but nothing is coming to me.

"And on my way back to the room, I found something interesting ..."

This is it. My last chance to stop him from finishing his story. What if I just blurt out that I knew he was in the North-east Wing? Or that I followed him into the kitchen? The problem is, if I do that he's going to deny it and still rat me out for wetting the bed. I've already been through this scenario a hundred times. The competition has to stay on. I have to keep my mouth shut.

"C'mon," Jess says. "Enough with the dramatic pauses, just tell the story."

Hudson locks eyes with me. "I found Flake here in the hallway locked out of the room."

Everyone stares at me, and I don't say anything because there are no words to say that are going to magically vaporize me from this situation and put me back in my bedroom at home, which is what I desperately wish could happen in this moment.

"You want to tell them what you were doing outside your room last night, Flake?" Hudson says.

"Not really," I say. "I don't think it's any of their business."

"I think it is," Hudson says. Oh my gosh, I want to punch him in his blond face so bad right now. Can I do that and not get booted from this competition? Probably not, but it still might be worth it.

"Lake, what were you doing sneaking around last night?" Laura asks with a concerned look on her face. It's then I realize that no one has any idea where this story is headed. They probably think I've got the stolen plans to the Microclimate Dome in my pocket.

"I wasn't sneaking around," I say, my face getting red. I can feel that I'm about halfway to bursting out into tears, but I'm determined to not let that happen.

There are a few more seconds of silence as Hudson milks the moment for all that it has. Eventually Haley says, "Guys, what is going on here?"

After another pause, Hudson sighs. "Okay, fine, I'll finish the story," he says.

"Someone was out looking for sheets because he wet his bed last night. Isn't that right, Flake?"

51

He said it. I can't believe he said it.

I want to be brave and defiant.

I want to own up to the accident and make it seem like it's not a big deal.

I want to chuckle about it and say "Oooh, my secret is out, Hudson," in a mocking tone to try and make him look dumb for picking on me.

But I can't do any of that. All I can do is stare at the floor and focus all the energy I have into keeping myself from crying. And I'm not sure I have enough energy to do that.

"Lake, is that true?" Jess asks.

I still can't look up.

"Really, Hudson?" Zig says in a tone I've never heard him use before. "How big of a jerk do you have to be to do that?"

"It's okay, Lake," Jess says to me, "I had a cousin who wet the bed until he was fourteen. It's not a big deal." My head is still down, but at least I'm not crying yet. I just wish someone would change the subject so everyone would stop looking at me.

"Is everything okay here?" says a squeaky voice behind me.

"Yeah, we're fine," Meatball says to Beardy. "When is breakfast going to be ready?"

"It's on its way out," Beardy says, and right on cue the servers appear from the kitchen with plates of food.

"Pancakes and sausage today, kids," Beardy says. "Make sure you eat up—we've got a big day ahead of us. Is everything okay with Lake?" he says, noticing my head is down.

"Yeah, he's fine, got something in his eye," Zig says, covering for me. "Is the next event happening right after we eat?"

"You'll find out soon enough," Beardy squeaks.

The servers put our plates in front of us, and as they do I feel a hand on the small of my back. It's Haley's. "I'm sorry," she whispers.

"Thanks," I whisper back.

"I peed my pants in third grade during an assembly," she says. "At least you were sleeping during your accident. I was wide awake."

I nod and smile. I know she's just trying to make me feel better. It's almost working, but I still want to dig a hole in the middle of the Great Room and crawl into it forever.

I force myself to eat as much breakfast as I can force down, all while looking in every direction but Hudson's. I don't know if he feels bad about embarrassing me or if he's still enjoying himself, and I don't really care, to be honest.

"Students, listen up!" Mr. Lincoln says from the stage as we finish eating. "As you all know today is big day. It's a busy day, in fact. We have a lot to do, and by the end of the day three of you will have earned scholarships to The Firestone School."

Despite everything that's gone on this week, and the craziness of the last twelve hours, I still get a rush when I hear him say it. The thought of winning a scholarship snaps me out of my little funk and reminds me that I've still got a mission to complete. This bedwetter is here to win.

"In a few minutes we will start our Firestone Fires exit interviews," Mr. Lincoln continues. "This is a tradition that we've had since we first started the Fires, and it's been something we've used to make the competition better and better each year."

"One by one, you'll be called into into the Southwest Wing, where we have a conference room set up for the interviews. These should only take ten or fifteen minutes each, so by the time we get finished with all ten of them it will be lunchtime. After we eat, our final event will start."

I look over at Jess. I'm so annoyed with her for not giving Hudson a hard time about being a jerk. I don't understand how she can be friends with him. I don't know about Laura, but I know Zig, Haley, and Meatball have my back. They wouldn't be buddying up to Hudson after he tried to burn me like that.

"Speaking of the competition," Mr. Lincoln says, "our last event of The Firestone Fires will once again be our scavenger hunt. The scavenger hunt will be played out in two separate stages, which I will explain more about in a minute. As you no doubt noticed when you walked in, there are ten locked crates here in the Great Room, each with one of your names on it."

I actually hadn't noticed that when I walked in because I was so worried about Hudson, but I see them now. There are ten wooden boxes, all spread out in the back half of the Great Room. They're big enough hat I could probably fit into one. Beside each one is a small chair with an attached desk.

"The first seven students to find their key and unlock their crate will move on from Stage 1 to Stage 2," Mr. Lincoln says. "The other three students will be eliminated."

My mind flashes back to Hudson's phone call last night. How did he know? He must have someone on the inside feeding him information. I scan the room to see how many staff are currently here, but other than Beardy and Mr. Lincoln, I don't see anyone else. No Dr. V, no Fiona Firestone. Could it be one of them? If it is, my money would be on Beardy, not Mr. Lincoln. Mom would probably agree.

"For the seven students who make it to Stage 2, you'll find a locked safe in your crate, along with clues that will help you figure out the combination to the lock. The first three students to crack the combination and unlock their safe will be awarded the scholarship they find inside."

So there it is. That's the final event. All that stands between me and The Firestone School is a locked safe inside of a locked crate. In a few hours I could be holding a piece of paper that will change the next six years of my life.

"That's the general idea of how things will play out," Mr. Lincoln says. "I'll go over a few specific rules and instructions after lunch. Any questions?"

Laura raises her hand and starts talking before she's even called on. "Will the entire school building be in play for the scavenger hunt, or will some areas be off limits, and if so, which ones?" she asks. Mr. Lincoln frowns.

"As I just said, specific rules for the scavenger hunt will be given to you after lunch. Are there any *good* questions?" he asks.

"That's rude," Laura says under her breath.

"Okay, then," Mr. Lincoln says. "Exit interviews will begin now and will be conducted in a random order that has already been drawn. When it's your turn you can find us in the Southwest Wing."

"Zig Simmons, you're up first."

52

Zig leaves for his exit interview, following Mr. Lincoln out the door to the right of the stage, while the rest of us get up to stretch our legs. I walk away from the table so I can have a few minutes to myself, and it's not until I sit down that I realize Haley followed me over here.

"Sorry again about Hudson," she says, sitting down beside me. "He is literally the worst."

"Thanks," I say, staring across the Great Room. I can see Jess and Hudson standing against the far wall, talking. "Seriously, what does Jess see in him?"

"I don't know," Haley says. "I mean, she knows he can be stupid sometimes, and I've heard her tell him to stop picking on you, but she says he's really not that bad if you get to know him."

"Yeah, I'm gonna pass on that," I say.

"Same," Haley says.

We sit there for a minute or so in silence, but somehow it's not awkward at all. I think we're both anxious to get this final event over with. This whole week has been so crazy, it's nice to just sit and chill with a new friend for a minute.

"You know what would be cool?" Haley asks, finally breaking the silence.

"Hudson, but if he was the exact opposite in every way?" I say, which gets her to bust out laughing.

"That would be cool," she says, "but not what I was thinking. I was thinking it would be cool if we both finished Top 3 today."

I try not to crack a huge smile, but on the inside I'm so happy to hear her say it. There are so many signs at this point that make it seem like Haley likes me, but I'm still having trouble believing it. This last one, though, I mean, she basically just kind of told me she does.

"So you *are* excited about coming here next year?" I ask.

"Yeah," she says. "I've always been excited about it, but it's still so sad to think about leaving a bunch of my friends. But after this week, I guess I'm excited about it now. Going to school here next year would be awesome. Especially if it was a couple of us."

We sit there for a few moments in silence before I finally break the ice. "You ready for this?"

"I'm ready to win," she says.

"Well, let's both win, then," I say. "How about this? I'll finish first, you come in second, Zig comes in third."

"Sounds good to me," she says. "I don't care where I place, as long as I'm Top 3."

"And as long as Hudson is bottom seven," I add.

"I don't know, Hudson always seems to be near the top of every event. He's gonna be hard to beat."

"Yeah, well ..." I start to say, but then stop.

"Yeah, well what?" Haley asks.

"Nothing," I say. I want to tell her that I think Hudson is about to go after the MCD files, not the key for his crate, but I know I should keep my mouth shut. Thankfully right then Zig emerges from the hallway.

"Hey look, it's Zig," I say as he walks up to us. "How'd that go?"

"I'm not supposed to say anything except this," he says, pointing to me.

"You're next."

53

I head in the direction Zig came from and follow his instructions. Take my second right and then straight through the door at the end of the hallway.

The door is closed, so I knock.

"Come in, please," I hear a familiar voice say on the other side. It's Fiona Firestone.

I walk in and I'm almost blinded by how bright the room is. The lights were on in the hallway, but this is a different kind of light. The entire back wall of the room is a giant window overlooking the South lawn.

A large table is sitting right in front of the window, and seated at it are Beardy, Mr. Lincoln, Fiona, and Dr. V. "Have a seat please, Lake," she says. I still think it's amazing that she even knows my name, and I fight to hold back a smile.

There's a single chair in the center of the room facing the table, so I sit down and take a deep breath.

"Congratulations on making the Top Ten, Lake, and good luck this afternoon," Fiona Firestone says.

"Thanks," I say. My one-word answer feels a little impolite, but I don't really know what else to say.

"Lake, the purpose of this interview is for us to collect any thoughts you may have on the competition," Fiona says, "and also to give you an opportunity to speak your mind about anything that you feel needs to be addressed with regards to your stay here this week."

"Okay," I say. Another one-word answer. More silence.

"Well then, my dear," Dr. V says, almost seeming annoyed. "What are your thoughts on The Firestone Fires so far?"

"I think it's ... I mean ... I'm happy that I'm still here, and you know, I think it's been good and I'm really hoping to win today because going to The Firestone School has been something I've wanted for a long time."

I realize that I'm not giving them amazing feedback on the competition, but I don't really know what else to say. This whole interview thing feels a little strange.

"Lake," Mr. Lincoln says, "you know that we are on high alert here at the school. Has there been anything in the last few days you've noticed that seemed off or not right?"

"Do you mean with the other students?" I ask.

"With anything," he says.

"I don't think so," I say slowly, pretending to rack my brain for anything out of the ordinary. I'm lying of course, but they don't need to know what I know. Not now, anyway. I'm so close to that scholarship.

"You don't think so, or you don't know so?" Beardy squeaks from the end of the table.

"I mean, I don't know," I say. "I've been really focused on trying to make it through each event, so I haven't really been paying attention much to the other stuff. I know we're supposed to be keeping an eye out, but I haven't really seen anything suspicious with regards to the MCD."

When I say this, I suddenly have everyone's full attention.

"And what, exactly, do you know about the MCD, sweetie?" Dr. V asks.

"Only the stuff I've heard and seen this week," I say.

"And what have you heard and seen?" Fiona asks.

I feel a bead of sweat forming on my forehead, but I try to stay cool. After all, it's not *me* that's trying to steal the plans. I haven't done anything wrong, here, so I've got no reason to be nervous. Just answer the question, Lake.

"I've heard some of the other kids talking about this technology that can basically keep it from raining in certain areas by building this weird science dome," I say. "You know, creating microclimates or something? And I guess it can control the temperature and do other things too, like make it snow in the middle of summer. Is that what it is?" I ask. "I mean, if I'm allowed to ask about it."

"You can ask about it," Fiona smiles. "And yes, what you've heard is the basic idea behind it. The technology itself isn't so basic, of course, but yes, that's what it does."

Fiona Firestone's smile puts me at ease a little, so I keep talking. "So what's the big deal about it being stolen?" I ask. "You just want to be the first to create it because it's gonna make you a lot of money?" Halfway through the question I realize how dumb it is, but unfortunately life doesn't come with a rewind button, so I can't take it back.

"Well, yeah, that's part of it," Fiona grins. "I do generally like to make money off of the things I create. But more importantly, in the wrong hands, this technology could do a lot of damage to the planet. In a worst-case scenario, it could be used to wipe out entire communities or be used as a weapon of war, which is obviously not what it is intended for."

"Why create it, then?" I ask. Suddenly you can't shut me up.

"Because there are thousands of potential uses for good," she says. "There are small wins like keeping outdoor weddings and golf tournaments dry, and there are big wins like preserving changing climates and protecting streams and rivers from localized flooding."

"Sounds powerful," I say.

"It is powerful," she responds. "And like most powerful things, it has the potential to do a lot of good or a lot of bad, depending on who controls it. That's why we don't want it to be stolen."

"Makes sense," I say, nodding.

"Does anyone else have any additional questions for Lake?" Beardy squeaks.

I'm hoping they don't. So far this has been pretty painless, and I'm ready to get back to Haley in the Great Room.

"One last question," Mr. Lincoln says. "I know you said you didn't see anything suspicious about your fellow students, but I'm wondering why you specifically singled them out. What about other people? Have you noticed anything suspicious about anyone here who is *not* a student?"

I pause for a second, wondering if it's possible that one of the three people sitting at this table with Fiona Firestone is secretly working behind her back.

"Lake," Fiona says, "if there's anything you want to say, no matter how crazy or far-fetched it seems, please say something. This is a completely safe place for you to do that."

Dr. V is staring me down like she has lasers for eyes. I look away, over at Beardy and Mr. Lincoln, who are doing the same thing. They want the truth. Well, unless the truth incriminates them. But they're not getting anything from me today. Not on the day that I win a scholarship to The Firestone School.

"No," I say, pretty convincingly. "Sorry, but I don't have anything to tell you."

"Okay, great," Mr. Lincoln says, rather quickly. "Please return to the Great Room and send in Laura Dickson."

And with that I'm out of my chair and out of the room before they have a chance to change their mind.

54

I head back to the Great Room and send Laura in, and then I hang out for the next hour or so while everyone takes their turn being interviewed.

Hudson is the last one to go, and it seems like his interview takes twice as long as everyone else's. At one point, right before he shows back up, I start to daydream that Fiona Firestone has figured out what he's up to and Beardy and Mr. Lincoln are wrestling him to the ground. Oh man, how great would it be for Hudson to come through that door in handcuffs right now?

But as quickly as it came, the fantasy vanishes when Hudson strolls back into the Great Room as free as a bird, with Mr. Lincoln and Beardy just a few steps behind him. Sadly, no one is in handcuffs.

"Okay, everyone," Mr. Lincoln says. "Chef Rachelle will be bringing in some of her famous brick-oven pizza for lunch today. I would like you to all take your seats at your assigned desk in front of your crate. You'll be eating alone today, and as soon as we're done, the scavenger hunt will begin."

I had already inspected the crates earlier, so I know which one is mine. The crates are set up in two rows of five, and I'm in the middle of the back row. I take my seat and think about the nine other kids in this room. Only three of us are going to be happy with how this afternoon turns out. I'm determined to be one of them.

There's Meatball, who is the only person here who might love Fiona Firestone more than me. From day one, way back when Hudson called him out for the meatball accident, he's made it clear that this is his dream. I bet he thinks he wants to win this more than me, but he has no idea how bad I want this.

Next to Meatball is Zig, who, other than Haley, is the one person I actually hope wins a scholarship alongside me. Truth is, I wouldn't have even made it past the first event if it wasn't for him forcing me to meet people on that first night. If I do win a scholarship, I'll always owe him for that.

Then there's Ryan and Britney—I still don't really know anything about them. I don't know if they like each other or if they're just friends, but they kind of seem to be in their own little world, whispering back and forth and making each other laugh.

On the far right, the last one in the first row, is Laura, who I can't really figure out. Just when I'm starting to like her, she does something super annoying, and then when I can't stand her anymore, she actually seems cool to be around. The whole Rogan Bosch fangirl thing was annoying at first, but she seemed to cool off with that a little bit each day.

The back row starts with Hudson, who may not even be trying to win a scholarship at this point. Does he think he can get through the scavenger hunt *and* steal Fiona's plans for the MCD? I have no idea, but I hope he fails on both counts. If he's not even bothering with the scavenger hunt and only focusing on looking for the flash drive, that's one less person for me to worry about. I hope he wastes all his time looking for the files in the Security Wing.

To my left is Erik, another kid I don't know too much about other than the fact that he sleeps in Room 6 with Zig and he needs to start shaving. Zig says he's always talking about the girls that are here and that he has a new favorite every day. Apparently he farts in his sleep, too. I'd make fun of him for that, but who am I to talk? I'd rather fart in my sleep than pee in my sleep any day. I'm just glad he's not in my room.

The last two people on my right are Jess and Haley. Jess has really annoyed me lately with her friendship with Hudson. It's confusing, because Jess is cool and Hudson is a jerkbag. Haley, on the other hand, seems kind of perfect. I mean, I know I've only known her for a week, but she's pretty, sweet, kind, and fun. That's a pretty good combination.

So, that's the Top 10, all hoping to be one of the three students who win The Firestone Fires and earn a scholarship to The Firestone School. Can't believe I'm one of them.

Servers come in with plates and pizza, and I grab two slices of pepperoni and a bottle of water. While we eat, Mr. Lincoln gives us our final instructions.

"Alright, students, here's how the scavenger hunt is going to work. Like I said earlier, it's broken down into two stages, and only seven students will move on from Stage 1 to Stage 2. The goal of Stage 1 is to find the key that will unlock your crate. The first seven students to find their key and unlock their crate will move on to Stage 2, the other three students will be eliminated."

"Stage 2 will start almost immediately after Stage 1 is done, so don't expect a big break. The seven of you who make it to Stage 2 will be released in the order you finished the first stage, in two-minute increments."

Interesting. So the first person to finish Stage 1 will have a head start on everyone else in Stage 2. A two-minute head start on the second person, and a huge twelve-minute head start on the seventh and final person. I finish my first slice and start on my second, enjoying every bite of the best pizza I've ever had. One more reason why I need to be a student here next year.

"The entire main building is in play for the scavenger hunt," Mr. Lincoln continues, "*except* for the Northeast Wing and the Security Wing. Those will remain locked and off-limits, as they always are. Does anyone have any questions?"

I glance at Laura, who usually does have questions, but she's sitting still with her hands on her lap.

"Okay, if no one has any questions, finish up your lunch and we'll begin in a few minutes." Mr. Lincoln walks out of the Great Room and leaves us to finish our pizza. I take another bite from my second slice and set my plate on the desk. I'm suddenly not hungry anymore.

A few minutes later Beardy walks around and hands us each a sealed envelope with our name on it. "Don't open it until we tell you to," Beardy squeaks at each one of us. Repeating himself ten times is totally unnecessary since we're all sitting about five feet apart, but that's just Beardy being Beardy.

Once we all have our envelopes, Mr. Lincoln gives us our final instructions. "Every participant has their own set of clues hidden on the property. Don't follow anyone else. Follow *your* clues to find *your* key."

I run my finger across my envelope, which says "Lake Mason—Clue 1 of 3," and a surge of adrenaline goes through me. This is the moment I've been waiting for.

Mr. Lincoln pauses for a second and the Great Room is completely silent. "Alright then," he says, "here we go. The final event of The Firestone Fires. On the count of three, you may open your envelopes. Best of luck to all of you."

"One ... two ... three."

55

I tear open my envelope and read the first clue:

CLUE #1

TOM CRUISE SAT IN ME FOR *TOP GUN*,
AND YOU CAN SIT IN ME TO WATCH IT.

Okay, I know *Top Gun* is an old fighter pilot movie that my mom loves, so I immediately make a break for the South Lawn where Fiona Firestone's helipad is. I need to remember to thank Mom for all those times she rambled about how handsome Tom Cruise was in that movie.

As I'm running I notice Laura and Erik are both sprinting down the Southwest Wing with me toward the lawn, as well, while everyone else has scattered in different directions.

As I turn the corner and head down the hallway, I wonder what I'm about to find. Is Fiona Firestone's helicopter still out there or is there a fighter jet out there now? That would be pretty amazing. Maybe the next envelope is in the cockpit?

I take another look at my clue as I get to the back door and stop in my tracks.

CLUE #1

TOM CRUISE SAT IN ME FOR *TOP GUN*, AND YOU CAN SIT IN ME TO WATCH IT.

Wait, if I'm gonna watch a movie I don't need a plane, I need a movie theater! I'm heading the wrong way!

"Crap!" I yell, and immediately turn and sprint back toward the Great Room. Every second matters right now and I just wasted almost a minute's worth of them. I turn left at the end of the hall, sprint past the bunk room hallway, and into the Rec Wing. The movie theater is at the other end of the wing, and as I approach it, Zig is running out with what looks like his second clue.

The lights are dim in the theater, but as my eyes adjust, I can see there are no clues on or around the screen. They must be in one of the rows, but which one? I look back at the clue.

CLUE #1

TOM CRUISE SAT IN ME FOR *TOP GUN*, AND YOU CAN SIT IN ME TO WATCH IT.

What did Tom Cruise sit in, exactly? Umm, a jet I guess. It must be one of the fighter jet names, but what are they? M-16? No, I think that's a gun or a firecracker. F-16? Yeah, that sounds like a plane and it might be a seat in this theater, too. I run up to row F and sprint across it to the other end. Only when I get there the last seat is 15. F-15? Is that a plane?

I open the folded-up seat and there's nothing in it. Crap. I open up the one beside it, F-14, and there it is. An envelope labeled "Lake Mason—Clue 2 of 3." I'm still in this! It's too dark to read the clue in here, so I sprint back to the hallway outside the theater, opening the envelope along the way.

I get into the hallway and unfold the sheet of paper as fast as I can without tearing it to reveal a periodic table of elements. Can't say I expected to see that. Scrawled across the bottom of the chart are the words, "TURN OVER." I flip the paper on and see the clue:

CLUE #2

CALCIUM - IRON

SILICON - NITROGEN - POTASSIUM

Is this some kind of code or combination? Do I need to know the numbers for those elements or their abbreviation?

I flip the paper over. Calcium is Ca, and element number 6. It takes me a few seconds to find Iron, but eventually I do. Iron is 26. Silicon is 14, Nitrogen is 7, and Potassium is 15—oh wait, that's Phosphorous. Potassium is ... where the heck is Potassium? It takes me what feels like an eternity, but twenty seconds later I find it on the very left side of the page next to the letter 'K' and the number 19.

So the numbers are:

6-26

14-7-19

Are they coordinates for a location? Dates? Letters in the alphabet? The sixth letter is F, and the twenty-sixth is X. FX NGS? That doesn't make any sense.

I hear a noise and see Haley racing my way. "Hey Lake!" she says as she races into the theater. "Better move fast, I'm about to grab my second clue!"

"Okay, but I already got mine," I say, smiling for the first time since this final event started. That's when it hits me. O-K. It's the K for Potassium that is part of the code, not the periodic number! I should have been thinking that from the start instead of looking for the most complicated solution.

I flip the paper back to the chart. Calcium is Ca, and for some weird reason, Iron is Fe. The first word is "Café!"

I flip it one more time to get the last three elements. Silicon is Si, Nitrogen is N, and Potassium is K. Sink! The café sink!

I sprint back toward the Great Room and take a left and then a right, heading down the north side hallway. Two more quick turns and I'm outside the front lobby café. This is the only café I know of at The Firestone School, so hopefully my clue is here.

I sprint over to it and pass Jess, who is heading out of the café back toward the Great Room. "Just found my second clue!" she says. I'm about to find my third, but I don't tell her that.

Once in the café, I run behind the counter and peer into the sink. It's filled with water, but down at the bottom in a sealed baggy is my envelope. I pull it out, dry my hands off, and rip open the envelope, which says "Lake Mason—Clue 3 of 3."

My heart stops as I read the clue, which is significantly longer than the first two I've received:

LAKE,

I NEED YOUR HELP STOPPING HUDSON. I KNOW YOU OVERHEARD ME TELL FIONA WHERE THE FLASH DRIVE IS.

YOU NEED TO GRAB THE DRIVE BEFORE HE DOES AND KEEP IT SAFE. IF ROGAN BOSCH IS WORKING WITH HIM, HE'S GOING TO FIND IT, BUT NOT IF YOU GET THERE FIRST.

DR. V

P.S. THE KEY TO UNLOCK YOUR CRATE IS IN THE CABINET RIGHT IN FRONT OF YOU. HELP ME WITH THIS, AND I GUARANTEE THERE WILL BE A SPOT AT THE FIRESTONE SCHOOL FOR YOU.

56

I t takes a few seconds to start breathing again, but even as I do my head still feels like its spinning. Five hundred questions flood my head as I skim the note a second and third time.

How did Dr. V know I overheard that conversation the other day?

Why didn't she say anything to me?

If they know what Hudson is up to, why don't they just kick him out of the competition?

Why do they need *me* to move the MCD files?

None of it really makes sense, but right now it doesn't matter. I need to unlock my crate to make it to Stage 2.

That's when a thought hits me. What if this is all fake? All this stuff about the MCD being in danger and the school security being compromised ... what if it's all part of The Firestone Fires? Am I being tested right now, to see how I handle chaos? Or what if this is a test of my character, like what Willy Wonka did to Charlie Bucket with the everlasting gobstopper? Do I only get a scholarship if I make the right choice? And what is the right choice? Is it to snitch on Hudson to save the MCD?

I open the cabinet in front of me, and just like the note said, there it is: my key. I shove the note in my back pocket, grab the key, and race back to the Great Room. There's no time to worry if this is some big trick—I need to get that crate open.

When I burst into the Great Room, I notice there's at least five other kids already there. I don't bother counting how many, but I do notice Haley, Zig, and Meatball. I get to my crate and fumble with the key for a few seconds before finally getting the lock to open. I pull it off and lift the lid of the crate to reveal my safe inside.

"Congratulations, Lake," Mr. Lincoln says from the front of the room. "You are student number six to complete Stage 1. There is only one spot left."

I breathe a deep sigh of relief that I'm moving on, and so are Zig, Haley, and Meatball. I also see Ryan and Hudson. My heart sinks a little when I realize Jess isn't here yet. There's one spot left, and she's going to have to beat Laura, Britney, and Erik to get it.

"Barely made it, Flake," Hudson says with a smirk.

"You too," Zig says to him from behind me. "Hudson just got here about thirty seconds before you did." I'm stunned, but I try not to let my face show it. I thought Hudson would be stealing the files, not finding his key. Did he give up on that to focus on a scholarship? Or is he going for the files during Stage 2? I reach behind me and feel the note in my back pocket that was in my final envelope, deciding not to do anything about it for now.

"When did you finish?" I ask Zig, trying to catch my breath.

"First one," Zig says. "Meatball and Haley were the next two, then Ryan, Hudson, and you."

So I came in sixth in Stage 1. That means I'll be sixth to start Stage 2, ten minutes behind Zig, eight minutes behind Meatball, six minutes behind Haley, four minutes behind Ryan, and two minutes behind Hudson. I glance over at him. He's looking the other way, so I stare for a few seconds and think about the note I just read.

If he is going for the MCD plans, he's going to have a two-minute head start on me. But does he know where they are? Does he know they're hidden in a notch on top of Fiona's office door? I don't think so, but I can't be sure.

The question is, should I even care? Should I abandon the thing I've wanted for half my life to try and stop him? Dr. V guaranteed me a scholarship if I could pull it off, but what if I can't? What if I don't stop him and I don't finish Top 3 either? Then the Microclimate Dome falls into the wrong hands and I'm back at Crapville Middle School next month waving TJ's taco breath out of my face on an hour-long bus ride to a school that's too cheap to buy computers for its students.

The seed of a possible plan pops into my head. What if I focus on the competition first and then try to stop Hudson? If my first clue for Stage 2 seems easy enough, maybe I can do both things at once? It's risky, but for the moment it seems like a decent option.

Before I have a chance to really think it through, a commotion on the far side of the room grabs my attention. It's Laura—she's racing across the Great Room with her key in hand, and about ten steps behind her, Jess is on her tail.

Laura gets to her crate first, but as she fumbles with her lock, she drops the key on the ground. By the time she picks it up, Jess is at her crate as well.

Both girls have their locks in hand, and seconds apart, both open up their crates to complete Stage 1. The finish is incredibly close, but not so close that I don't know who got to their safe first. The sadness that overtakes me confirms what everyone else knows and what Mr. Lincoln announces to the group.

"Congratulations, Laura," Mr. Lincoln says. "You are student number seven to complete Stage 1. Everyone else is eliminated."

Oh my gosh. Jess is done.

57

"We have our final seven," Mr. Lincoln announces. "As I mentioned earlier, we are going right in to Stage 2 without much of a break. Zig Simmons will be released first, and two minutes later Derek—or, Meatball, as he apparently prefers to be referred to as—will begin. We will continue this way until the seventh student, Laura, is released, a full twelve minutes after Zig has started."

Jess is now in the corner of the room, slouched down on the floor. I feel bad for her, but for now I have to stay focused on Mr. Lincoln, who is still giving instructions.

"That small safe you have pulled out of your crate contains a scholarship to The Firestone School. Your goal is to find the combination and unlock the safe. The first three to do so will earn the right to attend The Firestone School for grades seven through twelve. I don't have to tell you how valuable that is. For the other four of you, sadly, the journey ends here."

Ten minutes. That's how long I have to wait to start Stage 2. This is gonna be the longest ten minutes of my life.

"I'll reset the clock to zero and start it on my go. Your first clue is up here on stage with me. I'll hand it to you when it is your time to be released. If Zig Simmons would join me now, we'll begin."

Zig heads to the stage, and I take a moment to look around the room. This is it. This is why I'm here. Haley and I make eye contact, and when she smiles at me I let myself daydream for a second about what it would be like to be in class with her every day. Oh my gosh, that would be amazing, but don't get ahead of yourself just yet, Lake. A good secret agent never lets emotions get in the way of the mission.

I glance over at Hudson and wonder what he's planning. He'll be heading out two minutes before me, and I'm guessing he's going right for the Security Wing. By the time he realizes the plans aren't there, I might not only have my scholarship, but I might also be able to rescue the flash drive as well.

"Best of luck to everyone," Mr. Lincoln says. "Stage 2 begins ... now!" With that, he hands an envelope to Zig who rips it open, takes a few seconds to read it, and then bolts toward the west exit of the Great Room.

Ten minutes and counting until my turn.

Jess comes over to sit next to me, which is surprising because I thought she was off crying in the corner. I feel terrible that she's out of The Fires, but honestly, I kind of want to be left alone right now. This is the biggest moment of my life.

I don't know what to say to her so we sit in silence for a few seconds before she finally says, "This sucks."

"I know," I say, "I'm sorry." I want to add, "Why aren't you sitting with your buddy Hudson?" but that would be kind of mean, and I do feel bad for her right now.

"It's fine," she says. "On the bright side, at least it's probably gonna be three of my friends that end up winning this."

"Yeah, that is pretty cool," I say, "although wait, are you including Hudson in that three?"

She gives me a look. "Lake, I know he gives you a hard time sometimes, but trust me—he's not a bad person."

I would love to tell her what I know about him. About the

secret meeting in the middle of the night and the note in my pocket from Dr. V. I knew from the start that he was trouble, and for some reason Jess just can't see it. Maybe it's his blond hair and blue eyes.

"You don't believe me, do you?" she says.

"About what?" I ask.

"About Hudson," she says. "I'm sorry about all that earlier. It sucks that he made a big deal about your ... you know, your accident last night. That was so wrong, and I let him know that, too. I think he really did feel bad about it afterward, and he told me he was going to apologize to you."

"Whatever," I laugh, wondering if Hudson has ever said the word "sorry" in his life. "It's not even about the accident," I say.

"What it's about, then?" she asks.

"Nothing," I say, wishing I hadn't even hinted that I know more than I'm letting on.

We sit in more silence, which is finally interrupted by Mr. Lincoln announcing that Meatball is being released. Eight minutes until my name is called.

"Lake, wetting the bed is not that big of a deal," Jess finally says, breaking the silence.

"I know," I clap back at her a little too strongly, "it's not that."

"Then what is your deal?" she asks. "I'm the one out of the competition and you're the one acting all weird and sassy right now."

I look over at Hudson, who is waiting for his name to be called. This time he catches me looking, and he returns a smile so wide and devious that something inside me snaps.

"Okay, listen," I say, "I'm gonna tell you something, and you have to believe me that this is true. I swear I'm not making this up."

"What?" she says.

"Your buddy Hudson is the thief," I tell her. "You know how

Mr. Lincoln told us to be on the alert for anything suspicious? Well, I have been, and I know things."

"Lake, that's impossible," Jess says.

"No, actually, it's not and I have proof," I tell her, reaching for the note from Dr. V in my back pocket.

"No, it can't be him," Jess says with a confused look on her face. I feel bad doing this to her, but it's probably best that she knows.

"Listen, this has nothing to do with him being mean to me," I tell her. "Last night I followed him out of our room to a secret meeting he was having."

"With who?" Jess asks, confused.

"I don't know, it was on the phone. But they were planning to do something during this event. I heard it myself."

Jess looks stunned as I tell her this. She's not saying anything, but I can tell she wants to say something.

"I almost brought it up at the interview this morning," I say, "but then I was too afraid they would cancel the competition, and I really didn't want to blow my chance at a scholarship. But get this—just now instead of my third clue I got a note from Dr. V about Hudson. She asked me to stop him from stealing the MCD plans."

Mr. Lincoln announces that Haley is being released and she runs out of the Great Room with her clue. Six minutes away.

"It's not him," Jess says, seemingly fighting back tears. Is she really crying about this guy? Good grief, what is going on here?

"Jess, read this," I say, handing her the note.

Jess takes the note and skims it.

"Lake, this is not from Dr. V," she says.

"Yes, it is," I say.

"Trust me, it's not," she says.

That's when I realize what's happening. I thought I was the one withholding the important information in this conversation, but it's clear she's the one hiding something from me.

"Wait, is there something you're not telling me?"

She doesn't say anything. I sit there in silence for a few moments because a good secret agent knows when to shut up and listen. The problem is, I don't have time right now to wait her out. The clock is ticking.

"Jess," I say, "do you know something about the plot to steal the MCD files?"

"No! Of course not," she says.

"Then what?" I ask, raising my voice a notch while still whispering. "What are you not telling me?"

"I promised I wouldn't tell," she sighs.

"Jess, if you have information about the plans to steal the Microclimate Dome, you have to say something! There's still time to stop Hudson from getting away with this!"

"It's not Hudson!" she whispers, letting out a big sigh. "Ugh —I don't want to betray his trust."

I don't say anything, waiting for her to finish her thought. I can't believe she might know something about what's going on and she's not saying anything. The silence is broken by Mr. Lincoln announcing that the third student is being released. Ryan grabs his envelope and runs out of the Great Room. Four minutes left.

"Hudson's next," I whisper to her. "He's literally going to try and steal the files right now. If there's something I should know about what he's up to, you need to tell me now."

"Fine," she finally says, "but you can't tell anyone that I told you."

"I won't, I promise," I say.

"Hudson's not really in the scholarship competition," she says.

"What?" I say. "Yeah, he is."

"No, he's not," she says, matter of factly. "He works for Fiona Firestone on her security team. He helps her keep an eye on the students during the competition and also during the school year."

I'm floored and speechless for a few seconds. How could he

work for Fiona Firestone? He's twelve years old. Is that even legal?

"Are you sure about this?" is all I can think to say.

"One hundred percent," Jess says.

If this is true, the only thing that makes sense is why all of this has been so confusing. But it's such a curveball that I have no idea how to even process it.

"So wait, this note isn't from Dr. V, then?" I ask.

"Nope, it can't be," Jess says shaking her head.

"Because Dr. V is Hudson's boss, right?" I say, finally making the connection.

"She's not only his boss," Jess says, pausing for a second as if she's not sure that she wants to finish the sentence.

She looks down for a second and then back up at me again.

"Dr. V is his mom."

58

My mind is spinning a thousand miles an hour as I process what Jess just told me.

I keep thinking back to everything that's happened this week trying to find something that makes this news impossible, but everything sort of fits—even the conversation I overheard Hudson having last night.

So the distraction of the scavenger hunt wasn't about him stealing the MCD plans, it was so he could catch the real thief trying to do it.

"But wait," I say, "why would Hudson tell you that he works for Fiona Firestone? Why would he tell you that Dr. V is his mom?"

"I don't know," Jess smirks, "I think he kind of likes me."

Ugh. "Well, I don't care who he works for, he's still a jerk," I say.

"Yeah, but he's a cute jerk," she says, which makes me want to gag.

"So what else did he tell you about who's trying to steal the MCD files?" I ask her.

"Nothing. He wouldn't tell me about it," Jess says. "He said it would be better if I didn't know anything."

"Jess, are you lying to me?"

"No, I swear," she says. "What exactly did you hear last night during Hudson's phone call?"

I concentrate, trying to remember exact words as best as I can. "He said the scavenger hunt would provide the right amount of distraction so people wouldn't know what he was up to. They must think that the robbery is going to happen during the scavenger hunt?"

Just then, Mr. Lincoln announces that Hudson is released, and he races off as if he's desperate for a scholarship that I now know he doesn't even need. Two minutes until my turn.

As he runs out of the room, I notice that he does have the same wispy blond hair that Dr. V has. Now that I know they're related, it seems like an obvious clue I should have picked up on.

"But if it's not Hudson stealing it," I continue, "then it has to be Haley, Meatball, Zig, or ..."

"Laura!" Jess says, almost too loudly, and the moment she does, chills run up my spine.

"It couldn't be, could it?" I ask.

"Think about it, Lake," Jess leans in, "who was the one person who came into this competition openly talking about how she wasn't a fan of Fiona Firestone?"

"Yeah, that would be Laura," I say, "but wouldn't that be too obvious?"

"Well apparently not if we're just now realizing it," Jess says.

"Plus," I add, "she's been saying all week how she's coming around on Fiona."

"*Exactly*," Jess says. "It was all a cover."

Then I remember what Meatball told me about yesterday's party. "Did you notice that she didn't have any family or friends with her yesterday at the party?" I ask.

"Now that you say that, I don't remember seeing her at all," Jess says, starting to get angry. "I can't believe she's been lying to us the whole time."

I look over at Laura, who's on the other side of the Great Room, pacing nervously back and forth.

"Lake, she's getting released into the scavenger hunt two minutes after you," Jess says. "Should we just go say something to Mr. Lincoln now?"

"No," I say, "If we say something, I might not get my scholarship, and besides, I thought your boyfriend Hudson had this all under control."

"I don't think he knows who it is yet," Jess says.

"But he might," I say. "They might already know Laura's behind this and they're just waiting to catch her in the act. That's why we shouldn't say anything."

"But what if they don't?" Jess says, looking more serious than I've ever seen her before. "Lake, think about the note you just got trying to pin this all on Hudson. Whoever left you that note is two steps ahead of everyone else. They knew you were suspicious of Hudson, so they left you that note to keep you focused on the wrong person."

Jess is right, and I know it. There's a chance Hudson and Dr. V know what is going on, but they also may have no idea.

I squeeze the note in my hand. Ten minutes ago I thought it assured me a scholarship, hand-delivered from Dr. V if I could stop a thief. Now that I know it's a fake, it's just a worthless piece of paper that has left me more confused than ever.

I start walking toward Mr. Lincoln, who looks ready to call my name. When he does, I could head into the Northeast Wing before Laura gets there to make sure she doesn't steal the MCD plans. I have no idea if she knows where they are, but I have to assume she does at this point if she's working with someone else on the inside. The only advantage I have is the two-minute head start.

That's not my only option, though. I could just grab my clue, ignore all of this, and do my best to win my scholarship. I'm so close to trading in six years of Crapville for six years of The Firestone School.

"Lake Mason," Mr. Lincoln says, "you are released!"

And with that, I race up to him to get my first clue. As he places it in my hand, I get the first dose of clarity I've had in a while.

I know exactly what I need to do.

59

I grab the envelope from Mr. Lincoln and start opening it as I sprint out of the Great Room.

When I get out into the hallway, I pull the clue out. Only, instead of reading it, I fold it and put it into my back pocket. My mission is crystal clear. I know what I need to do, and it has nothing to do with opening up my combination safe.

I'm not sure if protecting Fiona Firestone's MCD technology will earn me a scholarship at the school or not, but this threat seems too important to ignore. Jess is right, I might be the only one who can stop Laura from doing this. I might be the only one who can keep the Microclimate Dome out of the wrong hands.

I run down the hallway, turn into the kitchen, and sprint back to the cold room. A few minutes ago I assumed that taking this secret entrance into the Northeast Wing would mean I was hot on Hudson's trail. But now that I know he's not the thief, I don't know what to expect.

Will Hudson be waiting for me in the secret entrance, thinking I'm the one stealing the plans? Or will he be standing in Fiona Firestone's office with Dr. V (his mom!), ready to put me in handcuffs? If he's not actually in this competition like Jess is saying, then who knows what he is up to.

I swing the door to the cold room open and weave around piles of boxes to make my way to the back corner. There are more boxes than usual in front of the hidden panel, but the adrenaline running through my body helps me slide them aside without too much of a problem.

This is it. There's no turning back now.

I press into the hidden panel with my shoulder and it slowly opens, filling the secret hallway with light. I make my way to the end of the hallway and find the small knob to the door that opens up into the closet. I pull it open and inch into the closet, pausing for a second to make sure I don't hear anyone inside the room beyond the closet door. Once I'm sure it's empty, I push open the closet door slowly, squinting as my eyes adjust to the fluorescent lights of an empty conference room.

I walk across the room, slowly pull open the conference room door, and peek my head into the hallway. It's empty. The whole Northeast Wing seems eerily silent.

For the first time during this whole week, I suddenly feel a shiver up my spine, a sense that I might be in danger. This isn't some fun mission at home to see if I can move mom's keys from her purse to the microwave. This is me trying to stop a legit thief from stealing what might be one of the most important inventions of my lifetime. I've never thought of Laura as dangerous, but I've been wrong about her all along. And if she's working with someone on staff, or even someone on the outside, that person might be the one I really have to worry about.

The crazy part is, this jolt of fear doesn't make me want to abort the mission. Instead, it's met with a surge of courage and resolve. I know what I need to do, and I feel strangely confident that I can do it.

I exit the conference room to see that I'm at the end of a

long hallway, and it's pretty clear that the office at the other end is Fiona Firestone's. It's lined with glass walls in the front, a huge desk to the left, and a leather couch on the right. Above the couch is a massive, framed photograph of what I think is a hummingbird. As I make my way toward her office door, I'm reminded that Laura was going to be released two minutes behind me. Has it been two minutes yet? I think so. She's probably on her way.

I try to open the door to the office, but it's locked. My ID Band wouldn't have given me access to anything in this wing, but it doesn't matter, because I'm no longer wearing it. I took it off and gave it to Jess before I grabbed my Stage 2 envelope from Mr. Lincoln. I've known that they can use the ID Band to track my location since the first day I got here, and that's the last thing I want right now.

There's a thin space between the top of the door where the flash drive is hidden and the underside of the doorway trim. From my vantage point, it looks too thin to get my fingers into, but there's a chance I can. If I can find a chair to stand on, it's worth a shot.

I race back to the conference room, checking every door along the way to see if any are unlocked, but none are. I grab the nearest chair, sprint back down the hall, and set the chair against the door. The chair gives me enough height to reach the top of the door, but there's just not enough room to get my fingers into the crack. I'm pretty sure I can feel the edge of the notch that Dr. V cut into the top of the door, but I just can't get my fingers in far enough to touch the drive.

There's no other way to get at the drive; I have to do what I've done hundreds of times at home just for fun. I have to pick the lock on this door.

I run back down to the conference room and rifle through the cabinets along the wall, hoping to find a paperclip, a bobby pin, or a set of tiny screwdrivers. Nothing. I check the drawers on the small desk beside the closet, but there's nothing but monitor adapters and power cables.

My last hope is the basket of pens on the table. I empty it out and there, among the pens and highlighters, are a handful of paperclips. I grab two of the largest ones I see, and race back to Fiona Firestone's office door.

Years ago when I told my mom I was learning how to pick locks she made me promise to never use it for a bad reason, and I never have. I got really good at it, but I've never tried to do it under this type of pressure.

I straighten both paper clips and insert the first one at the bottom of the keyhole, applying pressure downward and counterclockwise. With my other hand I insert the second paperclip all the way to the back of the keyhole and apply pressure upwards, feeling for the tumblers. I slowly pull the top clip toward me and feel the first two tumblers click. So far, so good. In fact, this whole thing almost seems too easy, and it leaves me with an unsettling feeling I just can't pinpoint.

I apply a bit more pressure, trying to snag the third tumbler when my right hand slips, and my thumb catches the corner of the keyhole, opening up a small but painful cut. "Dang it!" I wince, instinctively putting my thumb in my mouth to keep the blood from dripping.

I pull out my thumb to see how bad it is. The cut itself isn't even a quarter of an inch long, but it's deep enough that that the blood is starting to pool on my fingernail. I stick it back in my mouth for a few seconds to clean it up and hopefully help the blood start to clot, but I know I'm just wasting time.

I stick both paperclips back into the lock, carefully applying pressure with my bottom hand in a way that doesn't cause my thumb to drip blood. I once again get the first two tumblers to move easily, and though the third one gives me a bit more trouble, eventually it moves. The fourth tumbler slides with ease, leaving me one left.

I glance over my shoulder down the hall at the conference

room, expecting Laura to appear at any second, and that's when it hits me that she might not need to sneak into the Northeast Wing via the secret entrance. If she has an accomplice, she might have access to the entire building.

In fact, that's exactly what feels off about this whole mission. Why aren't alarms going off right now? Why am I not being chewed to death by robotic security dogs Fiona Firestone created in a machine lab? Should it really be this easy to break into Fiona Firestone's office?

No, it shouldn't. Something is wrong here, but I don't have time to find a whiteboard to brainstorm and connect all the clues. I need to complete this mission and get out of here as fast as I can.

I fidget with the final tumbler for a few seconds, my hands both starting to cramp from holding the same position for this long. The blood is pooling on my thumb again and starting to drip on the floor, so I lean down and lick off what I can get to on my thumb. And just when I think I can't hold on any longer, the final tumbler clicks into place.

I slowly turn the bottom paperclip counterclockwise, unlocking the door. I drop the paperclips, push the door open a few inches, and hop back onto the chair, running my hand along the top of the door. There, inside the small notch that Dr. V carved, is the flash drive.

I hold it up to the light for a few seconds and marvel at the power and potential that the information on the drive contains. It's nothing more than a tiny piece of plastic and metal, but I feel the weight of the world on it as I slip it into my pocket and head for my exit.

60

I close and lock the office door before carrying the chair back to the conference room. I don't know where Laura is, but she has to be looking for this flash drive. Hudson is out here somewhere, too. He's either looking for the thief or hiding somewhere so he can catch them in possession of the stolen drive.

Stolen drive.

I can't believe I'm the one stealing this, even if I am doing it for the right reason. I'm stealing it so it won't be stolen!

I decide to get back to the safety of the Great Room with the MCD files so I can figure it out from there. Maybe I'll go directly to Mr. Lincoln, explain what is happening, and hand him the flash drive. Or maybe I'll give the drive to Jess for safe-keeping, and then I'll see if I can still win myself a scholarship. I'm not sure what the better option is, but I'll figure it out when I get there.

I slip into the conference room closet, crouch down, and make my way into the secret tunnel, where I'm thankful that no one is waiting for me. I push my way into the walk-in fridge and weave my way back to the entrance to the kitchen, happy to no longer be in an officially "off limits" area. Granted, if someone walked in on me in this fridge right now, I'd have a lot of explaining to do, but technically no one said I wasn't allowed in here. I'd just tell them I was following my clue to get my combination.

My clue! I totally forgot that I haven't even looked at it yet. I consider stopping in the cold room to read it over, so I can brainstorm about the answer, but decide I can at least wait until I get into the kitchen where it's not so cold.

I burst through the cold room door into the kitchen, and when I do, I'm stopped dead in my tracks. The kitchen is dark, but there's just enough light for me to see that I'm not alone. Standing there, at opposite ends of the room, are Haley and Meatball.

"Lake?" Haley says with a confused expression on her face.

"Dude, what are you doing in the freezer?" Meatball asks.

I'm so stunned that the obvious answer I should give doesn't come out as quickly as it should. "I'm ... I was following my clue." I stammer. "Isn't that what you guys are doing?"

"Did you find it?" Haley asks, making her way over to me.

"Find what?" I respond defensively.

"Your clue," she says looking even more puzzled.

"Oh ... no, I mean, I don't think so, I mean, no." I say. "No, I didn't find it yet."

Meatball shuts the door to the cabinet he was rifling through and walks over to us. I'm trying to think of what to say to save this situation so I don't look like a total doofus in front of them, but nothing's coming. I just need to get back to the Great Room.

"Lake, what happened to your hand?" Haley says.

I glance down and see that the tip of my thumb is completely covered in blood and it's dripping onto the floor.

"Oh, shoot," I say, sticking it in my mouth again to clean it.

"Dude, what happened?" Meatball asks.

I could make up a story. Or I could just say "I'll tell you

later" and run back to the Great Room. But this might be the perfect time to let them know what I'm up to in case I need their help.

"Okay, listen," I say. "I can explain more later, but the MCD files were in danger and I thought it was Hudson trying to steal them for Rogan Bosch but Jess and I figured out it's been Laura this whole time. I had to grab them before she did."

"Laura was trying to steal the MCD plans?" Haley asks, not hiding the fact that she's having trouble believing me.

"Yeah, you know how she keeps saying she's coming around on Fiona Firestone? Well, she wasn't coming around at all. She was lying the whole time."

"So wait, *you* stole the plans?" Meatball says, wide-eyed. He seems impressed, like he didn't think I had it in me to pull off something like this.

"I didn't steal them, I'm saving them," I say. "But yes, I did."

Drops of sweat race down my back, and I wonder if it's the warmth of the nearby pizza oven or the predicament I'm in that's making me sweaty.

"Lake, if you knew it was Laura," Haley says, "why didn't you just tell someone? I mean, even when you thought you knew it was Hudson, why didn't you report it to someone?"

"I just figured out it was Laura a few minutes ago," I tell her, which is only partially the reason why I haven't said anything. I leave out the part about not wanting The Firestone Fires canceled because all I really cared about was winning a scholarship.

"And I mean, I thought about reporting Hudson when I thought it was him," I say, "but I didn't know who to talk to about it. You remember what Mr. Lincoln said. Everyone is a suspect. Honestly, I really think someone on staff here is in on it, too."

Suddenly a bright flashlight beam flicks on, momentarily blinding the three of us.

"Wow," says the squeaky voice behind it, "turns out you're a lot smarter than you look, Lake Mason."

The light switch flips on and the kitchen is suddenly bright.

It's Beardy, with a flashlight in one hand and a gun pointed at us in the other.

61

"I knew it!" I say.

"Shut up," Beardy squeaks. "You didn't know anything."

"I did!" I say. "I knew someone on staff was in on this, too."

"Well, congrats on your hunch, Detective Mason," Beardy squeaks. "The thing is, one of us has a correct hunch and one of us has a loaded gun."

I notice a set of kitchen knives about ten feet to my left, so I slowly start shuffling that way. I'm not really sure what I'll do once I get close enough to grab one, but I'll figure that out when I get there.

"No, no, no!" Beardy yells, noticing what I was doing. "A knife? Seriously? You were literally going to bring a knife to a gun fight? All three of you, close together in the middle of the floor *now*! Shoulder to shoulder, *let's go!*"

We squeeze together. I'm in the middle. Haley's on my right, Meatball is on my left.

"You're not going to shoot us," Meatball says. "We're just kids."

"Kids are scrubs," Beardy laughs, "but you're right, I'm not gonna shoot you. Lake knows what I want, and once he gives it to me, I will gladly not shoot you."

I reach into my right front pocket and run my fingers over the flash drive, unsure of what to do next.

"What do you got there, buddy?" Beardy says to me, "Is that the drive? Why don't you just give it to me, and nobody ends up with a bullet in their thigh."

"I can't give this to you," I say with as much confidence as I can muster.

"You can and you will," Beardy squeaks.

"If I give this to you, it's going to end up in the wrong hands and innocent people are going to die."

"First off, there's no such thing as innocent people, bud," Beardy says. "But honestly, I don't really care either way. I'm just doing my job and getting paid." As he says this a bead of sweat rolls down my face and it instantly gives me an idea. It's not the knives that can help me the most right now, it's the brick pizza oven. I take the drive out of my pocket and hold it up like I'm about to throw it.

"Let us go or I'll throw this in," I say, glancing over toward the wide mouth of the brick pizza oven.

"If you do it, I'll shoot you." Beardy says, his voice suddenly laced with a little fear.

"I think you're gonna shoot us anyway," I say, not sure if I believe that or not. My arm stays cocked in a throwing position.

"I already told you—" Beardy squeaks, his voice getting impossibly higher as he gets more angry. He pauses, takes a deep breath, and opts for a kinder voice. "I already told you, just give me the drive and I will let you go."

"Lake, just give it to him," Haley says.

"Listen to your girlfriend," Beardy smiles.

His eyes give away that he's scared he might not get the drive. I can feel the heat from the oven from five feet away. If I flick the drive in, it will probably start melting before it even lands.

"Okay, fine," I say, bringing my arm down a few inches. "Let my friends go and I'll give it to you." I make it a point to let Beardy momentarily see the drive in my right hand, before bringing my hands together in a praying motion for a split second. "Please, just let them go," I say, keeping my hands together and sounding desperate for effect.

"Okay," Beardy says, "so we're going to do this whole 'let my friends go' hero thing?" As he's saying this my hands come apart from the mock praying motion they were in. I immediately put my right hand back up into a cocked throwing position with my fist balled, ready to throw the drive into the oven. Only the drive isn't in my right fist anymore, it's now palmed in my seemingly empty left hand, which is down at my side. It's a sleight of hand trick I used to practice a lot, and I think I just pulled it off without Beardy noticing.

"Listen," Beardy squeaks, "your friends are going to be fine. I just told you no one's gonna get hurt—now give me the drive before I change my mind!" He takes two steps toward me, pointing his gun at my raised right arm.

"I swear I'll throw it in," I say, and as I do I feel Meatball digging his elbow into my left side. It dawns on me that he might have seen me move the drive into my left hand. If I can get it to him without Beardy noticing, we might be able to keep it from him just long enough.

"Just let them go and I promise I won't throw it in the oven. I promise I'll give it to you," I say, waiting for the right moment to slip my left arm behind my back so Meatball can grab the drive.

"Okay, listen," he squeaks. "I usually don't negotiate with scrubs, but I'm honestly not here to hurt you. I'll let your girlfriend and your buddy leave, but here's the deal. The moment the door closes behind them, you're going to give me the drive or I will shoot you in the leg."

"I promise," I lie.

"Lake, are you sure about this?" Haley whispers to me.

"Yeah, it's fine," I whisper back. "You need to get away from here."

"Hey, stop whispering," Beardy squeaks. "I swear, if you try anything, or throw that drive into the oven, you will experience the worst pain you've ever felt in your pathetic life. And maybe you'll be able to crawl far enough for help so that a doctor can save your leg, or maybe you won't. If you go back on your word, we'll find out."

As Beardy is delivering his squeaky monologue, Meatball and I have shifted toward each other just enough that our shoulders are now pressed tightly together. "Okay," I say, extending my still-clenched right fist toward Beardy, "that's the deal. Let them walk and you get this." While Beardy's gaze is focused on my right fist I feel Meatball's fingers behind me taking the drive out of my left hand. As soon as he has it, we inch away from each other. As I bring my left hand subtly back into view, I see Meatball slip the drive into his back right pocket out of the corner of my eye.

I'm betting on two things. One, I don't think Beardy wants to shoot us or he would have already. And two, if Meatball and Haley can get far enough away from Beardy before he realizes they have the drive, he might not be able to catch them. There's no way he can run as fast as they can.

Is he going to shoot me the moment he finds out I don't have it anymore? I hope not.

To my left, Meatball takes a few steps toward the door. "Alright, let's get out of here," he says.

I feel a slight wave of relief come over me as I realize he and Haley are about to escape from this situation unharmed. Only when Haley takes a few steps in Meatball's direction to follow him, he whips his head in her direction.

"Not you!" Meatball snaps at her, in a nasty tone I've never heard him use before.

"Are we all set here?" Beardy asks, keeping his gun pointed at me but turning his eyes toward Meatball.

"Yup," Meatball says, pulling the flash drive out of his back pocket and tossing it to Beardy. "We finally got what we came here for."

62

"Wait, Meatball?" I say. "You're the one working for Bosch?"

"Lake, you're a little smart," Meatball says shaking his head, "but not a lot smart."

"I don't understand," I say. "Why would you do this to Fiona Firestone?"

"Because she's the worst," he says. "She's the absolute worst."

My head is spinning, and I suddenly have a giant pit in my stomach that is somehow ten times bigger than my actual stomach.

"So you're working with Laura, too?" Haley says.

"Psshhh," Meatball laughs. "This has nothing to do with Laura."

"But I thought—" I start to say before Meatball interrupts me. "You thought wrong, dude," he says. "You had no idea what was happening this whole time. No idea. Turns out you're not just a bedwetter, you're a clueless bedwetter."

Ouch. I thought this kid was my friend, which must be why hearing him say that hurts as much as it does.

"Besides," he says, "Laura's a joke. She comes in here saying how much she loves my dad and a week later she's all 'Fiona Firestone is the best, I really misjudged her!'"

The stunned expression on my face has me momentarily paralyzed.

"Oh, did I not mention that at all this week?" Meatball says. "Yeah, my name is Derek Bosch. I guess I forgot to tell you that Rogan Bosch is my father. Minor detail. Didn't think it mattered."

My brain is buzzing with so much confusion I can almost hear a ringing in my ears. How did he even get into The Firestone Fires? How long have he and his dad been planning this? How did they get this past Fiona and Dr. V? How long has Beardy been in on this? So many questions, but all I know is this: the whole time Meatball was here to figure out how to get access to the MCD files, and I was the one who literally put them into his hands.

"I thought your name was Derek Rantelo?" is all I can think to utter.

"Oh, Rantelo's not real," he smiles. "I mean, 'Rantelo' is just the letters in the words 'not real' scrambled up and reorganized. It's called an 'anagram.' You'll learn all about it at Crapville next year, I'm sure."

"Ooh, now do my name!" Beardy grins.

"Mr. Hillit?" I ask.

"Evan Hillit," he says with pride. "Or 'The Villian' if you're good with anagrams. Which, apparently, nobody around here is."

They both have huge grins on their faces, and I've never felt so stupid.

"Why would you turn on Fiona Firestone, like this?" I ask Beardy. "You said yourself that she took a chance on you when she hired you last year."

"Kid, why are you still believing anything I've ever said," Beardy laughs. "This plan has been in the works for years. I never *turned* on Fiona Firestone because I never liked her to begin with, you moron."

He turns to Meatball. "Enough catch-up time, we've got a delivery to make. Let's put these two with the others."

They escort Haley and I out of the kitchen toward the Rec Wing. We stay silent and don't make any eye contact. Beardy and Meatball are about five feet behind us, and they have the two things that matter most in this scenario: the gun and the flash drive.

"Walk faster, lovebirds," Beardy chirps at us, before turning his attention to Meatball.

"Let's put these two in the gym closet with the others and then we're done here," he squeaks.

"How long of a drive do we have ahead of us?" Meatball asks.

"Oh, we're not driving," Beardy responds, "we're taking the chopper."

"Sweet!" Meatball says. "I can't wait to get off this stupid campus."

I know I should be formulating an escape plan right now, but I've got nothing. Beardy and Meatball are right behind us; just far enough that I could probably bolt away from them and around a corner before they could do anything, but there's nowhere to go.

The doors to the bunk room area at the far end of this hallway are usually locked, so this whole wing is essentially a dead end. And besides, what if Haley doesn't run with me? I'm not leaving her here with them.

The gymnasium is about twenty feet ahead, on the right, and just as I'm about to tell Haley that we're going to make it out of this okay, I notice a tiny shadow shift up ahead on my left. At least, I think I see something move? It was right in the entryway to the men's bathroom. I swear I saw someone's shadow, so I do my best to keep the same exact pace, knowing I'll be walking right by there in a few seconds.

I don't want to do anything to draw attention to myself, but I slightly tilt my head to the left over my next few steps, just enough so that I'll be able to see if there's anything or anyone in the entryway as I walk by. Three steps later I am even with the opening, and out of the corner of my eye I see Zig, pressed into the back corner of the entryway near the door hinges, with his index finger over his mouth telling me to keep quiet.

My heart skips a beat, but I somehow don't slow down or do a double take. Instead I put my head down and realize I have about five seconds to create a diversion to ensure that Meatball and Beardy don't see Zig when they walk by him. I don't have time to think of anything else, so I turn around, continuing in stride, and decide to do the only crazy thing that comes into my head.

Just as they're about to walk by Zig, I grab Haley's right hand, whisper "Just go with this" into her ear, and get down on one knee in front of her. I look up into her eyes, which are filled with tears and a sudden burst of confusion, and say, "Haley Jenson, this has been the best week of my life—"

"Hey, keep moving!" Beardy squeaks at us, but I stay down on one knee.

"—I know we're young," I say to her loud enough for everyone in the hallway to hear, "but I've never felt this way about anyone before. I don't know what these guys are going to do to us, so I have a question to ask you—"

"Are you proposing, you idiot?" Meatball laughs. At this point the two of them have walked past Zig without noticing him, and now they're just a few feet from us. As long as they don't turn around, they won't see him.

"I'm in love with her," I say to Meatball, continuing with the act. "Can you at least let me finish?"

"Um, *no*," Beardy squeaks. "Get back on your feet and keep walking. Someday you'll thank me that I just kept you from doing the stupidest thing I've ever seen anyone do."

"He was *proposing!*" Meatball cackles, barely getting out the words between belly laughs. "Oh my gosh, Lake. That is the most ridiculous thing I've ever seen."

"Shut up, Meatball!" Haley says, and for a second I wonder if maybe she didn't totally hate the fact that I was down on one knee in front of her. Then I remember that we're only twelve, and she was probably just going along with it for the act.

"GET UP AND GET MOVING!" Beardy yells, and this time I listen. I just needed to keep Zig in the clear and it worked, even if I completely threw away my dignity in the process.

"He got on one knee!" Meatball snorts.

"Okay, we get it," Beardy says, starting to get annoyed with him. "Let's not get distracted by Romeo the idiot."

Meatball walks ahead of us and leads us to the corner closet of the gym, while Beardy keeps his gun pointed at our backs.

"In here," Meatball says, opening the closet door with a key. The space is dark, but there's enough light coming in from the dim gymnasium to see three people tied to a beam in the center of room. As my eyes adjust, I notice that the closet ceiling is at least thirty feet high, and I can see that it's Fiona Firestone, Dr. V, and Hudson fastened to the beam with gags in their mouths.

"Don't tie them to the same beam," Beardy says. "Use that other one behind the volleyball net. And if they've got phones on them, throw them up on the balcony with the others."

"They don't have phones," Meatball says, waving us to the other side of the room. "Over here, let's go."

He grabs some rope and after setting us up back-to-back on opposite sides of the pole, he wraps it around us a half dozen times, pulling it so tight that it hurts. Beardy keeps his gun focused on us the entire time, but even if he didn't, I wouldn't run anyway. At this point I know my only option for getting out of this is not in this room. I just hope he's thinking the same thing and has a plan to get us out of here.

Meatball pulls out two old basketball jerseys from a cardboard box and twists them into gags. He wraps them around our heads and in our mouths so we can't say anything. They taste like stale sweat and dust.

"You guys missed it—Lake just tried to propose to Haley in the hallway!" Meatball says to the other three. "He's got a gun pointed at him, he doesn't have a ring, he's twelve years old, he's known her less than a week, and he *proposes*! Wait until my dad hears this one." He doubles over in laughter again, and I wish I wasn't tied up so I could punch him right in that stupid smile of his.

"Alright, enough," Beardy yells at Meatball. "Are they good?"

"Yeah, they're not going anywhere," Meatball says, testing the rope to show how taut it is.

"Alright, let's go," Beardy says. "We've got a delivery to finish."

"To the chopper!" Meatball says, causing Beardy to roll his eyes.

"What?" Meatball shrugs. "I've always wanted to say that."

They close the door and lock it behind them, and we are enveloped in darkness.

63

For a few seconds nothing happens.

There are five of us in the room now, but we're all bound and gagged. It's hard to make any noise when you can't move your mouth or any other part of your body.

I'm waiting for Zig to come busting through the closet door any moment now to untie us, but as the seconds tick away a realization hits me. Zig might not be coming. What if they found him just now? What if he ran the other way? There's no guarantee he's going to show up here.

Help might not be coming.

I wriggle my body back and forth to try and create slack in the rope, but all it's doing is giving me rope burn on my chest. I try to do the same with my wrists, but again, nothing is working.

I can't believe I'm stuck here in this closet while Beardy and Meatball steal what will probably be Fiona Firestone's most important invention right out from under her nose. Well, I guess technically I stole it and then they stole it from me, but what difference does it make? They're getting away, and none of this is working out. To make things worse, there's pretty much a zero percent chance Fiona Firestone even awards any scholarships at all this year, considering she's currently bound and gagged to a steel beam in a gym closet in her own school.

Just then there's a jiggling of the large double doors and the faint sound of Zig's voice: "Is anyone in there?"

All five of us do our best to make any sounds we can, but there's no way he can hear our muffled attempts through the doors.

"Hello!" Zig yells, still yanking on the locked doors. "Is anyone in there?"

We do our best to get louder, but the gags keep us from being heard.

"Get away from the door, I'm kicking it in," Zig yells, at which point we all stop grunting to hold our breath.

BANG! For a second, a splinter of light breaks into the closet as Zig's kick forces the locked doors apart an inch or so.

BANG! A second kick seems to weaken the lock even more, letting even more light in as the doors do their best to absorb the blow.

BANG! An explosion of light fills the closet as Zig's third kick snaps the lock, blowing the doors wide open. He races right over to Haley and me, pulling the gags out of our mouths before working on the knots securing me to the beam.

"Dude, what is going on?" Zig asks, while working the first of two knots free.

"Meatball and Beardy are the thieves," I say. "They're about to fly off the campus with the MCD files in the helicopter." Zig unties my final knot, and I'm free from the beam.

"Start working on those three, I'll get Haley," I tell Zig, who runs over to the other support beam and removes the gags from their mouths.

"We have to stop them," Fiona says between coughs. "We can't let them leave the campus with that flash drive."

"Don't you and Dr. V have copies, too?" I ask.

"Yeah, I have one hidden in my shoe," Dr. V says, "and Fiona's is hidden inside her belt."

"But if they have a copy, it doesn't matter." Fiona says, as Zig finally manages to set her free. "Once the code is out there, it's too late. We need to stop that chopper from taking off."

"Perhaps making three copies was a bit of an overreach," Dr. V says.

"No use in second-guessing ourselves now," Fiona says.

That's when I get an idea.

"Can you still control the MCD prototype that's here on campus?" I ask Fiona, as I loosen the last knot on Haley's wrist.

"I could if I had my phone," Fiona says, standing to her feet. "Why?"

"Because this would be the perfect time for a hurricane," I say.

"Unfortunately, our phones are up there," Dr. V says, motioning to a storage ledge twenty feet off the ground.

"We need a ladder, but I don't see one," Hudson says, as Zig finishes untying him.

"Actually, we don't!" Fiona says, stepping toward the open closet door. "WILBUR! ORVILLE!" she yells.

Seconds later, the two finches fly into the closet and hover a few feet above her head.

"My phone—up there," she says, pointing to the ledge.

The finches fly up to the platform and land out of sight. I'm watching in amazement, wondering if they actually understood Fiona and how they plan on carrying a phone that probably weighs five times more than they do.

"They're pushing it off the ledge!" Zig says, as one end of the phone slowly peeks over the edge of the platform.

As he's finishing his sentence, enough of the phone is hanging over the edge that it begins to fall. I start to move for it, but thankfully Haley is already a step ahead of me. She catches it in her cupped hands a split second before it hits the concrete floor.

"Thank you!" Fiona says, grabbing the phone from her.

"Okay, wind and rain on the max settings. Let's see what this dome is capable of."

"C'mon, we might still be able to catch them," Hudson says, sprinting out of the closet.

"You okay?" I ask Haley, as we follow him out.

"Yeah, I'm fine," she says.

We're all free now, so the six of us head out of the closet, and as we do, I grab Zig's arm. "Hey man, thanks for getting us out of there. I don't know what we would have done without you."

Zig smiles. "People need people."

I crack a smile, but only for a second.

Everything is still hanging in the balance.

64

The six of us sprint through the hallway and into the Great Room, which seems unchanged from when I left it twenty minutes ago. But when I was last in here, the sun was shining outside. Now, through the windows, I can see sheets of rain pouring down.

Jess and a few other students are sitting along the far wall, and Mr. Lincoln is lounging at a table near the stage. No one in here has any idea what is going on.

"Did they come through here? Where are they!" Fiona shouts at anyone listening.

"Did *who* come through here?" Mr. Lincoln asks, getting up out of his seat.

"Meatball and Mr. Hillit!" I yell. "They have the plans for the MCD!"

"What?" Mr. Lincoln says, confused. "Why would they have the plans?"

"No time to explain," Fiona says, turning to Dr. V. "Take Hudson with you to the Security Wing, in case they're trying to leave with more than just the drive. And call the police on your way there—we need backup."

Hudson and Dr. V head toward the far end of the Great

Room, while Zig, Haley and I follow Fiona out of the South exit toward the back patio. Just as we're getting near the door to the outside, the booming sound of a helicopter engine almost stops us in our tracks.

We race out onto the South Patio and immediately we're soaked from the heavy rain. Across the lawn, about a hundred yards away, we see Beardy and Meatball seated in the chopper.

"We need to stop them!" Zig yells over the noise of the rain and the chopper blades.

"Will they be able to fly out in this storm?" I ask.

"It won't be easy, but they're gonna try," Fiona says. "But what else can we do? We can't get over there in time to stop them."

That's when it hits me. We won't get there in time, but I know something that might.

"Fiona, can you unlock the drone shed?" I ask.

"Why?" she asks.

"Because that's how we're gonna stop them," Haley says, catching on.

Fiona swipes her wrist against the door and pulls it open. "Wait," she says, "you're going to take down my helicopter?"

"It's either that or they get away!" I say, grabbing the HLX-2500 as Haley pulls the remote off the shelf.

"That's not going to work!" Fiona says.

"It's our only chance," I say.

"The HLX-2500 isn't big enough," Fiona says. "You're gonna have to use the 5000."

"But I thought it wasn't ready to be flown yet?" Haley asks.

"It's not," Fiona says, pulling the sheet off of it, "but it's our only shot."

Once the cover is off Haley and I reach down and pick it up. It's so heavy that it takes both of us on either side to carry it out of the shed and onto the patio. We set it down as carefully as possible and step back. It somehow looks even bigger outside the shed.

"Here's the remote," Fiona says, handing it to Haley.

Wiping the rain out of her eyes, Haley powers on the drone. As she pulls back on the left lever to lift it off the patio, Beardy and Meatball start taking off from the helipad.

"They're lifting off!" Zig yells.

"Here goes nothing!" Haley says, taking the drone up above our heads and speeding it toward the helicopter. For a few seconds I watch in awe, as it seems like Haley knows exactly what she's doing despite this being the 5000's first flight. But as it moves across the yard it keeps dipping and flying too close to the ground.

"What are you doing? Keep it higher!" Fiona yells.

"I'm trying!" Haley says. "I don't think the propellers are big enough for how heavy it is!"

Beardy and Meatball are about ten feet off the ground at this point, and slowly climbing with each second. Maybe using the MCD to create a hurricane was a bad idea. If they can navigate it with the chopper but Haley can't with the drone, they're going to get away.

"There's too much wind!" I yell. "Should we turn off the storm?"

"No," Haley says, "It's not the wind, it's the weight!"

"We don't have time to disassemble it," Fiona says.

"I know," Haley says. "I have a better idea."

Haley banks the drone ninety degrees to the right, keeping it only a few feet off the ground. That's when I think I realize what she's doing. "You're going to crash it into the fire pit?" I yell.

"Just the landing legs," she says. She doesn't even look at me as she says this, her focus completely on what she's doing. I'm not even sure she's blinking right now, she's so locked in.

As the HLX-5000 approaches the fire pit we all cringe. She's coming in too low and it seems like she's going to destroy the entire drone. But at the last second, she pulls back and lifts it up. As it races by the fire pit the landing legs catch on the lip of the fireplace, pulling them off and sending the drone awkwardly straight up into the air and then back down again.

"It's gonna crash!" Fiona screams.

Haley doesn't respond—I'm not even sure she heard Fiona. As the drone dips closer to the ground, Haley pulls back and swings her arms around, as if willing the drone back into control. Just as it looks like she might not be able to keep it up, it levels off and then starts climbing again.

"Got it!" she says, and immediately the drone banks back to the left toward the helicopter, which is now twenty feet in the air.

"Is the chopper too high?" I yell.

"Nope, I got it," she says, as the drone races toward the climbing helicopter. It's clear that Haley's hunch about the weight was right, because the drone is flying much better than it was before she took the legs out.

"Almost there!" yells Fiona, as the rain and wind intensify, to the point that I wonder if she just cranked up the hurricane setting from a Category 1 to a Category 5.

"Here we go!" Haley says, flying the drone just above the cabin on the chopper, directly into the orbit of the propellers.

BOOM! Sparks fly; brilliant flames and thick smoke shoot from the helicopter as the HLX-5000 catches the propellers. Shards of metal fly in every direction, causing us to take cover, and the helicopter starts violently shaking and falling.

Beardy is trying to control the helicopter, but the damage is too great for it to fly. It sputters and falls, tilting briefly to the right and then back to the left, and eventually, when it's dropped to about eight feet above the ground, it does a nose dive, crashing to the earth with a violent rumble.

65

The four of us rush down the steps and across the yard toward the smoking helicopter, unsure if the thieves survived the crash.

As we get closer to the chopper, I realize we're not alone outside. Everyone inside the school has emptied out onto the South Lawn to check out what's going on. In the distance, police sirens are getting louder by the second as the rain continues to pour.

"They're still moving!" Haley says as we arrive at the wreckage. "Should we pull them out?"

"No!" Fiona says, "let the police do it. If they're injured, we might only make it worse."

"Fiona, the drive," I say, pointing to Beardy. "Check the inside pocket of his jacket."

While Beardy groans and tries to open his eyes, Fiona slips part of his jacket out from under the seat belt restraint, reaches inside, and pulls out the flash drive.

She holds it up for a second and makes eye contact with me, before slipping it into her pants pocket. She mouths the words "Thank you," to me, and I nod back. "Thanks to all of you," she says, this time to Zig, Haley, and myself.

Beardy finally opens his eyes, as does Meatball, but it's clear they're going to need to spend some time in the hospital to mend whatever is broken. And from there, they'll probably move straight to their new home in a jail cell for an extended stay.

As police cars pull up in the driveway, I exhale more deeply than I probably ever have before.

I can't believe this is all over. The hunt for the thief, my week with Haley, and The Firestone Fires. It's all done.

I'm not sure what was happening inside the school during the last half hour. I don't know if anyone got through The Fires and was able to unlock their safe and grab their scholarship. And if so, I don't know if Fiona Firestone will honor it or not. The funny thing is that, considering what just happened, I'm not sure I even care.

"Let's get back inside," Fiona says, which sounds like a great idea.

I wipe the rain from my eyes and my body shivers as the wind whips it back into our faces. We head back up to the building and, despite how cold and wet I am, I feel strangely calm and at peace.

The Microclimate Dome plans are safe, and so are Haley and Zig. And honestly, that's all that matters to me right now.

Nick is never gonna believe this one.

66

I'm lying in my bed.

My very own bed in my very own house.

Honestly, it's great to be back home.

A full week has passed since that crazy day at The Firestone School, but it seems like seven years ago, not seven days.

It's just after lunch and Nick and T.J. are on their way over to hang out for the day. We'll probably play some PS4, get some pizza, and talk about school, which starts back up in a week and a half.

I never thought I'd say this, but I think I'm okay with going to Crattville this year. Yes, I'm still going to have to deal with the same troublemakers in my class who always give me a hard time, but after dealing with Hudson for a week, I feel like I can handle them just fine.

I've also been texting with Haley, Zig, and Jess a bunch since I got back, and having them as new friends is going to help me get through the school year. We're already planning a weekend get-together at Jess's house over Thanksgiving Break.

More than anything, I've realized how great it is to have good friends. I'm thankful for old friends like Nick, and my new friends, too. I'll never take that for granted again. And believe it or not, I'm even finding myself enjoying time with T.J. as well. He's not that bad of a kid, really, even if every time he talks all I can smell is Taco Bell.

The doorbell rings, but I decide to stay in bed and let my mom let them in. I pull the bedsheet up over my face and lay in silence waiting for them to push open the door. I notice that the sheets don't smell like fabric softener, which is a good thing. They haven't been washed since I got back, because I haven't wet the bed all week. Maybe I've done that for the last time? Gosh, I hope so.

"Lake, you've got some friends here to see you!" Mom yells out from the living room.

"I know, send them up!" I yell back.

"I think you actually need to come down," she says with a hint of something in her voice that I don't quite recognize.

I reluctantly pop out of bed and head downstairs, and a few steps from the bottom I'm stopped dead in my tracks.

Standing there in my living room are Fiona Firestone, Dr. V, and Hudson.

"Good afternoon, Lake!" Fiona Firestone says. "Good to see you again."

I'm so stunned I don't know what to say.

"Lake, you remember Dr. V and Hudson," she says, as if somehow I would have forgotten about them.

"Yeah" is all I can muster up.

"What's up, Flake?" Hudson says.

"Hey, Mudson," I respond instinctively. Shoot, why didn't I think of calling him that during The Fires?

"Lake, we only have a few minutes," Fiona says, "but we wanted to stop by to see you in person to thank you again for your bravery and help in protecting the plans for my Microclimate Dome. Because of you, the files are on lockdown and the technology never leaked."

"Well, that was the first rule of The Firestone School, right?" I say, recalling what Fiona Firestone had said to us the first morning of The Fires. "We're better together than we are on our own."

"We are," Dr. V says, "and we couldn't have saved the tech without your help. But, you really should have come to us earlier with what you knew."

"I know, and you're welcome," I say. "So I guess you officially canceled the scholarship competition, right?"

"Unfortunately, with what happened during The Fires we're not giving out any competition scholarships this year," Fiona says. "We have quite a mess to clean up at the school before the students come back in two weeks."

"*If* they come back in two weeks," Dr. V interjects.

"Right. At this point, we may have to delay the start of classes," Fiona says with a sigh.

"So, my dear," Dr. V says, "when is your first day at Crattville?"

"A week from Tuesday," I laugh, slightly puzzled that she knows the name of my middle school off the top of her head.

"How are you feeling about it?" Fiona asks.

"I mean, good, I guess," I say. "I wish summer was longer, but whatever."

There's an awkward pause that hangs in the air for a few seconds. It's finally broken when Hudson says, "Well, ask him or I'm going to."

"Ask me what?" I say.

He looks at Fiona, who finally speaks up. "Lake, we're not giving out any scholarships through The Firestone Fires this year, but Dr. V and I have been talking, and we were so impressed with what you did this week, that we'd like to extend you a special offer."

My head starts buzzing and I turn to my mom, who smiles back at me like she knows something I don't.

"Lake, we are officially accepting you into the Firestone School by offering you a full six-year scholarship," Fiona says.

"If you haven't been too traumatized by what happened last week, we'd love to have you."

My mouth is wide open in stunned silence, and just as I'm about to say "Yes," Dr. V speaks up. "There is one condition," she says. "You have to agree to a work-study program where you intern in my security department for a few hours a week. I think we can learn a thing or two from a budding secret agent like you."

"How do you know about that?" I ask, instinctively embarrassed that someone other than my family or Nick knows about my secret career ambitions.

"Your mom told us when we were doing a little background paperwork on you earlier this week," Dr. V says.

"Mom, you knew about all this?"

"They told me a few days ago," she says. "It's been torture keeping it to myself, but I wanted to let Fiona Firestone be the one to break the news to you. I'm so happy for you."

"Will I have to work with him?" I ask, pointing at Hudson.

"Yes, of course," Dr. V says. "You'll be working directly with him on quite a few projects."

"Hmm," I mutter out loud. "How long do I have to decide?"

"Really?" Hudson says in disbelief.

"I'm kidding," I laugh, finally breaking my straight face. I'm still a little salty about how he treated me during the week of The Fires, but now that I know he was trying to sniff out a thief, I've mostly gotten over it.

Just then, a tinge of sadness hits me when I realize this means I won't be going to school with Nick this year after all. I know he and T.J. will be bummed, but they'll be so happy for me. I can't wait to tell Zig, Haley, and Jess, too.

"Alright, Lake, we have to go," Fiona says. "But we're looking forward to seeing you at the school in a few weeks. We'll be in touch."

"Thank you so much," I say. "I can't wait. Have a safe trip home."

"Well, we're not going home yet," Hudson says.

"We have a three-hour drive to Silver Pass ahead of us," Fiona adds.

"Wait," I say. "Silver Pass? Are you going to see Haley?"

"Look at Flake getting all excited about his fiancée," Hudson says. "Did you put a ring on her finger yet, or are you waiting until you're both thirteen?"

Fiona ignores Hudson. "We're about to make the same offer to Haley that we made to you."

"Really?" I say, not even trying to hide my excitement.

"Yes," Dr. V says. "And last night we met with your friend Zig and offered him a spot as well. Even though we didn't have official winners, you three showed yourselves to be honest, brave, intelligent, and loyal throughout the entire week. Exactly the type of students we want at The Firestone School."

"And don't text Haley about this yet, dear," Dr. V says. "Give us a few hours to get there and surprise her, and then we'll tell her to reach out to you."

"Okay, sounds good," I say, still smiling like an idiot. With each second my mind processes what is happening more and more. I'm going to The Firestone School. I'm going to be interning in their Security Department. I'm going with Zig and Haley!

"I can't believe it," is all I can think to say. "I just can't believe it."

"Well, believe it, Lake," Fiona Firestone says as she turns to leave. "And welcome to The Firestone School."

67

The car is packed.

Mom is in the driver's seat, and Viv is riding shotgun.

Nick and T.J. are in the back seat with me, making the trip with us to move me in.

Mom said we're making a surprise stop on the way to the school, but I already know we're going to eat at Dexter's. I snuck onto her phone and scrolled through recent searches when she wasn't looking. A secret agent's work is never done.

Zig just texted me that he's already at the school. He got there an hour ago and he's setting up our room. *Our room!* How amazing is that?

Haley is on her way; she'll probably get there around the same time we do. The three of us are making plans to grab pizza tonight and maybe catch a movie.

I get into the car, settle down between Nick and T.J. in the back seat, and buckle up my seat belt. Maybe mom was right after all. Maybe friends really are the secret to a great life.

"To The Firestone School we go!" Mom says, starting the car.

"You sure you don't want to just go to Crapville Middle School with us?" Nick says. "Last chance to change your mind."

"Nick, you know I don't like it when you say Crapville," Mom says.

"Sorry, Mrs. Mason," Nick says.

"You guys are going to crush it at Crattville," I say. "But Fiona Firestone is kind of expecting me, so I can't really let her down."

"Your loss," Nick says.

The funny thing it, it does feel a little bit like a loss that I won't be classmates with Nick this year. It's about the only downside to all of this, but we both promised to stay in touch as much as possible, and I know we will.

Same goes for Jess and Laura. They admitted in our group text that they were jealous about the offer the three of us got to go to Firestone, but they promised to come visit at least once. Jess said she'd visit even more to see Hudson, which almost made me gag. I'm still not sure how I feel about working with Hudson, but at least I know now that he's one of the good guys. Maybe he'll actually start acting like it at some point.

"Mom, can we stop at the sporting goods store on the way home?" Viv asks. "I'm thinking we should turn Lake's room into a workout area."

"No way," I say. "Mom, tell her she's not allowed to touch anything in my room."

"You'll never know, anyway," Viv says. "When you come home on break you can just sleep on the couch. Or you can just move in with Nick and never come home again."

"Guys, be nice to each other," Mom says as she pulls out of the driveway. She turns left to head north, on our way to my next mission.

There's nothing really secret or dangerous about this next one as far as I can tell. I'm an incoming seventh grader at The Firestone School with a cool internship and new friends ready to take this journey with me. The biggest question mark I have at this point is if I've wet the bed for the last time. It's been over three weeks since my last accident, so maybe I'm finally over that, too. Man, I hope so.

Any good secret agent will tell you that the thing about missions is that they never go the way you think they will. You come in with a plan, and then you adjust on the fly.

What's about to happen on this one? I have no idea. But with some good friends by my side, I'm ready for whatever is about to come next.

ABOUT THE AUTHOR

Bryan Allain is a large-nostrilled mammal. He was born and raised in Massachusetts and now lives in Lancaster County, PA. He enjoys playing golf, writing books, and eating sharp cheddar cheese—but not all at the same time because that would be hard.